Sanjoy Chakravorty has written several books of non-fiction on subjects like inequality, industrialisation, immigration, and land. His last book, *The Price of Land*, was shortlisted for the 2013 Crossword Award. *The Promoter* is his first work of fiction. It was written in Philadelphia and Calcutta, the gorgeously crumbling twins born a decade apart, where he spends most of his time.

# The Promoter

Sanjoy Chakravorty

OM
Om Books International

First published in 2015 by

OM
Om Books International

Corporate & Editorial Office
A-12, Sector 64, Noida 201 301
Uttar Pradesh, India
Phone: +91 120 477 4100
Email: editorial@ombooks.com
Website: www.ombooksinternational.com

Sales Office
107, Darya Ganj,
New Delhi 110 002, India
Phone: +91 11 2326 3363, 2326 5303, 4000 9000
Fax: +91 11 2327 8091
Email: sales@ombooks.com
Website: www.ombooks.com



ISBN: 978-93-85031-73-1

Printed in India

10 9 8 7 6 5 4 3 2 1

To Paula,
this is another way…

**Caution:** All the characters and most of the facts in this story are made up. If any of this had actually happened (though it probably didn't), it would have been in the recent past.

# Contents

# The Happiest Day

Late in the evening on the second Friday in June, when a moist blue dusk had settled in after a long day of patchy rain, a small contingent from Lake police station arrested Bodhichitto Banerjee from his flat in Selimpur. Bodhi—also known as Bodhi babu, Bodhi sir, Mr Bodhi, and BB—was ready for this. He had waited all day with the anxiety and impatience of a prisoner whose hanging had been delayed by red tape. He had put fresh bandages on his hands and worn loose and comfortable cotton clothes. He had tucked a large hand towel in his hip pocket. After a brief internal debate, he had chosen to wear a pair of his more expensive shoes. He didn't know what he was about to step into, so he had opted for safety over frugality. His feet felt hot in them, but he needed to be ready for anything. This shameful thing that was about to happen was going to happen one way or another. There was no way to avoid it. Bodhi just wanted to get it over with.

The news of Bodhi's arrest spread with the rapidity and virulence of a dengue epidemic among the dozens of people that were his friends and relatives and the hundreds of people that lived in flats constructed by him. Bad news always travels fast, and in this case the speed was accelerated because his arrest was a public event.

The arrival of the arresting party with flashing lights and blaring horns drew dozens of curious young men to the scene in his neighbourhood. They stopped whatever they were doing. Some were playing carom. Some were playing teen patti. Several others were going through cleaning rituals—scraping dirt from their toenails or yanking overgrown nose hair or inspecting boogers rolled up between forefinger and thumb. Their conversations darted from one topic to other—the sexual availability of the women walking by, the political origins of the bandh that had just taken place, Katrina, Kareena, and sundry Khans and Kapoors, and similar topical issues. Then there were some men who were doing nothing useful at all. All these people—the carom and teen patti players, the toenail and booger scrapers, and even the idlers—rushed to the gate of Bodhi's apartment building when the police jeep arrived with flashing lights and blaring horns. Three of these young men had mobile phones with video cameras. How they managed to possess such expensive objects without any official source of income is a question of some socioeconomic significance, but not one that can be indulged now. What matters is that they had the phones and filmed the arrest from various angles.

These videos were soon acquired by Breaking News, a TV channel of more repute than reliability, for two bottles of Royal Stag and a can of Heineken. They edited the combined material into a montage and overlaid it with a soundtrack of impending disaster. *Doom doom doom doom.*

The footage showed Bodhi in handcuffs, his face covered by the hand towel he had thoughtfully tucked away in his hip pocket, being bundled into the backseat of a police jeep. Breaking News ran the story all evening, as a five-minute segment every fifteen minutes. Since they had exclusive footage of the arrest, this was their big news of the day. *City Promoter Arrested from Luxurious Home*, their headline tag announced. *Dispute over Heritage Building Leads to Deadly Violence*, said the subheading crawl.

By nine in the evening, when the most-watched half-hour of the day was aired, *Breaking News* had obtained interviews with neighbours who said with one voice that they were very shocked. Bodhi's father was a pillar of the community, they said, and they had known the boy almost from the day he was born. Very sad, very sad, these were very dark times. But, the neighbours had to admit, the possibility of something like this happening had always existed, because, after all, Bodhi was a promoter, and who didn't know that promoters were the vilest men in the city.

It's fair to say that the general populace didn't expect ethical behaviour from anyone, certainly not from business people whatever be the business, and least of all from people in the real estate business. Public sentiment on this subject was consistent—the whole business was dirty, and any man, like Bodhi, who joined it of his own free will, was a compromised man to begin with. Bodhi's arrest led people who knew him to recall the classical sayings—that one cannot swim in the river without getting one's hair wet; at the same time that one cannot stay in the river without having an amicable relationship with the crocodile; and, above all, that one cannot dance the khemta while being decorously covered by the proverbial ghungta. One can be a khemta-dancer or a ghungta-wearer, but not both, not simultaneously. Plain-spoken people didn't care for these oblique proverbs. You work in a landfill, they said, you must be covered with shit.

But for Bodhi specifically, the flesh and blood Bodhi that people knew, this was an unexpected turn of events. Even his outraged clients couldn't believe that a man like him could do a thing like this, whatever it was that he had done. The fact was they had trusted Bodhi…more or less, and most of the time. He was an educated man, like they were, and he spoke and behaved as educated men should. He was exactly like them, his clients thought, and while they themselves may not have been pure of heart and intent during every waking minute of their lives, they weren't criminals either. Sure, they stretched the truth as far as they could on their tax returns, and had shivers of lust when young buttocks shimmered by in ever tighter pants and ever tinier skirts. But who didn't and who wouldn't? The world was full of temptations. More and more every day. But they had never tried to grab what wasn't rightfully theirs. They knew how to keep their animal instincts in check. They were the moral backbone of society, its solid middle-class. Civilised gentlefolk. Bodhi, they were sure, was exactly like them. How could he have done this?

It was a sleepless night for many in the city.

His clients were worried. Bodhi had built the flats they were living in, and now that his criminal tendencies had been exposed, they began to speculate on how much cement he had replaced with sand and how many bars of steel he had neglected to put in. After midnight, when their neighbourhoods were quiet enough that they could hear the hidden life of their buildings—refrigerators humming, water gurgling through walled-in pipes, cockroaches and geckoes playing hide and seek—numerous people, generally older than average, began to hear their floors creak and walls crackle. Their hearts began to race and they sat up in bed in a cold sweat.

Inside his own flat, Bodhi's father clutched his side-pillow like a koala on a eucalyptus tree and tried to force himself to sleep. For seven or eight years he had been taking a single shot of self-prescribed Calmpose every night at ten-thirty to make sure that he would be asleep by eleven; but that night the pill failed to do its job. Baba was a natural worrier. Fast-moving things like buses and trains had always worried him, minibuses in particular, but now even slow-moving things like low pressure systems over the Bay of Bengal and five-day test matches were causing anxiety. These worries, however, were mere distractions; jellyfish on a beach, litter on a footpath. They couldn't compare to the magnitude of what had just happened.

His son was in jail! Surely because he deserved to be.

The Banerjee family, utterly respectable if not quite illustrious, that had produced freedom fighters and communists and teachers by the dozen, had been disgraced. Being arrested was not the problem. Bodhi wasn't the first Banerjee male to be arrested. But, according to family lore, whenever a Banerjee male had been arrested before, it was for a noble reason like fighting for liberty or justice or equality. Now Bodhi had been arrested as a common criminal. And what was worse, Baba's own brother-in-law may have been responsible for his arrest. Baba didn't know what to think or do. He castigated himself for having failed as a parent. He had been unable to impart proper values to his son. Bodhi had wanted things that were beyond his reach, and as the ancients had pointed out, there was no good or honourable way of doing that. Baba had failed to guide his son's thoughts in acceptable directions, and then had failed to protect him when his improper thoughts and actions had put him in danger of getting arrested. Thank goodness the boy's mother wasn't alive to see this day. If she wasn't dead already, this would have killed her for sure.

After two hours of palpitation, Baba took a second shot of Calmpose.

His brother-in-law, Bodhi's uncle Chhotomama, the man who indeed was responsible for putting him in jail, tried to read himself to sleep in his government flat. He turned the pages of volume twenty-three of the *Collected Works of Lenin* without enthusiasm or focus. Most nights, a paragraph of this would soothe him into a dreamless sleep. But tonight, the memories of events from the last few weeks kept bouncing around inside his head. He tried to identify points at which he could have done something different that would have averted this calamity—and for him the calamity was far larger than the mere arrest of his nephew—but couldn't see how he could have stopped this. He had done what he had to do, what needed to be done, what any man of conscience and integrity would have done. The fault was not his but in Bodhi's nature and in the nature of the times they lived in. Neither was what it should have been, neither was what it used to be when Chhotomama was young. He had moral clarity, he was not to blame; it was the world, and Bodhi with it, that had become muddled.

Bodhi too couldn't sleep that night.

It wasn't because he was afraid to face the morning and his family and the criminal justice system and the blame and shame that would be slapped on him like cow dung patties on a mud wall. It wasn't because his bony pelvis was poking through the chapatti-thin mattress and rubbing painfully against the concrete floor of the lock-up in Lake thana. It wasn't because the numerous bedbugs in the chapatti-thin mattress were feasting on his meagre flesh with the enterprise of small-town baniyas. It was because Bodhi was too excited to sleep. He was shivering with elation. His humiliation and terror earlier in the evening had been replaced by something like bliss.

All things considered, that first night in jail was the happiest of Bodhi's life.

# Part I
# The Assignment

In which Bodhi accepts a task that he is entirely unsuited to accomplish but can't refuse

# 1

In the beginning, there was a compliment.

Bodhi felt it coming moments before it arrived, like an itchy nose before a sneeze. He couldn't predict whether it would be a compliment or a critique because he was never sure how these things would go. Mr Dikshit, the man about to deliver the judgment, was one of Bodhi's clients. He sat across Bodhi's desk and began tapping it with a pen in his right hand. *Tuk tuk tuk tuk.* Then he began scratching the back of his head with his left hand. A few flakes of dandruff flounced out of his thinning hair, dyed eagerly black earlier that morning, and swirled in the eddy of a draft created by the barely-cold air blowing out of the AC in the window. It was clear to Bodhi that his client was agitated at the prospect of taking a bold step and his body was reacting as if it was about to parachute into Pakistan…alone, in the middle of the night.

Appearances can be deceptive. Who, for instance, would have expected Napoleon to be a great conqueror? Or elephants to be so timid? But it took an active imagination to associate Mr Dikshit with boldness in any form. Bodhi had known the man for close to three years now, from the day he had stepped into his office, this room they were sitting in now, to inquire about the flat he ended up buying. They had had many conversations over these years—about Mr Dikshit's stomach condition, his elder son's turbulent career in the mobile phone industry, his daughter's tranquil comforts in suburban New Jersey, his soft corner for the working class, and his devotion to Ma Kali. Bodhi, a sensitive and observant man, felt that he understood this client of his, not merely as a representative of a large social category—a sarkari naukar who wouldn't hurt a fly or move a file without written authorisation from a superior—but as a singular individual made of real meat and bones and feelings.

Mr Dikshit was thin and bent, like a question mark, and his sallow, sunken face was a canvas marked by a lifetime of misery. His mother had diagnosed him with amoebic dysentery in his early twenties and prescribed a lifelong regimen of Podophyllum. Mr Dikshit was in his mid-fifties now and had accumulated three decades of health and job-related sufferings as a result of being shuttled arbitrarily between the towns of Patna and Giridih and Gomoh and the departments of Animal Husbandry and Horticulture and Milk Output in the Bihar government. None of these well-staffed institutions had left a visible mark on society. Mr Dikshit saw this now with the lucidity that only impending retirement can provide. This blooming realisation—that his was just one among millions of lives lived in vain—had raised his spirit in recent years and made him noticeably less irritable, so much so that his wife had remarked more than once about a certain devil-may-care attitude in his behaviour. She saw signs of the young man she had married, who had hair on his head but not in his ears, a man who had not yet been felled by amoebic dysentery and used to think nothing of eating two bowls of creamy red yoghurt after a tumbling plate of biryani.

The Dikshits had bought a two-bedroom, 840 square foot flat from Heavenly Homes Ltd., the firm that Bodhi co-owned. It was the only property the family had ever possessed. Today Mr Dikshit was in Bodhi's office to pay the final five per cent instalment. The family had done a restrained but meticulous grihapravesh in the new flat the week before with two dozen guests (Bodhi among them) and the prescribed quantities of coconuts, incense sticks, and basil leaves. They had installed a sofa, a sunmica dining table with a brass flower vase on top, a clay statuette of Ma Kali with an orange tongue hanging down to her navel, framed photos of Ramakrishna Paramhamsa and Mother Teresa, and some pots and pans in the kitchen. Their dream had come true. They were in possession of their flat. Now that Mr Dikshit's business dealings with Bodhi were almost over, he felt an irresistible urge to bring closure to their brief but eventful relationship. Bodhi had seen several clients go through this phase, this urge to end things with a summary judgment, to have the last word on the subject (or so his clients thought until they had to come begging back to him for favours).

"Bodhi babu," Mr Dikshit said, "words cannot express how happy I was to be dealing with a trustworthy man like you. Don't mind it, but I think so that this line of yours is full of liars and cheats. And criminals. I feel like I can talk to you openly about this because you seem to be so broad-minded. But this is no secret. Everyone knows."

Bodhi was relieved that it was a compliment. It could very easily have gone the other way. In his six plus years as a real estate entrepreneur, Bodhi had been called a liar and a cheat, a criminal, a fraud, a conman, and a swindler too, but never, according to him, for good reason. He tried to forget these words and names as soon as he heard them. Being cursed at was part of the job. These simple people had no idea how this business worked. They thought they knew, but they didn't. What they knew was what they had heard from others, and those people too had heard from yet others. It was like a game of Chinese Whispers. Someone says 'Gandhi*ji*,' and after a few rounds someone else hears 'Gavaskar'.

But he remembered the compliments. He valued these unsolicited character certificates and following a habit he had developed even before pubic hair, kept a running list. Bodhi maintained many lists—of goals, books, songs, movies, foods, enemies, and compliments. On his list of favourite things to do, making lists was close to the top. This compliment was the third this year. Mr Sinha had provided the first ("You are a man of your word Mr Banerjee," he had said, "a rarity these days."). Mrs Ghosh-Dastidar had provided the second ("A good man like you should find a good wife soon.") The Ghosh-Dastidars had two daughters of marriageable age—Rimli, 25 and Jhimli, 22—so Bodhi wasn't sure whether hers was a compliment or an invitation to an alliance. He had made a note of it on his compliment list anyway.

Though Bodhi looked forward to receiving compliments, he didn't quite know how to deal with them. They were new to him. He hadn't grown up in an environment in which people complimented each other. His family members were generous with critiques but miserly with words of praise. Criticism builds character, they said, turns boys into men. Praise leads to complacency, they said, and complacency leads to decay. So every fresh compliment threw him into a fluster. Sometimes he tried to look nonchalant. He waved a carefree hand in the air and said that he was only doing his job and nothing more, heh heh. This response came naturally when the compliment was too effusive to be believable. Then there were the grudging ones like Mr Dikshit, people who laced their compliments with the mild poison of reproach. You're a good man sir, but only in comparison to the degenerates you associate with; all your friends are daylight dacoits sir, and thank goodness you're just a petty thief.

In these situations Bodhi felt his face settling naturally into a sad and empathetic smile. It was a sincere smile. He had genuine empathy for people like Mr Dikshit and the problems they had to endure because of people like him. Had he not been sitting on this side of the table he could very well have been on the other side, a man like Mr Dikshit, mistrustful of everyone but powerless to do anything when the mistrust turned out to be well-founded.

"The missus and I were so much terrified," Mr Dikshit said, "that we would be swindled out of our life's savings, or we would get something that was substandard or dangerous. It's a blessing of the goddess that we came across an honest promoter like you."

Bodhi smiled again, sadly and empathetically.

~

Cookie happened to be passing by at the moment of Mr Dikshit's confession. He acted as if he hadn't heard anything, but Bodhi saw his big belly trembling like a plastic bag of mustard oil. He was thankful that Cookie had the good grace to keep the laughter silent. But it'd be too much to hope that Cookie would forget about what he had overheard and never mention it again. That wasn't Cookie's way. He couldn't wait to tell Bodhi what he thought about Mr Dikshit's feelings.

They had lunch together later that day. It was one of their rituals. If both happened to be in the office during lunch hour and neither had a meeting at that time, they had lunch together, usually in Cookie's office because it was larger and had two ACs to Bodhi's one. Cookie had a tiffin-carrier delivered from home. As usual, it contained four chapattis, a reasonable portion of egg-tadka, two small peeled onions, and a tablespoon of aachaar. Pinky, Cookie's wife, was forever trying to make him eat less and lose weight. It was a doomed project. She knew, as Bodhi knew, as did everyone who knew Cookie, that every evening he more than made up for the meagreness of lunch with an assortment of finger foods (fish fry, momo, chicken lollipop) washed down with impressive volumes of alcohol. Cookie was more proud of his ability to drink without looking drunk than anything else he had achieved in life. Bodhi had one of the office boys pick up something Chinese—chilli chicken with fried rice or prawn hakka noodles with gravy.

"You look quite pleased with yourself, Mr Trustworthy Banerjee," Cookie said, chomping noisily on an onion.

Bodhi produced a pragmatic grunt, like an old man getting out of a chair.

"You shouldn't be," Cookie said. "I don't think it was a compliment."

"Well, I do." Bodhi had to respond because he knew that Cookie wouldn't let go until he did. Cookie was the sort of man who made sure that if he had a point to make, it didn't remain unmade.

"What Mr Dikshit means," Cookie said, "is that you look incompetent. These clients of ours, these scared-of-their-shadows noodle-dicks, they all assume that any competent person, anyone with any brains or balls, anyone who looks like he has more money than them, which is all of us, must be a crook. But because you look incompetent, like a vegetarian bachelor, they assume that you're not a crook."

"I'm not a crook," said Bodhi, who was a bachelor but certainly not a vegetarian and was disturbed by the suggestion that he looked like one.

"Ha, ha," Cookie said, "they all say that, don't they."

"You're just jealous," Bodhi said, "because no one's ever told you that you look trustworthy."

"And they bloody well shouldn't," Cookie said, "because I'm not."

Cookie kept his hair very short at all times and wore bright shirts as tight as banana skins. Their stripes and patterns emphasised his fleshy belligerence. Like an overfed bull. He had the pink, puffy face of an alcoholic, and piggy, observant eyes. He laughed a lot, but smiled not as much. Cookie didn't do things in small scale, like smile when he could laugh out loud or speak softly when he could rumble. He was a big man with a big body and big gestures and big ideas.

He was the enforcer in their business, the person who shouted at underlings like suppliers and contractors, demanded payments from clients when they were late or evasive, denied client requests to change this or that, and made the hafta payments to the police and local netas and their goondas. He went drinking with these netas and their goondas when mere cash wouldn't do but had to be supplemented with social recognition. Cookie did most of the unpleasant stuff and did it with relish.

Bodhi dealt with the official types, the babus and clerks whose expertise was in getting in the way and slowing down an already comatose process, like speed bumps on choked roads, but had more or less known rates. Most of them were, in any case, too squirrelly to require intimidation and much preferred to deal with a cultured Bengali gentleman like Bodhi.

Cookie was the mace and Bodhi the lotus in Vishwakarma's hands. Thank goodness, they said to each other whenever they sat down to count their blessings, that their skills were so perfectly matched. They made a very efficient team.

"And you aren't trustworthy either," Cookie continued. "We know that, don't we, you and me, even if others can't tell by looking at you?"

"Ha, ha," Bodhi said. It was a carefully modulated sound, designed to indicate nothing, certainly not hilarity, and neither agreement nor disagreement. He had been practising it for years. Cookie had seen him perfect the sound through those years so he understood exactly what Bodhi meant. There was little Cookie didn't know about Bodhi, including things Bodhi wasn't sure of himself.

"Don't bray like a donkey, saaley natwarlal," Cookie said. "You want to be a good man in this dhanda of ours and you want people to like you and say: oh, that Mr Banerjee, he's such a nice fellow, na! Not like those other promoters always so much lying and cheating. As if you're better than us. Like Sita in Ravan's den. Pure and unspoilt among all the horrible rakshashas. I tell you, one of these days you're going to twist yourself into a knot that you won't be able to get out of. Don't expect me to help then."

Bodhi stared into the middle distance, like a poet looking for the right word to rhyme with *dilemma*. He had lately begun to compare his condition to that of Yudhisthir, the righteous but conflicted eldest Pandava brother, and the many tricks he had used to stay technically righteous while skating really close to the far edge of morality. They were spiritually alike, he and Yudhisthir, always pondering the big moral question of all time.

How to do good and be right and win at the same time?

Bodhi had written a poem to express his inner conflicts. That he had been motivated to write anything at all was itself commendable. This wasn't how things used to be when he was a teenager. Then, a dozen and more years ago, the injustices of the world and his own regular humiliations in it used to disturb him with great frequency, and, in response, he had written many poems of love, longing, and loss. His ambition in those days was to become a full-time poet and win a Nobel Prize in literature, or, failing that, a Sahitya Akademi Award. This recent (untitled) composition said—

The field of my dreams
bloomed
with daffodil and daisy

pure and promising
like a newborn baby
Now it is overrun
with machinery
Tractor and truck and bulldozer and crane
drilling
into a mind going insane

In Bodhi's own assessment of artistic merit, the work was passable. He could see its deficiencies—that it was a little too literal and not sufficiently allegorical. But there was a bigger problem with the composition, a problem that Bodhi could barely admit, even to himself. It was insincere. It spoke about feelings he thought he should feel, not the ones he really did. His truest thoughts weren't on subjects appropriate for poetry, or poetry of the kind that people he admired accepted as poetry.

~

Bodhi and Cookie ate in companionable silence for a minute as the material world went about its ordinary noisy business. The two ACs in the office whirred away. This drone mixed with the muffled hum of motorised traffic from the main road in front of the office and provided an ambient base, like a tanpura for a khayal singer. On top of this base were layered many other sounds. One of the two ACs needed repair and every time its compressor shut off, it coughed—*khok khok*—like Devdas dying of TB. Random melodious notes were added by the heavy clanging of trams turning into a depot around the corner and the clinking warning bells of rickshaws and bicycles. Loudest of all was a song playing on a scratchy mike at the impromptu shrine that had sprung up on the pavement across the road some four or five years ago. It was time for the afternoon prayer. *Govinda aala re aala...*

"So, what's this evening about?" Cookie asked at the end of a small but satisfying burp. "Why has Chhotomama called the two of us to a meeting? At the club, of all places."

"The club was my idea," Bodhi said. "Chhotomama wanted to talk to us both and I thought why not the club. I'm paying for it every month and hardly get to use it."

"Chhotomama at the club. Ha ha. It'll feel like torture to that old communist."

"No, no," Bodhi said. "Nothing like that. He's an important man...he's on TV all the time...and I'm sure he goes to places like this quite often. Not that he enjoys himself, but he wouldn't enjoy himself anywhere nice anyway."

"What's the meeting about then? What did he say?"

"Not much. He was quite vague. All he said was that this is very important and he needs to talk to us soon."

"Does he want to buy a flat?"

"I doubt it. He's not into buying things. You know how he is. High above all material desires. And even if he did want to buy a flat, why would he need you? He could just ask me."

"Maybe he doesn't trust you."

"And he trusts you more than me? Not even your wife does that."

"That's a good point. Maybe he's getting married and wants our blessings."

"Cookie! Don't be stupid. The man is at least sixty years old. Have some respect for his seniority, yaar."

"What, sixty-year-old men can't get married? There's a law against that? And you know what...I have the greatest respect for men who marry at sixty. Those are real manly men. You and I will be lucky if we can get it up when we're sixty."

"What bakwas. How many men do you personally know who got married for the first time at sixty? Not one I bet. This is India, my friend, not America. We have certain values. I think he just wants to smack you on the head for being a stupid sardar. That's why he wants to see us together. He wants me to hold you down while he smacks you on the head."

Cookie laughed in short rolling snorts. *Frooth frooth frooth*. Bodhi scrunched his morose face into an expression that people who knew him would recognise as a smile. Strangers were likely to think that he had pulled a muscle.

"Is anyone else coming or will it be just the three of us?" Cookie asked.

Bodhi hesitated. "Neera will be there," he said.

"Why she? Why for?"

"Well, she's Chhotomama's assistant."

"Then it's something to do with his work."

"That's what I said, didn't I?"

"No, you didn't."

"Yes, I did."

"*Aha*, now I understand all. That's why we're meeting at the club. To impress your girlfriend. Finally you're learning some style from me."

"She's not my girlfriend," Bodhi squirmed.

"Of course she is. You, on the other hand, are not her boyfriend. Not yet."

"Maybe never."

"Very possible. In fact, very likely. You act like such a goody goody around her, chhupa rustam, you'll never get what you want."

"Yeah…but…"

"You have to ask for what you want, Bodhi, otherwise no one's going to read your mind and give it to you. Do you understand how horrible the world would be if people could read each other's minds? Everyone would know what everyone else was thinking. No one could lie. No one could have impure thoughts. Oye, bada kabootar, disaster. That's why god gave us tongues. To speak. Thinking is no good. You have to say it."

"What'll I say? I don't know what to say."

"Just listen to yourself. Are you a man or a hijra?" Cookie was exasperated. "Do I have to do everything for you? Run your business *and* declare love to your girlfriend? I'm not your bloody servant, scarecrow."

"This isn't funny, Cookie. You don't know what I'm going through."

"Then don't tell me. Sob stories bore me."

~

Cookie, unlike Bodhi, had never read a poem that wasn't on a syllabus. His legal name was Naveen Singh Arora. He was a Sikh who had cut his hair at eighteen and married a Bengali woman at twenty-three. This dual identity gave him license to insult both communities at will. His views on Bengali work habits were brutal, best left unsaid. He advocated a ten-year moratorium on Rabindrasangeet and all songs that had to be accompanied by harmonium or included any of the words 'mahi' or 'rabba' or 'maula.' He argued that if during that ten-year moratorium Sikh men cut their hair like other normal men, saving themselves at least one hour each day during which they wouldn't be required to clean and dress and tease all that unnecessary material into patkas and pugris, the increased productivity would by itself turn India into a first world country. "Imagine," he said, "how much more efficient our government could be if the prime minister didn't have to spend an hour each day taking care of his hair. Such a stupid waste of time! So many more laws we could make, so much more development we could have."

To put it in a nutshell—Cookie was a theorist. His uncomplicated mind saw the core of the thing, the heart of the matter, and his simple language was able to describe what he saw with precision, clarity, and vulgarity...as needed. A casual observer could be fooled into thinking that he was a semi-literate country bumpkin. Many people had made that mistake and suffered for it.

Bodhi and Cookie had been friends from the day they met, on the last bench of geography in class eight. Cookie used to be thin then and used to wear a patka, but was almost as pushy and outspoken as his adult version. After high school they had ended up at the same place—Benimadhab College near Park Circus, an institution renowned in the city for the quality of the mutton cutlet served in its canteen. It had some famous alumni—a TV personality who was beginning to become a film star, a winner of the national *Dance Your Arse Off* contest, and a rising member of the opposition in the state legislature who had acquired a reputation for integrity by slapping policemen—but only students of Benimadhab College knew that these luminaries were from their alma mater. For the rest of the world, the reputation of the college rested on its mutton cutlet, much as Shaktigarh's rested on its lengcha and Barddhaman's on its sitabhog.

Bodhi got a B.Sc. (Botany Honours) and Cookie got a B.Com (Pass, No Distinction). Then, after poking around at this and that for a couple of years, selling everything that could be sold—photocopy machines, water purifiers, inverter units, vacation time-shares, advertising space on hoardings and in newspapers, life insurance—they had become business partners.

~

Cookie was a practical man. He came from a family of practical men. His father had started working at fifteen, first as an apprentice and later as a regular truck driver hauling coal between Dhanbad and Durgapur. By the time he was twenty seven he had acquired his first truck by using an assortment of illegal but necessary procedures, including assault and procurement of women. Eventually, he came to own half a dozen trucks plying the coal corridor. But because it was an exceptionally dirty and violent business (and who knew better than he?), even by the standards of Bihar, Cookie's father moved to the city and began converting his trucks into a line of rocket buses running from here to Digha and Siliguri. Cookie's older sister and her husband had taken over that business. His father had initially demoted Cookie when he cut his hair and then had cut him out of the family business altogether when he married a Hindu girl. This romantic decision of Cookie's—to forsake money for love—had shocked everyone, Cookie most of all.

It was saccha pyar, he said, that had driven him to become a promoter. In other cities Bodhi and Cookie would be called real estate developers or builders and given the respect due to real estate developers and builders, but here they were called promoters, and treated with suspicion by all, including their own friends and relatives. Their firm, Heavenly Homes Ltd., constructed flats for the upper crust of the lower middle-class in the city, in ordinary neighbourhoods far away from the posh areas. Many of their clients were older people (like Mr Dikshit) buying their first homes in anticipation of retirement; many were government workers from departments in which they had little or no access to off-the-book-and-under-the-table payments; all of them wished they had more money and could buy something bigger and better located, but then they would be different people with different lives who wouldn't need to buy flats from Bodhi and Cookie.

Heavenly Homes Ltd. had nine full-time employees and enough work to keep them busy most of the time. In the seven or so years that their firm had been in existence, Bodhi and Cookie had become well-to-do men. Not really rich, or even rich enough, because the finish line, the standard at which they could call themselves rich, had kept shooting further ahead, like a bank robber on a crime spree, during the same years that they had been moving ahead in life. When they were born, a lakhpati was considered rich; when they were in high school, a crorepati was considered rich. Now no one knew what was rich and what wasn't. But this must be said—both were far better off than either could have imagined when they began their business.

For Cookie, this wasn't a new condition. He came from a moderately successful business family after all. For Bodhi on the other hand, the son of a retired history teacher in a Bangla-medium government high school, this was like winning a lottery. Heavenly.

But one man's heaven is another man's hell, like tutti-frutti sundae for a diabetic. The family elders had a tendency to view Bodhi's financial success with scepticism or scorn. His father held a dim view of Bodhi's definition of heaven and his method of attaining it. Senior Mr Banerjee was an amateur theologian (and an armchair Marxist, as well as a prolific film critic in the oral tradition), who, after comparing the merits and demerits of the religions of the world, and mortified by the opportunisms of the Brahman caste he had been born into, had come to wish that he could have been a Buddhist. He couldn't convert because his wife, Bodhi's mother, never authorised it. In exchange, he had been given the naming rights for the children.

His older child, his only daughter, was named Bisakha, after the first female disciple of Buddha. His younger child, his only son, was named Bodhichitto. The name was given with high hopes—that he would become the possessor of a soul like Gautam Buddha's, a soul that strives for enlightenment, not for selfish reasons like attaining moksha and going beyond the endless cycle of birth and death and rebirth, but to enable the welfare of all living beings. His theological investigations had left Bodhi's father least impressed by dhyan and tapasya and aggressive renunciation and all the other self-centred hermit methodologies recommended by the holy books. What good is enlightenment, he asked, if its core motive is selfish—to get a sweet deal for oneself? What's the point of seeing the light if all you do with it is escape, alone, from darkness?

It had become apparent to his father that his hopes for and the name he had given his son were both unfashionable. Bodhichitto had become Bodhi. That was understandable; disappointing but understandable. Even if they knew how to pronounce his name, which most people didn't, they didn't have the time to utter all four syllables in Bodhichitto. But the dropped *chitto* appeared to have taken with it the very soul that his father had hoped for. Bodhi the man was turning into the opposite of the Bodhichitto he had been named after. He seemed to worship money (though he was much more interested in earning than spending it), and like every other man without *chitto*, appeared to have dedicated his life to gaining status and upward mobility. What disappointed Bodhi's father most was the utter ordinariness of his son's desires.

# 2

Bodhi rushed into the bathroom as soon as he returned from work. He showered and shampooed and sprayed cologne on his underarms, and after worrying for a few seconds about the stinging that would accompany it, his crotch. He was going to see Neera that evening, and though he had no reason to think that she would sniff his crotch (or, for that matter, his underarm), he saw no reason not to be ready by looking and smelling good...all over. Bodhi had thought of little else all day. That he would see Neera and she would see him and he had to look his best and say clever things, but not so clever as to appear shallow. It was a fine line and Bodhi was never sure which side he was on.

He wore a well-ironed blue shirt with a pair of white crossed swords embroidered on the breast-pocket that he had decided to wear the minute he learnt that he would see Neera that night, with his form-enhancing, wrinkle-free khaki trousers, and his major indulgence—the best loafers from the most expensive shoe store in the biggest mall in the city. Bodhi didn't like to waste money, far from it, but he had a justifiable weakness for quality footwear. He felt that he had earned the right to wear comfortable yet sturdy shoes because of the long hours he had to be on his feet, many of them at construction sites where his toes had a tendency to find the sneaky steel rods and hidden-in-plain-sight chunks of concrete that others seemed to be able to avoid.

Bodhi needed to dress with care, especially on an evening when the pulsating desire of his life would be present, because—there's no delicate way to put this—he was not a handsome man. Bodhi was painfully aware of this reality. He had concluded early in life that his looks couldn't be improved. He had scrupulously listed his plus points—he was (a) not short, and (b) not fat. A couple of years ago, after the comparative evidence from men of his age could no longer be ignored, he had added one more point: he was (c) not bald, nor going bald. But the virtues of what he was not were overwhelmed by what he was, the negative-negatives on his original list, features that had gotten more pronounced over the years. He was: (a) goggle-eyed, (b) bobble-throated, and (c) bungle-some.

He did his best to hide his protuberances; the goggling eyes under a pair of thick-rimmed glasses and the bobbling Adam's apple under a beard that he wished would grow more luxuriantly than it did. A thicker beard would have allowed him to brand himself—as a gangster or a rock star or an intellectual (he would have preferred the latter)—but as it hung haggardly from his cheeks and chin, like a beggar's rags, its thinness made him look perpetually apologetic. There are beards that define men—like Karl Marx and Kabir Bedi—so much so that without them they look naked and weak, like furless poodles. But, not he. He would have looked much the same without his beard.

But there was little Bodhi could do to hide his clumsiness. People couldn't see it as long as he stood still or made slow, cautious movements. Since that wasn't always possible, people found out soon enough that he had a tendency to bump into, or trip over, or drop, or topple things. Depending on whether he did any damage—broke a glass or a lamp or overturned an ashtray or spilled a drink—this sometimes annoyed but more frequently amused people who knew him. People who didn't know him found this feature reassuring.

Cookie never tired of telling Bodhi that people liked him precisely because he looked like a discarded scarecrow, or a vegetarian bachelor, or a sad clown on stilts. As with everything else, Cookie liked to be frank about Bodhi's physical limitations. That's what friends are for, he said, to tell you when your fly is unzipped or your girlfriend is a phoney. Cookie tried to convince Bodhi that his clumsiness worked to his advantage. Men who stutter or stumble or limp or gulp or goggle clearly had a head start, Cookie said, over men who did none of these things and at the same time weren't handsomely chiselled either. The latter weren't interesting. They were nondescript, like whitewashed walls, whereas ugly men like Bodhi were like graffiti. At least there was something to see.

Cookie's argument was not entirely without merit. Bodhi's supposedly negative attributes actually gave him some traction, not so much that he could ever become the centre of attraction for squealing teenagers, but sufficient to make women of more discerning tastes take a second look. "At least he doesn't look like a wife-beater," was a common thought. "He might be handy in the kitchen," was another. Bodhi dearly wanted to be athletic and intimidating, like a

Pakistani fast bowler, and didn't fully understand that this lack of coordination was one of his biggest business assets. The more he bungled the more his clients trusted him and the healthier became his bank balance.

But a sexual magnet he was not. No, Bodhi was sure he had to look better than nature had intended, and given the circumstances and time limitations that evening—it was a working day after all—he felt he had done as well as could be done with the raw material he had to work with.

~

Chandan, Bodhi's driver, hadn't turned up at work that day with some excuse about his daughter's health (or was it his son?). This had been happening so frequently that Bodhi had stopped paying attention and begun to think that he should get a different driver, someone with more robust children, or better still, none at all. He felt mean for a moment for having such an uncharitable thought, but then one had to be realistic. Drivers come and go. There was no point getting attached to any one of them. The moment of self-recrimination passed.

So he had a decision to make. Drive or take a taxi? He lit a cigarette.

There was no question of taking a bus. Bodhi hadn't been on one in years. He didn't know what the fares were these days. He did use rickshaws now and then to carry out local errands, buy groceries and medicines and whisky, but that was only on Sundays, when Chandan had the day off officially and Bodhi didn't feel like taking the car out. Truth was, he never felt like taking the car out by himself. He had learned to drive five years ago, using his own car (because Baba had never owned one), a hulking white Tata Sumo. The man who taught him to drive was a driver he had hired when he bought the car; not Chandan, but an earlier edition who had been fired for extending his visits to his village by weeks for flimsy reasons like dying uncles and dead grandmothers.

Bodhi was a timid driver in city full of fearless ones. Traffic in the city terrified him and parking the Sumo into tight spaces was an art he had never mastered. And the Sumo itself was decidedly mid-market, nothing to be proud of. Bodhi had been thinking of getting an upgrade to a foreign brand, maybe a Honda City, something more in keeping with his rising position in society. If only he could learn to enjoy driving. Bodhi couldn't decide whether the benefit of being seen in a superior car was higher than cost of watching someone else have the pleasure of driving it. He decided to take a taxi. At this rate, he told himself, he would soon forget how to drive. Add to the list of things he was forgetting how to do—(a) read books, (b) write poetry, (c) play bridge, (d) take afternoon naps, (e) take aimless walks, (f) waste time. It was a long list, growing longer.

This was another moment of self-recrimination, but it too passed. Then he had a final moment of self-recrimination for having too many moments of self-recrimination. This wouldn't do, this wouldn't do at all. That was the old Bodhi, and he knew where that loser was headed, didn't he? A grumpy, skimpy, brat-infested lifetime of lower middle-class inconsequence was exactly where that Bodhi had been headed. In the same direction as all the men in the Banerjee lineage…including the freedom fighters and revolutionaries, who, by the time they were forty, were grumpy and skimpy and brat-infested, and indistinguishable from their cousins who had never fought for freedom nor rebelled against the oppressive state. Time turns red to pink and black to grey. Bodhi resolved to avoid any thought that could lead to even a moment of self-examination, which, he was well-aware was the first step on the slippery slope to self-recrimination.

Taxis didn't wait around in his short and narrow dead-end lane, so he had to walk about two minutes, turn right where his lane met an equally narrow street, through the curve on that street, then left on a wider road to the main artery, and across it to be in the correct direction of vehicle flow. If he caught a taxi facing the wrong direction—which meant the taxi would have to make an U-turn at an impossible intersection ahead—it would cost him at least ten minutes and twenty rupees more. The money wasn't anything, not any longer, but Bodhi's habit of counting every rupee was deeply ingrained.

It was seven and traffic was snarled like a bowl of overcooked noodles. D. Club was only four kilometres from his neighbourhood, but at that time of the evening it would take at least half an hour to reach. The taxi moved like a corralled animal released in a herd, bellowing and barging into any space that opened ahead, separated by no more than a finger width or two from the other equally frantic vehicles around it. Every release at a traffic signal was accompanied by a discord of horns—peals and bleats and blasts of impatience and habit. Bodhi was used to this and his principal problem was what to do with the window?

Keep it rolled up and suffocate in the heat or roll it down and be assailed by the sounds and smells of the evolutionary experiment around him. He had gotten used to travelling in AC cars and normally didn't need to deal with environmental issues like temperature and smoke and sound. He remained preoccupied with the window for much of the ride.

The taxi driver was a young man wearing a yellow T-shirt that identified him as a *Palm Beach Bunny* in thick pink letters. He had red sleepy eyes and a three-day stubble, like a movie star. Who's imitating whom, Bodhi wondered. A plaster cast figurine of a goddess he couldn't recognise was on the dashboard, framed by twinkling red and blue toony bulbs. The goddess had the requisite four arms with blessings and weapons, but her animal companion, the usual clue to identification, was indeterminate. It could have been a big rat or a small tiger. *Bipodtarini Ma*, Bodhi concluded; according to his driver Chandan, who was his primary informant on the working class, she was the goddess in form.

The radio was tuned to a station bubbling with inane deejays. They were playing hit songs from Hindi films. Mr Palm Beach Bunny tapped his finger to the thumping bass.

Yeah sexy!
Sexy lady on the floor
Keep you coming back for more
Stolen it, have you? Hey!
Taken my heart, have you? Hey!
Put a spell on me, have you? Hey!!
Have you? Hey!
Have you? Hey!!

I can't sleep, and I wander
Your memories make me wonder
As you shake your booty, hey!
Made me crazy, have you? Hey!
Made me crazy, have you? Hey!!

~

Bodhi wondered whether the writer of the song knew Neera? Not the shaking booty part as much as the driving crazy part. Now that the time to meet Neera had neared, Bodhi was beset by insecurities. How would she behave tonight? Would she flirt with him and encourage him, or be indifferent? Maybe she would be both. Encouraging at first, getting his hopes up, getting him to say or do something stupid, and then turning tepid and indifferent. His palms became slippery with a cold sweat. He knew this was not the sweat of summer but of anxiety. It smelled like kerosene.

He tried to anticipate what fresh information he would receive that evening.

Perhaps she would bring him up to date on her spiritual growth. Unlike Bodhi's father, Neera felt that the path of spiritual progress ran through renunciation. She said she abhorred materialism and the all-pervasive culture of consumption. She was always looking for things to give up and maybe tonight she would announce something new she had renounced. Neera had been a pacifist and animal-rights enthusiast for years and had become a vegetarian about a year ago. She had adopted one of its more rigorous forms and ate nothing that had eyes, which meant fish and meat, or had the potential to have eyes, which meant eggs. But she was beginning to waver. Someone had told her that animals were handled by India's poorest people and by refusing to eat meat she was contributing to a financial squeeze, however tiny, on those who could least bear it.

How could one compare the pain and suffering of animals with that of humans? How did one figure out this moral calculus? Neera had confessed to Bodhi that she was finding it hard to find a cause that was unalloyed in its purity and goodness. There always appeared to be at least two sides to any argument. She had recently begun investigating the issue of Tibetan rights and was increasingly drawn to the personality of the Dalai Lama. Bodhi had begun to think that Neera had a problem with commitment, not just to him but everything.

Nonetheless, he looked forward to receiving these titbits on Neera's inner world. Her outer world, the one she presented to him, most of the things she said were so vague and unrevealing, like statements from the Chinese politburo, that he had to spend significant time deciphering them. Unlike the Americans, who had think-tanks devoted solely to the task of decoding the utterings of the Chinese politburo, Bodhi had to figure out Neera all by himself. This work occupied most of his free time, and on occasion, took up time that he should have been and, to unobservant eyes, seemed to be spending, on more tangible tasks like making money.

Most people in Bodhi's circle found quasi-mystical leanings of the kind Neera exhibited to be signs of a lazy and self-indulgent mind. "*Nakhrebaazi*," said Cookie, the capitalist. "*Nyakamo,*" said Chhotomama, the communist. This was a matter of general principle for both. Bodhi didn't think that Chhotomama meant it to apply to Neera, though he was beginning to suspect that Cookie did.

Bodhi agreed on this principle about other people—that quasi-mysticism was nothing but woolly-headed vagueness—but made an exception for Neera. Instead of intellectual laziness he saw openness to new ideas, instead of self-indulgence he saw self-denial. Like men in love from the beginning of time, Bodhi found ways to imbue the object of his love with superior qualities; he was able to interpret the data in ways that matched his belief.

Though it could appear that way, it didn't mean that Bodhi was delusional. The condition Bodhi suffered from, along with billions of others, was more properly called ideology. A person without any ideology (if such a person could be found) could say that what he saw was what he believed. However, in reality, what people already believed was what they saw. If one preferred cats to dogs, one saw the good qualities of cats (they ate less, they were clean) and the bad qualities of dogs (they barked, they expected to be played with). The preference came first. It had no inherent meaning; it was all about taste, which was just another word for ideology.

Love was an ideology. Evidence and reality had nothing to do with it.

The other update Bodhi was likely to receive, the one he wasn't at all looking forward to, was on Neera's special friend in America. Bodhi hadn't met the gentleman in the five months he had been hovering around Neera, but had learnt a great deal about him, except the nature of his exact relationship with Neera. The special friend liked Bengali sweets (the dry kind, not syrupy), foreign films, whirling dervishes, and fast cars. He hated (just hated) hangovers, hairy armpits, and politics. He was a neuroradiologist (or was it radioneurologist?) doing advanced work at a quite famous university hospital in America. Bodhi had forgotten its name, but he had been assured by Neera that it was quite famous.

The special friend played sarod and rugby. "Why *sarod*?" Bodhi had asked innocently, "Are his arms too short for sitar?" Not at all, he had been told, the special friend was tall and fair and had a full head of curly hair. He had to take Neera's word for it because he hadn't seen a picture of the special friend yet. The man refused to be photographed... on principle. He was in psychic convergence with the wise and ancient tribes of Africa who believe that if you take a man's image, you capture his soul.

These details had been given to Bodhi in dribs and drabs, leaving him the responsibility of stitching these fragments into whole cloth. He had had to manufacture impressed-looking expressions when the special friend had surpassed himself; the time, for example, when he bungee-jumped twelve times in an hour. Bodhi typed banjee, bunji, bunghi, and behn*ji* before he got the spelling right to look up its meaning online. He had had to emit sympathetic-sounding noises when the special friend neglected to write or call Neera, or when he was cruel or aloof.

These past few months had been quite an emotional roller-coaster for Bodhi. What made the situation worse for him, made it unbearable at times…the thought that pushed him to the edge of reason, was the possibility that for Neera those months had been a serene time, that not for once had she lost sleep thinking about him.

# 3

The main entrance to D. Club was through a tall six-panelled glass door into a spacious marble foyer, framed with three large aged sofas of dark burnished mahogany, each upholstered with an ornate calico fabric of blue and orange patterns. The walls of the foyer were covered with enormous oil portraits of past club presidents. The names listed the chronology of authority in the city beginning in 1903, the year the club had been established. McPhersons, Hamiltons, and Jessops ran up to the nineteen-fifties, followed by Mukherjees, Dutts, and Chowdhurys till the eighties, and Ahluwalias, Singhanias, and Neotias after that. All were grim-looking men, most appeared to have had problems with hair retention.

The foyer split into two wings. One passage led to the indoor sports amenities: badminton and squash courts for the physically fit and a billiards room for others. The second passage led to food and drinks. There were two dining rooms—one Indian, one multi-cuisine; and two bars—one indoor, with red leather stools and chairs and cosy dimly-lit tables, and the other on a long colonnaded patio overlooking a well-tended lawn with a swimming pool on one side and six tennis courts across it.

Something was happening at the club that night and at first Bodhi couldn't understand what it was. There were many more people there than he expected to see on a normal evening and most of them were even more dressed up than he was. Sherwanis and silks and tight black dresses as far as the eye could see. Shining hair, glittering clothes, and layers of prosperous necks and waists like turtles hatching on a beach. Had he brought Chhotomama to the club on the night of a party? He hoped not. That would make Chhotomama uncomfortable and he wasn't a man who tolerated discomfort with stoic dignity.

Bodhi wasn't sure of what to expect at the club on a normal evening. He was one of the newest members here and unfamiliar with the routines and rituals of the place. The decision to become a member hadn't been easy. There was the matter of the compulsory donation of three lakh rupees. He still got a twinge in his lower abdomen when he thought about the donation and the pleasure he would have gotten by having that money send him monthly updates from the safety of a fixed deposit.

Then there was the matter of which club to join. The D. Club was known for its kebabs and biryanis and affordable whisky. But the R. Club, which specialised in golf and Salisbury steak, was tempting too. Bodhi had never played golf but didn't see that as a handicap. There were many things he hadn't done before the last few years—like own a car and ride an airplane and dance at weddings and use hair gel—and learning golf would simply be one more of those. One moved up in the world, one did new things.

His father didn't approve of clubs. Not just this one, but each and every one. They not only cost too much, he said when Bodhi announced his decision to join D. Club, but he would never associate with the type of person who went to one. You mean, Bodhi said, those persons wouldn't associate with you. It's mutual then, Baba said, they have their world, we have ours. As during most recent conversations with his father, Bodhi felt that his values were being questioned. How can you pass judgment on something that's out of your league, he asked, you don't even know what it is? How can you refuse something that's not even being offered to you? It's like claiming to have a complete lack of interest in being the ambassador to France. You're an idiot, was his father's closing statement on the subject.

~

Chhotomama arrived a few minutes after Bodhi. He was rumpled, as usual, and utterly mismatched to the environment. White kurta, white pajama, and a black cotton bag drooping from his left shoulder. The only concession was his footwear. Black sandals instead of his usual thin-sole chappals. The old clubs in the city maintained dress codes—no shirts without collars, no jeans, and no slippers. One was allowed to wear formal "native" clothes, but not without strapped footwear. "The worst combination of British and Brahman snobbery are your bloody clubs," Chhotomama had snorted when Bodhi had reminded him about the code the day before the meeting.

Chhotomama was allowed and expected to dress the way he did. He was an intellectual. And now that TV channels frequently sought his views on topical issues—elections, abductions, Muslims, malnutrition, corruption, poverty, censorship, potholes, budgets, rapes, gang rapes—he had become something of a public intellectual. On most subjects he could be relied upon to represent the view of his obsolete breed—the communist intellectual.

If the city's clubs had their dress codes, so did its communist intellectuals.

Chhotomama was the director of the Bengal International Culture and History Institute. Anyone who knew about it knew it as 'The Institute.' But few did because it was small and highly specialised, and invisible to all who weren't already aware of its existence, that too typically because they knew one of the two dozen people—scholars, administrators, and fourth-class staff included—that worked there.

The insignificance of the Institute didn't however diminish the fact that Chhotomama was a significant intellectual. He had been a communist in his soul from his mid-teens and a Party member for almost thirty five years. Again, just because there were millions of communists all around didn't diminish the fact that Chhotomama was one, more so because he became one before it was fashionable and convenient, and even more so because he remained one even though it was beginning to be unfashionable and inconvenient now.

Chhotomama was Bodhi's mother's brother, younger than her, the youngest of three siblings. All the Chhotomamas of the world didn't have to be physically small (after all, the familial name was derived from birth order, not genetic content) but his was. He was a short man, no more than six inches over five feet, and thin and stooped.

He wore glasses with a thick black frame and gloomy lenses which magnified his big round eyes to paani-puri size. Bodhi had the same goggling eyes, his inheritance from maternal genes. The rest of Chhotomama's face was covered by a bushy unkempt beard that hadn't been trimmed or groomed after the last elections for the state assembly. His head, in contrast, was almost completely bald, with a big open space on top that resembled a helipad for jungle guerrillas. The few remaining strands were arranged like a laurel wreath on a Greek god, curling over his ears and the back of his neck, giving him the look of a character actor in a theatre company.

"How's your father?" Chhotomama asked. He had an unexpectedly big voice for a small man. It was mellow like a monsoon wind and cultured like a mango jam. Nature had not been entirely unkind.

"The same. Nothing changes with him," Bodhi said.

"He should try to get out more. He's just seven years older than me, but to look at him you'd think he's my grand uncle." Chhotomama was about sixty and had looked as if he was sixty-five for as long as Bodhi could remember. "He should get a hobby. Or do some social work. The man is turning into a boiled potato."

They found seats on the colonnaded patio, overlooking the back area of the club where the tennis courts had been covered by a temporary stage and a shamiana over it. In front of the stage was a makeshift semi-circular dance floor, around which about fifty people sat in scattered clusters among several rows of plastic bucket chairs. Other groups had moved these chairs further back, on to the lawn, from where they could observe the action on the stage, when it began, without having to devote too much attention to it.

On stage a band was tuning instruments. An electric guitar cried out sharply and stopped abruptly, like an infant given a nipple. There were murmured conversations of drum rolls. 'Hello, hello, check, check, one, two, three,' said a solemn voice.

A bearer brought their order—beer for Bodhi, Royal Challenge for Chhotomama, and fish fingers—and placed it on the small round table between them. The patio was full, but when a young man wearing a leopard skin hat and knee-high boots asked for the extra chairs at their table, Chhotomama didn't yield. "There are others coming," he snapped.

"This is why I don't like going to clubs," he said to Bodhi. "First, they dictate what I can wear. Then, if there's something going on, it's all fashion shows and Bhangra nights and nonsense, and so many people jostling around that you can't really enjoy yourself. Can't even have a drink in peace. *Chhih*!" Bodhi was afraid that his uncle was going to spit in disgust, but all those years of education must have had some effect because he didn't.

"I'm sorry about this," Bodhi said. By then he had remembered the reason why so many people were at the club. "I didn't realise that they're having Baisakh Bash tonight. Otherwise we would have met someplace else."

"So this is what it's come to. Hah! Now we celebrate the Bengali new year the same way we do the Christian new year?" Chhotomama said as if he had never heard of these types of events before. "With a bash. No traditional songs of harvest, no songs welcoming the new year, no Rabindrasangeet, but a bash! Hah!" Again he didn't spit, but a few tiny bubbles of saliva floated away on their own, refracting cute little rainbows when the light caught them, some to other tables and people, and the remainder on to Bodhi's clothes and into his drink.

~

Bodhi looked around to check whether Neera had arrived. She hadn't and his wandering eyes were drawn toward a navel winking out of the fleshy folds of a dark waist draped in a transparent blue sari. When he looked up, the face didn't match the navel. It was middle-aged and powdered white and its smiling eyes were locked on his. Bodhi's ears turned purple and he swivelled his head back to his uncle's face. Oh god, he thought, I need to fuck someone soon.

This was a thought that Bodhi had been having for over fifteen years. Never had the thought been followed by action. He had had a girlfriend in college, a thin and solemn student in the philosophy department who always wore her long and straight hair in a severe braid. Tight. They used to have deep conversations about the meaning of life and the nature of reality. Bodhi used to read poetry to her, some of it his own output, and she would read out her favourite passages from Hegel. She was quite taken by the idea of thesis and anti-thesis and the circular relationship between them. She would let him hold her hand now and then, but only for a few seconds and only when she was sure no one could see them.

Months of pleading for intimacy from Bodhi had had no effect on her. She heard his appeals like a judge at a hanging, wearing a curiously revolted expression, but never yielded.

Her parents had wanted her to get married, to Bodhi if he was genuinely interested, but really anyone of Bodhi's age and family background would do, but preferably with better job and income prospects. They were afraid (and national statistics would show that they had good reason to be afraid) that their daughter would find it very hard to catch a husband worth catching if she hadn't done it by the time she was twenty five. They had found a suitable match for her in Bangalore with some SAP or JAVA specialist during the months that noncommittal Bodhi was working as a travelling salesman of photocopy and fax machines. There was no sign yet of the entrepreneurial initiative and gurgling cash flow to come.

After college, Bodhi had visited a budget-class brothel in Khidirpur with friends, but hadn't been able to summon the nerve to pay for any of the overweight women in brightly coloured polyester saris he could have afforded at the time. Just looking at the windowless and airless rooms in which the whores did their business suffocated Bodhi. Their indifference to his personhood insulted him. He was sure that he wouldn't like how they smelled even if every one of them had taken the name of a flower—Jui, Shefali, Daisy, Rose. He was afraid that they would take his money and then his pride. He had heard about the tricks these whores would play on inexperienced customers like him, feigning intercourse and making them ejaculate between their capacious thighs. The thought that he could be duped disturbed him greatly. There was something deeply wrong about this. If he was going to go through the shame of paying for sex, the least he would expect was actually to have sex, even for a minute.

Picky dicky, his friends had jeered, wussy pussy.

Bodhi was sure that he wasn't the only thirty-year-old virgin in town. The man sitting across him—Chhotomama—was a permanent bachelor and Bodhi found it hard to imagine him in bed with anyone. Chhotomama in a whorehouse or Chhotomama with a girlfriend! Chhih! Both were ridiculous notions, not simply because Chhotomama was old and sexless now but because he seemed to have been old and sexless from his youth. He was like a mythical creature—like Garuda or Golem—that exists in a single life-stage. It doesn't age and doesn't have a before or after. The idea of Chhotomama with a whore or girlfriend was no less ridiculous than trying to imagine him or Garuda or Golem masturbating or watching porn, both of which Bodhi did as frequently as his busy schedule allowed. His time was late on the nights when he hadn't had too much to drink, and his father had drifted off with his sleeping pill, and the neighbourhood night-guards hadn't started their irritating stick-beating rounds, and the night-dogs were just beginning to howl. That was Bodhi's werewolf time. His joyless jerk offs were as secretive and uncertain as the rest of him.

Once, at a small gathering of friends, someone had asked the question—if you had one superpower to choose, which one would it be? To fly or be invisible? Bodhi was the only who chose invisibility.

That invisible Bodhi was indiscriminate in his search for wantonness. He looked for exposed navels and plump cleavages and painted toes with the expertise of a man who had been doing this for a long time, like a connoisseur of classical art, and further imagined that it would be possible to have transcendental sex, sex with no consequences, with the owners of these navels and cleavages and toes. All these wanton women would want would be sex, not love, and all Bodhi would want would be to reciprocate. The prospect of handling real female flesh, kneading and caressing and licking and biting breasts—it didn't matter whose—or intercourse—in any position—made him swoon with lust. Sometimes he felt that he had reverted to his teenage years, so uncritical was his desire. It didn't matter whether the women were young or not-so-young, tall or short, thin or plump, fair or dark, long-haired or short, in saris or in pants. Big innocent eyes were nice, but hooded come-hither eyes were just as good. Sharp nose, flat nose, small or hooked nose, none of that mattered.

With the light switched off
they were all the same
Flesh upon flesh
from rundi to grand dame

The buzz in the city was that wanton women were everywhere. Categories didn't matter. They came from the ranks of the married and the unmarried, the divorced and the widowed, the fertile and the childless, housewives and their house-servants, and society ladies and society's dregs and everyone in between. All one needed to do to get between their legs, he heard, was to ask. It wasn't even necessary to ask politely. Neither was it useful to take rejection seriously.

All the rules of sex had changed, his friends told Bodhi, Satisavitris were out, Munnisheilas were in. The black-and-white distinctions between heroine and vamp in the black-and-white era were gone. Good and bad were passé, as old-fashioned as typewriters and Keo Karpin. Heroine was vamp now, vamp was heroine. Women contained multitudes. Dance, dance, dance, dance, dance, dance, dance.

But Bodhi didn't ask. He was too Bodhi, too goggly and gangly. They would say yes to everyone else, but no to him. They would laugh at him. Or rub their thighs and make him come. They would point their fingers at him, waggle their thin long red nails, and cackle with glee, like witches at a haunting. *Hee hee hee hee.*

He had convinced himself that his failure to ask was not because he lacked courage but because he wanted to be faithful to Neera. Because he believed in love. Cookie took great joy in pointing out that this may have been an adequate defence for the last few months that he had known Neera, but quite unacceptable for the eight years after college that he hadn't known her. "The fact is, baiju bawra," Cookie said, "you know nothing about women. You can't learn how to swim without getting in the water." But how could he, Bodhi protested, if he was never allowed to get close enough to learn? How could he, if every time he looked at a swimming pool, the water evaporated in an instant, or if he jumped in, the water turned out to be a mirage, and he ended up flat on his ass? It wasn't his fault that he didn't understand women; they refused to be understood by him. He was like a student who avoided a teacher—initially because he hadn't done some assignment, and after that because he had avoided the teacher when he hadn't done his assignment. Cumulative causation. A spiral of decline. One failure leading to another and another. Nothing succeeds like success, and nothing fails like failure.

All this fear of rejection had created an even bigger fear. Now, Bodhi wasn't sure whether his penis would be up to the job when the time came. He was afraid that penises come with expiry dates—*Use By Thirty or Discard With Contents in Commode.*

Would Neera be impressed by his virginity? Would she see it as a prize and therefore be more inclined to capture it for herself if somehow Bodhi found a way of letting her know without embarrassing himself? Probably not. She would probably laugh at him, exactly like the wanton women of his imagination would laugh at him if he ever dared to want sex from them. Waves of jealousy and anxiety submerged Bodhi when he had visions of Neera's sex life. She must have had lovers. Possibly, several of them. Maybe she had one even now. There was that special friend in America, and didn't everyone know about the sexual predation of Americans, even second-hand ones. No, Neera couldn't possibly be a virgin. He didn't know for certain that she wasn't, but he was sure that she didn't radiate an aura of virginity, whatever that aura was supposed to be. So here she was, sexually experienced yet single and very likely expecting lovemaking of superior quality from whomever she chose to favour. With feathers and leathers and mirrors and oils. *Whoo!* Bodhi's head spun. He felt as inadequate as a lion-tamer's apprentice on his first day of training.

# 4

Cookie arrived with the pomp and show of a prince visiting his subjects. Between the time he stepped on the patio till the time he reached Bodhi's table, Cookie shook hands with, high-fived, back-slapped, and/or embraced at least six people, not one of whom was known to Bodhi. Chhotomama, to his embarrassment, also received a hug.

"So, Chhotomama," he said, "shall we try to get some work done now, before it gets too loud? What did you want to talk about?"

Chhotomama arranged his sad, scowling face into a serious, earnest one. After the muscles had settled into their new alignments he leaned forward. He placed his elbows on the table and cupped his palms ten inches apart, holding his thoughts like a goalie preparing for a dropkick. "Let me ask you this. How's your business doing? Are things going well?"

This was unexpected. Chhotomama didn't approve of their line of work and this curiosity about their professional well-being was odd. Surely he wasn't making small talk.

"Not too bad," Cookie said. "There are ups and downs."

"Hmmm...," Chhotomama's furrowed eyebrows wanted to know more.

"To tell you the truth, it's been a little down lately," Bodhi said. "There's a lot of competition. More every day, it seems like."

"It's not a high skill job. You must expect competition." Ah, this was more familiar, this crinkled-nose disapproval.

Cookie grinned. Bodhi grimaced. Both knew Chhotomama's views on these things and prepared themselves for a lecture on their, especially Bodhi's, failings. The working assumption about Bodhi in his teens had been that he would become a teacher, like his father and numerous other relatives. Perhaps, a college professor. He would write obscure texts and be discreetly well-regarded. He had disappointed everyone, first by failing to get a master's degree and then by failing to become a teacher. He had compounded those disappointments by becoming a promoter.

"You boys could have tried other things," Chhotomama said. "There are so many careers possible these days. In computers, in media... We had none of these opportunities when we were your age."

Bodhi thought about telling the truth: that his father's and Chhotomama's generation claimed to be morally superior to his and Cookie's, more ethical and more upright, but in reality were uptight and judgmental hypocrites; that he and Cookie and their like were made out to be greedy corrupt leeches compared to the high-minded older bunch that had driven the city to its knees and every job out of it. He could have said that Chhotomama's generation never understood anything beyond how to get in other people's way and stop things, that it never understood money and made a fetish of poverty, that it was as greedy for power as it accused others of being greedy for money, and that it was wrong about everything that mattered, especially money, which mattered most of all. But they were in a public place, a civil setting, so circumspect Bodhi, who avoided conflict if he could, didn't say any of the true words of their world as he saw it.

Instead, he said mildly, "The housing business is a career too, Chhotomama. There are many people making a living from it."

Chhotomama was used to having the last word on most subjects. "Not as much as promoters like you," he said.

"I don't think you're being fair, Chhotomama." Bodhi couldn't hold himself back any longer. For years he had mentally rehearsed a rousing but rational speech to counter his family's disapproval of what he did for a living, but had never been able to deliver it. Most of the time he was outnumbered, and when he did find one-on-one or two-on-one situations when he could hope to get a few sentences in without interruption from his garrulous and opinionated relatives, his stomach turned queasy with apprehension. Bodhi knew that if the recipient of his speech brought up the subject of how he began his career as a promoter, he would be stumped.

Every great warrior has some fatal weakness. Bodhi had two problems. Not only was he not a great warrior, but everyone in his family knew his weakness. Any one of them could shut him up with one word.

~

But that night was different. Chhotomama looked a little smaller than usual and a little more defensive.

Plus, there was the booming support of Cookie. To him, Chhotomama's words were deeply provocative, like a chest-baring challenge to a filmy hero.

"I have to butt in, Chhotomama," Cookie said, "but this is a big industry. There are many more people than just us promoters. We may be making a bit of money, but that's because we're taking the biggest risks. Think of how many people are making a good living from this business. Just for starters, there are all the people directly connected to the construction side of things—us and the architects and interior designers and landscapers."

Chhotomama made a face like a Kathakali mask on hearing 'landscapers' but before he could interject Bodhi jumped in. "Then there are the local goons who supply sand and stone chips. They'd be ganja-addicted burglars without this work. There are all the services a house needs; carpenters, painters, cable TV operators, plumbers, electricians. Plus servants. New houses need new servants. So your beloved working class is taken care of. And don't forget the Party. Your Party makes money from every sale, every piece of land that changes hands. The bigger the project the better it is for the Party. Your people couldn't run an election without this business. Have you thought about your precious Party, what they would do without this bonanza?" Bodhi ended with a flourish.

Chhotomama was stunned by his volubility and aggression. Normally, he would be the one giving the speech and Bodhi the submissive listener. The hair on his cheeks straightened with tension, like streamers stuck to a blowing fan. But just as he opened his mouth to say something,

Cookie spoke up. "And the banks. Remember the banks. They plead with people to get them to borrow. You've seen the slogans—*Don't think twice*! *What are you waiting for*! They call you on your mobile. They show up at your door. Surely the banks are not in the business of losing money."

Like Ali Akbar and Ravi Shankar in jugalbandi, the promoters pressed on toward a climactic jhala. Bodhi said: "And who's moving into these new flats? Mostly young families desperate to get out of joint families. Hardly your capitalist imperialist class. So, Chhotomama, it's not just me. It's not just us. It's everyone."

There was a silence as wide as the Brahmaputra in September.

"That may be," Chhotomama finally found his voice, "but you can't deny that every building you make results in the destruction of at least one old one."

"Yes," Bodhi said, by now fully energised by Cookie's magnificent resistance, "and you have seen what's being destroyed, right? By the way, just because I'm using your word—destroyed—it doesn't mean I agree with it. You know what I mean. Improved is a much better word. All those old buildings...they're all rubbish. The ugliest things on earth."

"Heaps of cow dung," Cookie elaborated.

"With warts and moles and hair growing out of them," Bodhi explained further.

"I'm not so sure, Bodhi," Chhotomama shook his head dubiously.

"Our work is fine, Chhotomama. In fact, it's important. It's necessary. I know why you're upset. You're simply not comfortable with all the changes that are happening. You and Baba and your generation. You all think alike."

~

The basic arguments were well-established, so they didn't need to fight over fundamentals. According to Chhotomama, their city and society and country had gone mad. Everything was for sale. Parks and ponds and wetlands were for sale. Sidewalks and underpasses of bridges and flyovers were for sale. Roofs were on sale for mobile phone towers. Gardens were on sale for advertising banners. Decades old structures were being demolished to make way for shopping malls and apartment buildings. Layers of history and art that were inscribed in these structures were being peeled off. The city was losing its character, its history, its communities and networks, the basis for its sustainability. The middle-class was being pushed out of the city and the moneyed class was taking over. And promoters like Bodhi were the primary agents of this horrible change.

Bodhi and Cookie had a very different perspective. The city badly needed a facelift, they said, this ancient junk had to go. The city had been so poor for so long that for decades nothing had changed. Few new structures were built. The old ones weren't maintained. Wherever one looked, one saw run-down old buildings with crumbling roofs and faded paint and chipped walls covered with political graffiti fading and spreading like tattoos on retired sailors. Replacing these eyesores with modern new structures wasn't a bad thing at all. The people who were selling their old houses either couldn't afford to maintain their properties, or had had them subdivided into tiny cubicles between feuding brothers and uncles and nephews, none of whom had sufficient living space, or had renters who paid fifty-year-old rates, less per month than it cost a family to see a movie at a multiplex, or being non-residents simply didn't care. And, by selling, the landowners made a lot of money. More than they had dreamed of. More than they deserved. Everyone was happy. The sellers were happy. The buyers were happy. The middlemen were happy. If this wasn't progress, what was? Promoters like them were the primary agents of progress in the city.

"This is a frenzy, boys," Chhotomama said in a softer tone, "and in every frenzy, major mistakes are made. These mistakes can't be corrected later. Once you destroy a hundred-year-old building, it's gone. It's impossible to bring it back." Did Chhotomama mean frenzy or revolution? The effects sounded the same to Bodhi.

"Sure, maybe there'll be mistakes, Chhotomama," Cookie said. "But there are mistakes in everything we do. You have to look at the net result."

"Yes. The rich get richer and the poor become angrier." Chhotomama said this more in sadness than anger. He had a tendency to see class conflict in everything. He was also impatient for the peasants to get their act together and organise a revolution before he died so that he could have the satisfaction of saying *I told you so* to the increasingly smug faces that told him he was irrelevant and obsolete and had been so for his entire life.

Bodhi leaned back in his seat, a little flushed, inwardly jubilant that he had finally managed to make his speech, at least part of it, but disappointed that he had missed a couple of important points, including an especially spiteful one on land grabbing by the Party. Had he known that he would get a podium that day, he would have brought notes.

He didn't want to quarrel with Chhotomama and had no intention of getting into an argument. He liked and respected his uncle. He had been a mentor on many matters. He had introduced Bodhi to some of the finest things from cultures around the world—poetry, music, films—very cultivated things that Bodhi didn't have time for now. The most time he could manage now was to think about what he no longer had time for, and that didn't happen frequently either. But when it did Bodhi felt sad. *Those were the days my friend*. Someday, he told himself, he would become rich enough to not worry about becoming rich and would go back to the things he used to like when he wasn't rich. He would go back to doing things he was forgetting how to do—(a) read books, (b) write poetry, (c) play bridge, (d) take afternoon naps, (e) take aimless walks, (f) waste time.

Lately, Bodhi and Chhotomama hadn't been able to have a conversation that didn't turn high-pitched. Their conversations teetered between Bodhi's growing bank balance and Chhotomama's eternal infallibility. They disagreed on America and China, Rabindrasangeet and Ratan Tata, trams and rickshaws; whether to call Bombay, Mumbai and Madras, Chennai. And what to call their city.

"Boys, let's not argue," Chhotomama said. "Let's start over."

"If you wish. You're the one who wanted to meet... apparently to listen to your lectures again." Bodhi was gruff.

"Let it go, Bodhi," Cookie said, in an uncharacteristic display of moderation. "You've made your point."

"Actually, I called you to get some advice and help," Chhotomama said. "Lecturing is an old habit, what can I do? Though, I must say, today I was at the receiving end, no?"

Bodhi managed a wan smile.

"Tell me, what do you know about architectural preservation?" Chhotomama said.

Cookie and Bodhi looked at each other. "Almost nothing," Cookie said. "But why..."

"What's the setup? Who are the preservationists? Are there any? Is the government helpful?"

"We don't know Chhotomama, we really don't." Cookie again. "You know we're not in the preservation business. Quite the opposite. Ha ha. But Bodhi can find out. He's the artistic one between us. A very refined Bengali. Ha ha."

"Can you do it soon?"

"Maybe...I don't know," Bodhi said. "But what's this about? You're being quite mysterious. What do you have to do with preservation? Is this for some research project?"

"No, no. It's more complicated than that. You probably know that I'm retiring in a few months." Bodhi nodded. "We've just appointed the man who'll replace me as the Institute's director. He's going to be here tonight. His name is Bankoli. He is from the Sunderban forest area. Studies the settlement of the dozens of small islands in the Bay of Bengal. He seems to be a capable fellow. But I don't know much about him. That's why I called you here. I want the two of you to meet him."

Would Chhotomama never stop talking in riddles?

"I'm hoping that all of us can work together," Chhotomama continued.

"On what?" Bodhi said. "I'm afraid I still don't understand."

"Yes." Chhotomama hesitated. "I'm telling you this confidentially, but pretty soon people will know. It's about the Institute. We're moving out of Raniganj Mansion."

"Oh." This was a surprise.

"Yes. It's been brewing for a while now. We've been trying for years to get more space for the Institute. I don't need to tell you how cramped we're at Raniganj Mansion. You've seen how we operate. More than half the space is taken up by books and journals and supplies and things. Very little is left for the staff. The junior scholars don't even have space for bookshelves in their offices. So, I thought this would be my last big project as director, getting more space I mean, or that's what I thought when I started making the rounds and begging powerful people. It's taken me three years of pleading with ministers and bureaucrats. Every time I came close, either the secretary would be transferred to Delhi or the minister would be moved to a new portfolio. It's been frustrating." Chhotomama paused to sip his whisky. "You must have seen the new building coming up on the bypass. It's going to be...what are they calling it...The World Trade Centre. It's opposite the Windsor Castle complex."

The promoters nodded. They knew precisely which building Chhotomama meant. It was their job to know these things.

"The government has given us a whole floor in that building. More than double the square feet we have now. The entire institute will move there. The building is almost complete so it'll probably happen soon, maybe in a few months."

"Wow," Bodhi whistled. "That's a big change. I can't imagine the Institute anywhere but in Raniganj Mansion."

"Me neither," Chhotomama said and looked up at the ceiling. "What did Tagore say? *I want what I should not want; what I get, I do not want*. The old man was quite perceptive. You know, when I was younger I used to think that all this Tagore worship was nonsense, just a lot of nose-scraping at the altar of..."

"So what'll happen to Raniganj Mansion?" Cookie interrupted, trying to contain the rising tide of Chhotomama's musings before it immersed the island of possibility that had peeped out. Bodhi and Cookie were curious and excited. Both smelled a big business opportunity.

"That's why I wanted to talk to you. I want to keep Raniganj Mansion the way it is." This was the last thing they wanted to hear. But Chhotomama was always going to be Chhotomama. "My goal is to preserve the building, keep it as a memorial of the best of early twentieth century Indo-British architecture. The way things are going, it may turn out to be the only surviving example. Nothing seems to be safe from you promoters."

Chhotomama sighed. He was a historian of nineteenth century Bengal and had written two books on the popular culture of the period. *Songs of the Boatmen: The Language of Love and Revolution in Colonial Bengal* and *The Petit Poets: An Anthology of the Literature of the Ganges Traders*. Both books had received positive reviews in prominent scholarly journals. 'Exhaustingly detailed' wrote one reviewer about his first book. 'Densely argued by a historian's historian,' concluded a reviewer of his second book. Chhotomama's knowledge of the language of that period was believed to be unmatched. His collection of mid-nineteenth century vulgarities was reputed to be the envy of linguists and philologists from far and wide.

"Who owns the building?" Cookie asked the most basic question before Chhotomama could launch into a detailed exposition on the fine points of Indo-British architecture. "Doesn't the Institute own it?"

"It's complicated. We're still trying to figure it out. It was a gift, that much we know, a bequest of some sort. But the Institute may not be the owner. I'll know for sure by next week."

"That's prime land Chhotomama," Cookie said. "How much is it? 30 *kathas*? 35? It must be more than half an acre. And that location. Well, well, well. There's going to be quite a scramble for it if it's on the market. And we'll be first in line." Cookie grinned at Bodhi.

"That's exactly why I need you. I want Raniganj Mansion to be preserved and I need you to help me do it. Who better than a friendly fox to guard the chicken coop?" Chhotomama said seriously.

They didn't question this idea. Why they? Why not someone else from among the innumerable people

Chhotomama knew in the Party and the state bureaucracy whose job it was to do exactly this sort of thing, who claimed to be ideologically aligned with exactly this kind of goal? Was it because Bodhi and Cookie were known to be foxes whereas the others would pretend to be chickens or the guardians of chickens but in reality were foxes too? Was it because everyone was a fox? Some like Bodhi and Cookie were openly so while others wore chicken masks to hide their basic foxiness.

Bodhi and Cookie agreed to do what they could. They couldn't have refused to his face because that would have been impolite, but in hindsight this was the moment for Bodhi to have stepped aside. He didn't know it yet, but after this evening his fate and the fate of Raniganj Mansion would become intimately intertwined, like a yogi's legs during a combination Utkatasana-Garurasana, and would, in a matter of days, lead him to jail. This was when he could have said, "No Chhotomama, I don't think I can do it because I have a conflict of interest. It'll be hard for me to be a friendly fox because I want that chicken as much as anyone else. In fact, that's exactly the kind of chicken I like most of all. Fat and juicy. It looks like chicken I've never had and heaven knows we all love the birds we've never had."

But Bodhi didn't say anything then because he wasn't thinking about the temptations of Raniganj Mansion. After Cookie and he had had their magnificent debating triumph over Chhotomama, Bodhi's attention had begun drifting. He had been listening to Chhotomama but not paying as much attention as he should have. There was a much bigger temptation on his mind. All he could think then was—*Neera, Neera, Neera,* this means I can spend more time with her. I don't have to make excuses, I don't have to manufacture reasons, I can see her wherever I want.

# 5

Chhotomama wanted to say more, discuss details, but couldn't because the rest of his group arrived at this point.

"Let me introduce you," Chhotomama took care of the formalities without getting out of his chair. He had consumed two large pegs already and didn't want to test his legs. "This is Bodhichitto Banerjee, my nephew." He swivelled his head in Bodhi's direction. "Cookie Singh, my nephew's business partner. He does a have a more proper name, but you have to ask him for it. My old grey cells have misplaced it. Ho ho." Cookie smiled, but didn't provide his name. "Dr Bankoli, my colleague at the Institute." He directed an expansive wave toward a stout, dark man in a grey safari suit, about fifty, with thick brushed-back greying hair and a French-cut beard. "And all of you know Neera, of course."

Bodhi tried not to goggle. Of course, he knew what Neera looked like, but every new sighting was a jolt and raised his pulse as if he had run a hundred-metre dash. She was tall and pale with a long, flat face under a mass of unruly, curly hair that didn't quite reach her shoulders. It was her most striking feature, most likely because these weren't natural curls. One expected silken straight hair to go with that face that had a pointed chin, a small nose, big

Buddha ears, and thin eyebrows above light brown eyes that slanted down toward her big ears—not enough to make her look Chinese but enough for a stranger to guess that she had family roots in the hills of the Northeast, maybe Assam or Meghalaya, maybe even Nepal or Burma. She was a hill-person among plains-people. She never wore much make-up other than a line of kajal and a touch of lipstick, and always wore spectacular earrings of absurd shapes and sizes, sometimes several at the same time in the many punctures in her big ears. Bodhi had never seen her wear a bindi. She almost always wore a sari to work and almost always wore something else—salwar-kameez or skirt-blouse or shirt-pant—outside work.

Neera had opted for a Benazir Bhutto look that night. She wore a white churidar under a long black kameez, both with many folds and creases, and a silvery muslin scarf wrapped once around her head and draped back over her shoulders. Rebellious tendrils of her permed hair had escaped from the gauzy enclosure. Neera was patting them back with long fingers tipped with black nail polish. She gave Bodhi a quick sideways smile. His gall bladder shifted uneasily, as it always did when she smiled at him, as it had done the first time he had seen her.

For Bodhi, it had been love at first sight.

That was about five months ago. He had gone to Chhotomama's office to drop off a packet from his father. The packet had some family photos and a couple of books Baba had unearthed for his brother-in-law from a footpath vendor in Golpark. Bodhi had stopped to light a cigarette when he saw this vision of a frizzy-haired mop-top in a pale blue sari stride toward the gate of Raniganj Mansion. He couldn't see her face from that distance, but there was something about the combination of that pale blue sari and that stride—flatfooted but jaunty, bold but unsure—that made his heart do a cartwheel.

This wasn't the first time Bodhi had fallen in love with a stranger. He had done it several times. It was, in fact, his only method of falling in love. The philosophy student who had been his girlfriend in college was no exception. He had fallen in love with her while standing in line to pay tuition at the college registrar's office. Later, after she had married someone else, Bodhi had concluded that he had never really been in love with her. It was time-pass, not true-love. But that was revisionist history, convenient for the revising historian.

Bodhi had fallen in love in buses (when he still used to ride buses) and airport lounges and from the insides of taxis. Once he had fallen in love from a rooftop under construction by Heavenly Homes Ltd. with a woman on a rickshaw a hundred feet away. On a couple of occasions he had puffed out his chest and contrived a dashing smile and followed these lovable strangers for a few minutes till he felt weird and concerned that he would be caught as an eve-teaser (or worse) and publicly humiliated. Love at first sight was a safe method of falling in love as long as there was no second sight.

But that day when he went into Chhotomama's office to deliver the books, Neera was already in the room. They were introduced. She looked concerned when he tripped over a chair-leg reaching out to shake her hand. Most women would have laughed out loud, or, at best, tried to smother the laughter with a palm (Bodhi knew this from experience), but not Neera. She had been concerned. Sweetly and enchantingly concerned. Genuinely and endearingly concerned. Bodhi had walked out of Raniganj Mansion a changed man, with a bounce in his step and a song on his lips. He had found an excuse to come again the next day (more books for Chhotomama), and then another excuse to come yet again (wrong books last time). The third time they met they had an impromptu lunch (carefully plotted and timed by Bodhi) at a Madrasi joint around the corner from Raniganj Mansion. Bodhi was so nervous that he couldn't generate enough saliva to masticate his crunchy dosa. Most of it lay forlornly on his plate, like a lonely housewife taking an afternoon nap. That day they talked mostly about gender issues and the status of women in society and a little bit about Aamir Khan.

Neera started mentioning her special friend in America during their fifth meeting, between the hot and sour soup and vegetable manchurian. It was too late to stop by then. Bodhi was too far gone.

Now, five months later, Neera was almost as much a mystery as she had been on that first day. Sure, Bodhi knew things about her that he hadn't known then, but even those details added to the enigma. She was close to his age, almost thirty. This he had calculated from the date of her school graduation which she had let drop in a casual conversation about having seen *Dilwale Dulhaniya Le Jayenge* after her higher secondary exams. Unless she had failed a class or received a double-promotion she would be thirty sometime next year. She was not married and had never been married. Bodhi wasn't one hundred per cent certain of this, but assumed it since she never mentioned a husband or ex-husband. He knew that married women mention their husbands as soon as possible to strangers and divorcees mention their ex-husbands even more often to friends. Bodhi was a stranger at first and now a friend, if not more, and one way or another he expected to have heard something if there was something to hear. He had been told that she came from a broken home, or as Neera put it, 'a progressive family.' She lived with her father. Her mother was married to some other man and lived in some other state. Bodhi didn't know much more and was hesitant to probe. Who knew what would emerge?

Neera loved animals. She had two beagles named Pomo and Poco. Poco was eleven and Pomo eight. She was kind. She was earnest. She was generous, far more so than Bodhi, who was stingy both with money and words of appreciation for others. She was moody. She would switch her face off every now and then, rarely for a reason Bodhi understood. She could take on a little-girl persona and giggle like a feather-brain about inane things. She could look through people. She could command people with her eyes. She always spoke slowly in a low voice. Sometimes it was hard to hear her. These things Bodhi knew.

He also knew that she came from a lot of money. Neera had spent time abroad, in Europe and America, but Bodhi couldn't tell for how long. Maybe months, maybe years. She had certainly studied abroad. Not for a full-fledged degree (because he knew she had graduated from Loreto College in the city) but some sort of short course in printmaking or music appreciation or something like that. Every now and then she would express a wish to study more, get a master's degree in something, she wasn't sure what, maybe women's studies, maybe art history. Her special friend in America had been strongly encouraging this line of thinking. The bastard.

She had a car and driver at her disposal at all times. She came to office in it, a black Toyota Camry with leather seats and eight speakers, and it stayed with her all day. Her salary couldn't be much higher than the cost to maintain this luxury. Obviously, she didn't pay for this. Her father, who was in the advertising business, did. Bodhi didn't know how rich her father was, but from all the circumstantial evidence he had been gathering, it seemed as if Neera's father was richer than anyone Bodhi knew or had known personally. He didn't belong to the industrialist class. He didn't have houses on three continents or a private plane. Those people didn't live in this city. But he did seem to be part of the upper echelon of the city's trader/entrepreneur class and appeared to be quite a bit richer than Cookie's father, who owned twelve AC rocket buses and was the richest person Bodhi had known up to that point.

Neera was indifferent to money. It was like a ring she had worn on a finger many years ago, that was always with her, on her body, visible to anyone who cared to pay attention, but whose presence she was never conscious of. She didn't know the price of anything. Bodhi made it a point to know the price of everything, remember those prices, compare them when comparative situations presented themselves, and make judgments of value based on price. He couldn't imagine a life in which price didn't matter. He was finding it very hard to get inside a mind in which price didn't matter.

Bodhi had never known anyone like Neera. She was like a foreign country to him. At a basic level everything was familiar—foreign lands had roads and houses too—but at another level nothing was—their traffic drove on the right, their houses had sloping roofs with tiles, their women wore hats, their squirrels were black. It was bad enough that Bodhi found Neera impenetrable, what made it worse was his constant longing to be with her impenetrability, baffled all the while by her ambiguities; he was confused, insecure, a bungling wreck. All Bodhi knew was that he wanted Neera. He didn't understand why, he didn't understand her, but want he did. Understanding would come later, he told himself. Like the Tata Sumo he had learnt to drive after buying, understanding could come after he got what he wanted. It had to, otherwise why would he want her so much?

~

Dr Bankoli was oblivious to the quivering tension between Bodhi and Neera. "Delighted to meet you Mr Banerjee," he said in a loud, cheery voice. "We have a lot to discuss as your uncle must have told you."

The solemnity of Bankoli's French-cut beard was tainted by the appearance of uneven, oversized teeth when he spoke. In silence he looked like a colourised version of the stern but fair-and-loving patriarchs in black and white films from the sixties. A pipe and a dressing gown would have completed the picture. The benevolent dictator of everyone's dreams, whose decisions were always good because they were based on a judicious consideration of every interest except his own. But when he spoke he was transformed into a more shadowy character; not overtly villainous but faintly malevolent, someone who lusted after teenage nieces, for instance, or embezzled little sums at work over many years.

Cookie mouthed the words 'Party member' to Bodhi with a slight cock of his head to signal resignation. Bodhi blinked his eyes in assent. There was no doubt that Bankoli, like Chhotomama, was a member of the Communist Party. Otherwise, he couldn't be in line to succeed Chhotomama as director of the Institute. The Party didn't like to share power, even at a microscopic level. Bodhi couldn't tell much else about Bankoli because whether he was a member of the Party or not didn't say much about the person. The Party was like air and mud, an entity so abundant in their ecological niche that membership in it indicated nothing at all.

Cookie had theories on a wide range of subjects, from sociology to international relations. He argued, for instance, that it was better to vote for a criminal for parliament, who'd fight, on your behalf, the other criminals already in parliament, than a social worker with impeccable ethical credentials; he calculated that 1 beef-eater = 3 fish-eaters = 5 wheat-eaters = 10 rice-eaters, and its corollary theorem, 1 Christian = 3 Muslims = 10 Hindus = 100 Sikhs on the scale of the history of murder; and he insisted that there was something in the water of Bengal that gave every single

Bengali man amoebic dysentery and/or a love for leftist politics. Of course, not everyone was afflicted by both conditions. One could be a leftist without having amoebic dysentery and one could have amoebic dysentery without being a leftist, but it was impossible to find a man who suffered from neither condition.

"Why, khote sikkey, why?" Cookie had asked Bodhi many times, usually after a third peg. "Why does this only happen here and nowhere else?"

Cookie felt he could demand an answer because Bodhi was a leftist too. He had to be. He didn't have amoebic dysentery—not yet—therefore by Cookie's theorem, he had no choice. It would have been hard for him not to be a leftist. All the men in his family leaned left. Some leaned so far that they had toppled over and become members of the Party. Chhotomama wasn't the only one; there was another uncle (from Bodhi's father's side) and a first cousin (from his mother's side). Bodhi too had been tempted to sign up in college and had even participated in a couple of rallies organised by one of the several student communist parties. One was against ragging in the college hostels and the other against American adventurism in the Middle East. But he never joined the Party. He was not a joiner. He wanted to be invited where he didn't belong but he wouldn't join what he could, where he would be welcomed.

Bodhi preferred not to think about the contradiction between his political belief and his professional life as a promoter. He was afraid to acknowledge the contradiction because it would leave him vulnerable to Chhotomama and his father and their unending lectures on the contradictions and dialectics and inevitable crisis of capitalism. But of course they knew. They had seen the boy and now they saw the man. "You're just muddled, Bodhi," Chhotomama liked to set the record straight. "You think you can be on both sides at the same time, but you can't. Nobody can." Bodhi would look away. He didn't say, though he could have had he thought about it, that everyone was muddled. It was the curse of the middle-class—the muddle class—that it wanted irreconcilable opposites, to be wealthy and ethical, to be powerful and just. Equity and efficiency, truth and harmony.

Bodhi would try to defend his Bengali brethren and try to answer Cookie. "Because it's heavy, man," he would say, "because of the exploitations and injustices of the past." Or—"Because of the education, man, because we're a cultured people, and cultured people are sensitive people who always feel empathy for the BPL people." But never could he identify what was special about Bengal that this ingrained love of leftism happened only here and nowhere else. Unlike every other place on earth—not just India, but the whole globe—Bengal chose—willingly—to be ruled by communists for over three decades. They didn't have to be beaten or jailed or oppressed. It wasn't a police state. There was no Stalin to banish them to Gulags, no Mao to send them for re-education to the villages. They elected to. There had to be something in the water.

Bodhi had heard somewhere that Eskimos had a hundred words for snow and that Americans had over two hundred forms of Christianity. It made sense to him, for the same reason that it made sense that Bengal had dozens of leftist political parties. It was a product in demand and therefore widely available in a range of choices. The local market for leftism offered many brands.

An outsider usually found it hard to distinguish between all the brands—the plain Marxists from the Marxist-Leninists or the plain Maoists from the Maoist-Marxists or the Stalinist-Maoists, and all of them from the Opposition party that didn't have Mao or Marx or Lenin in its name but behaved as if it did. It was possible that the people who had joined one group instead of another understood the differences. Were they for peasants or factory workers? Or both? Did they specialise in tribal rights or resistance to global capital? Did they prefer cultured civil disobedience with singing and dancing or violent revolutions with guns and bombs? Swadesi guns or imported ones? Did they support East Bengal or Mohun Bagan? Did they approve of women wearing pants? Did they support teaching English in primary school? Which books would they like to ban? What were their feelings about Trotsky? What about Gorbachev? Was Deng Xiaoping a deep revolutionary or a reactionary renegade? Was Stalin a monster or hero that had had been slandered by American imperialists and their bourgeois stooges?

Chhotomama was a doctrinaire Marxist. He could quote passages from the 18th Brumaire of Louis Bonaparte from memory, and given an opening, often did. His intellectual positions had evolved over time, and now, following an established tradition in Indian philosophy, were defined by what he didn't like. *Neti, neti, not this, not this*. He was anti-religion, anti-sexist, anti-imperialist, anti-revisionist, anti-globalisation, anti-liberalisation, anti-market, anti-Congress, and anti-BJP.

On the other hand, one of Bodhi's most reliable informants on properties that could be persuaded to come on the market was one Bablu Das, a mahogany-muscled brute who wore two gold chains round his neck, eight rings on his ten fingers, each topped with a magic stone designed to ward off a specific hazard, and an inch-wide hibiscus-red tilak on his forehead as a mark of his devotion to Ma Kali. Bablu Das was a Party worker and appeared to be as devoted to it as he was to the goddess.

Bankoli had shown up in a safari suit, so he wasn't a Party member of the intellectual variety (which would have required him to wear kurta-pajama, like Chhotomama). He wasn't wearing a tilak on his forehead, so he wasn't a Party supporter of the thug variety either. He belonged somewhere between Chhotomama and the informant Bablu Das, this Bodhi was sure of, just as he was sure that time would reveal the exact location.

~

Chhotomama wasn't in favour of further shop talk that evening. These were serious matters, he said, and this atmosphere of frivolity wasn't conducive to the seriousness the issue deserved. Baisakh Bash had ruined his plans. He ordered a refill of Royal Challenge with soda and ice. Bankoli ordered Black Label on the rocks. Bodhi's fingers instinctively reached for his wallet, not to pull it out, but to touch it, to make sure it was still there. These were his guests and all this would be billed to his account. He had the money, of course, but wasn't used to it yet, even after six years of plenty, and frequently forgot that he had the money and had panic attacks about losing what he did have.

On stage, a beauty contest had begun. A dozen girls were competing for the title of Miss Baisakhi. Chhotomama and Bankoli preferred to talk about the show, its hermeneutics and semiotics, words they were familiar with, rather than watch it. They stayed in their seats on the patio. Cookie wandered off to high-five the friends he had missed on the way in. He probably knew half the people at the club that night. Bodhi could attach names to a few faces, not because he knew them personally but because they were prominent people in the city.

"Let's get closer," Neera said. Bodhi's flash of elation subsided when he realised that she meant the stage.

Neera turned out to be quite knowledgeable about the contestants. They and their families were familiar figures on TV reality shows, she explained, and she watched when she could. She provided a running commentary. Bodhi made a mental note to add one more item to the list of things he didn't understand about Neera.

They stood to a side, leaning against a column of bamboo poles holding up the shamiana. Their shoulders touched and then moved away like paper boats in a bathtub. Bodhi's throat felt like a dry inkwell and he could feel his tongue swelling up and swirling back into it. He prayed that he wouldn't be required to speak but was afraid that Neera was about to provide new information on her special friend and would demand his participation. She had done this before, talked about her special friend at the very moments she had allowed her body to come tantalisingly close to his. She did it once while touching elbows in a movie hall ('he loves art films from the seventies'), and another time at a restaurant, immediately after wiping away a dangling morsel from the corner of his mouth ('what he really misses are kalakands from Mouchak').

Bodhi thought about making a pre-emptive strike. But he couldn't imagine what he would strike with. What would he say? Where would he begin? 'Do you love me?' 'What's going on with your special friend?' 'Do we have a future together?' What if she laughed in his face? Called him a jealous, old-fashioned fool for thinking that just because she had gone to a few restaurants and movies with him didn't mean she loved him, or just because she talked about another man, she loved that man either. Just because she had plucked a bread crumb out of his beard it didn't mean that she was willing to spread her legs for him. And even if she did spread her legs for him (out of pity or curiosity or generosity) it didn't mean that she was ready to trot seven circles around a sacred fire with him. What if she accused him of being so hopelessly middle-class that he couldn't comprehend that men and women could be friends without being lovers? That they could touch each other without sexual intent. That would be the end of the affair. He would know she didn't want him and he could never go out with her again. Better to suffer in ignorance than to suffer with knowledge. Silence and non-aggression were the only strategic options available to Bodhi.

"He's coming on vacation soon," Neera whispered conspiratorially, "maybe as soon as the monsoon starts and the weather gets a little cooler."

Bodhi was startled. His body jerked without his bidding and he tried to cover up his surprise by smacking at a non-existent mosquito.

"What if he asks me to go to America? He says that it won't be too hard to get admission in his university. What should I say?"

Bodhi slapped at another non-existent mosquito.

"He says that there's no scope here for the kind of cutting edge work he does. I have to agree, I must say. I mean, look at the condition of the hospitals here. How can anyone possibly use a polycardiograph, which is what he has to do like twenty four-seven, what with all the load shedding and voltage fluctuation here? And that's just one of the technical things he's specialised in. Some friends of his came back from the States, with good jobs in big hospitals, but they couldn't stick it out. He doesn't think he can either. BB (she had a private name for Bodhi), are you listening?"

"*Unghh*," said Bodhi, trying to visualise the size of a polycardiograph. It sounded bigger than his Tata Sumo.

"Do you think this is unpatriotic? Living abroad forever. I mean one doesn't have to be patriotic in a Bhagat Singh kind of way...with sacrifices and all...you know what I mean. But, he says that with the rupee to dollar rate being what it is, it's more patriotic to earn in dollars and send money back. Improve the nation's foreign exchange reserves and all that. I never thought of that angle before. What do you think, BB?"

"*Grrth,*" said Bodhi, still trying to pull his tongue out of his throat while trying to think cogently about Neera's question. One of the many things about Neera that puzzled Bodhi was why she remained in the city. She belonged to that class whose men and women had almost completely abandoned it. Bodhi wasn't familiar with that class—they didn't attend Benimadhab College with him, nor did they buy flats from him—but was aware of its existence. Many of the women had gone abroad, either as students or wives. Others had left for the more exciting pastures of Bombay or Delhi or Bangalore. Why then was she still here? Just to tempt Bodhi into reaching for something that was beyond his grasp and would forever remain that way? Just to remind him of his limits and teach him a lesson on knowing one's limits? Bodhi intoned some lines from a poet dead for more than a century—

Oh hope, you sorceress
bless your treachery and illusions
that enthral us mortal fools

"I really need to know what you think, BB," Neera said. "I know you want what's best for me?"

The militarised border where their arms and shoulders were touching became a full scale war zone. Tingles of sniper fire were replaced by cluster bombs and bunker busters spreading an untameable inferno. Bodhi was afraid that he might lose his arm for good if he didn't pull away immediately. But he couldn't. He could neither say anything nor move away as the inferno jumped from his arms to his neck and face, the redness spreading like a spit of paan parag on a freshly whitewashed wall.

Fortunately for Bodhi the beauty contest came to an end then, relieving him of the responsibility of saying anything. One of the girls won. Bodhi couldn't tell who it was despite the detailed information provided by Neera. They returned to their table.

Bodhi got another tall beer for himself, his third of the evening, and a second glass of wine for Neera. "Are you trying to get me drunk, BB? Are you planning to take advantage of me?" she teased. They were sitting across each other. The physical distance, the fact that they weren't touching any longer, helped calm Bodhi's nerves. He could speak again. Nothing very intelligent—"I don't think you can get drunk on two glasses of wine" was what he said—but at least they were recognisable words in a known language.

Chhotomama and Bankoli came back after a stroll through the attractions of the club. Cookie had disappeared into more enjoyable company. Bodhi suggested they listen to at least a few songs from the band that had been tuning up earlier. This wasn't just a ruse to spend some more minutes being tortured by Neera. There was a time when Bodhi used to be up to date on musical trends in the city, and tonight, like a phantom limb amputated long ago, those memories had twitched back to life. It was probably an effect of the beer.

The band's name was *Alphabet Curry* and it had a reputation for acute social observation. Four young men in bandanas and jeans and bales of shampooed hair bounded to the stage. The title of their first song was, 'I Can Be the Lover You Want'.

What shall I sing for you my love?
Shall I remember that old tune
with harmonium and sarangi
My lament of lost love
I wasn't good enough for you
It was my fault for loving you
I'll always worship you from a distance
Or shall I sing my new words
with electric guitar and drums
Take me as I am honey
or hit the road
And while you're at it
change
into something more comfortable
Like a tank top
And please lose some weight
Choose your song my love
I can be the lover you want

Neera beamed questioning looks in Bodhi's direction. Bodhi couldn't understand her unspoken questions, or why she had questions, or why he was the one being asked to answer them. "Ask your special friend," one part of him wanted to say, while another part wanted to drag her by her hair and shout, "Stop! Enough of this nonsense you witch! (He couldn't call her bitch, even in his imagination, even when drunk.) You're coming with me and that's the end of it!" He had been drinking steadily through the evening and was feeling lightheaded and dry-lipped and looking to escape before the words inside his head burbled uncontrollably out of his mouth. What he wanted now was a long taxi ride home, by himself (Bankoli and his pretentious French-cut beard had brought Neera here and they could take her home *dammit*), with the windows rolled down and a cool breeze on his face.

"Last round," he said. "Let's leave after this one."

~

Bodhi turned back for a moment at the entrance to the patio and took a last look. *Alphabet Curry* struck the opening notes of *(I Can't Get No) Satisfaction*. The dance floor had been largely empty till then but now began to fill with middle-aged bodies. Everyone knew this song. The night was about to turn into a dance party.

Bodhi knew what he would see if he stayed—an exhibition of what Cookie called the 'dance of the shapeless.' Plump, prosperous bodies wriggling and twisting into positions they had never taken when they had been young. 'Dance of the shapeless' was a distinct form, derived from but independent of the 'dance of the clueless' which could be seen at any gathering of the city's high-net-worth youth. Those were of a different order entirely. Enjoy yaar, Bodhi would hear pimple-faced, gel-haired, jewellery-bedecked, barely-men in chinos and half-buttoned silk shirts yell at each other. Enjoy, enjoy, enjoy, would shriek the bleached and hennaed, fake-tattooed and underarm-shaved and poufy-haired girls above the tremendous din of mechanical music.

Bodhi looked at these people with considerable fascination and not a little repulsion, as if they were aliens popped out of pods. Just in the last decade these pod creatures had descended on the city and, in the way that aliens have, multiplied and taken over its established watering holes and created innumerable new ones for their exclusive use. One night they were at a private club, the next night they were someplace else—a nightclub, a seven star hotel, in Singapore, or someone's country estate. The city had never seen anything like them—youngsters, reeking of money, shamelessly, from their ten-thousand rupee shoes and twenty lakh rupee cars to two thousand rupee haircuts and five thousand rupee sunglasses.

How much money does one have to have and for how long till one reaches this state of obliviousness? When does a person cross over from a state of merely having money to always having had money? Bodhi was convinced that this transition wasn't possible in one generation. Therefore, he himself could never become a pod creature. He was too old already, and thanks to Baba and Chhotomama and the gene pool that had spawned him, irredeemably and immutably middle-class.

His shirts were middle-class, even when they were blue and embroidered with white crossed swords. The blue was invariably the wrong shade and the embroidered swords might as well have been a label that read 'middle-class pretender.' His best pants screamed middle-class; faker, arriviste, aspirational, *jaali*, they said, with the minty-sulphurous smell of new money wafting through the zippers and stitches. His Tata Sumo...the same. Predictable, boring, and the same. His flat—all of its 950 square feet chopped into three bedrooms and two bathrooms and a drawing-cum-dining hall—was the very embodiment of his middleclassness. His class stuck to him like the smell of blood on a butcher. No amount of washing could wring it out.

If he made serious money, if Heavenly Homes Ltd. succeeded far beyond what seemed likely, if such success continued for a couple of decades, it was possible that he would be able to produce pod creatures like these. But did he even want to? Would he have anything to say to a pod creature even if it carried his name? What language would the pod creature speak in? What accent would it use? There were so many to choose from these days. What would irredeemably middle-class father and congenitally pod creature child talk about? What did pod creatures talk about? Did they even have conversations? They looked so physical and active and bursting with good health that Bodhi found it hard to imagine that pod creatures wasted time with conversation. They probably frolicked all the time. And who would he produce the pod creature with, who would provide the other pair of chromosomes? Neera? The mere thought vibrated and warmed remote parts of his body.

During his first hours in jail, it was the memory of this moment that kept coming back to Bodhi, the moment when he was about to leave D. Club and felt completely out of place. The questions that he never allowed himself to ask himself, the questions that he refused to answer for his father, overwhelmed him. Why was he so desperate to get to that place where he didn't belong? Why did he want to be a man whose own children would feel like aliens? What existed in that place and state that attracted him so? As always he had no answer, only a justification. He was no different from everyone around him. All of them, all the men he knew that were old enough to desire and young enough to hope wanted to get to that same place, some knowing full-well, others not, that they wouldn't belong. They couldn't all be wrong, their entire generation, and if they weren't then the impulses that drove them must be natural. It was very ordinary, this desire, as common as frogs croaking and dogs fornicating in August.

It was the doubt that was unwelcome. Bodhi was training his mind to ignore doubt. He was teaching his head to dispel discomfiting questions as soon as they entered. So, that night, by the time Bodhi returned to his flat and threw his tipsy body into bed, he had forgotten all about the disconcerting moment at the club. Over the next few minutes, till sleep seeped up from his toe-tips to his eyelids, he experienced a half hour of pure bliss with his favourite fantasy. It was on par with opening the batting for India, close to winning the Nobel Prize for literature. He was on a world tour with Neera. They flew first class to Paris, eating lobster and caviar all the way. Bodhi had never tasted caviar, he didn't know what it looked like, but he was sure that he would love it if he got a chance. They took a luxury liner to New York and waltzed in a titanic ballroom to *The Blue Danube* performed by a live orchestra. Bodhi had never seen a real person waltz and the real Bodhi would surely trip over his own heel in the first minute if he tried to do it, but the Bodhi of Bodhi's dreams could dance anything. Samba, Cha-Cha, Gangsta. They played volleyball on Copacabana Beach; Neera in a striped bikini, Bodhi in Bermuda shorts, and someone else's, a tennis player's, body. They floated in a hot air balloon over the Grand Canyon, rode a bullet train from Tokyo to Kyoto, and walked hand-in-hand on the steps of the Great Wall near Beijing. They spent the night in Angkor Wat, curled in each other's arms inside the main temple hall, while a heavy rain drenched the dense forest outside and kept the real world and real people far, far away.

# 6

Chhotomama called an emergency meeting of the Save Raniganj Mansion team at eight-thirty at Raniganj Mansion itself. Bodhi arrived a few minutes early, hoping, with no luck, that Neera would do the same. It was Sunday morning and the affluent neighbourhood near Elgin Road, one block removed from the main avenue, looked and sounded languorously awake. Rickshaws rattled by carrying elderly men and their servants on the way to or back from shopping for the big meal of the week. Vendors pushed bamboo carts loaded with vegetables through the side streets and called out their wares: "aalooo...baygooon... jhingaaa." There was a din in an auto mechanic's shop at the end of the street. Bodhi could hear the faltering cough of a malfunctioning muffler and the vulgar whoops of the teenagers working on it. TVs were on in several nearby houses. Snippets of songs in many languages fluttered in the air. They had to compete for attention with the voices of little girls practising their scales...ni ni ga ga re re ma ma.

Raniganj Mansion was enclosed within a boundary wall five feet high. The left side of the wall was plastered with posters advertising services for sex doctors and Bollywood dancers and miracle cures for amoebic dysentery and erectile dysfunction. The posters covered some but not all of a faded red slogan, maybe five years old, that ran the length of this side—*Long Live Chairman Mao! Long Live the Worker's Revolution!* At the centre of the wall was a wrought iron gate eight feet high. To its right were posters selling tutorial services for Higher Secondary and Joint Entrance exams and a Bangla film currently in theatres—*Who Dares Wipe Away My Sindoor!* This side was dominated by a makeshift tea stall, twelve feet by eight, blocking the entire width of the pavement.

The stall was a black tarpaulin sheet held up by Raniganj Mansion's wall at one end and tied with two plastic strings to a telephone junction box and a lamp post at the other. Underneath the tarp a coal-burning oven had been fashioned out of a metal drum. A large aluminium kettle sat on it, blowing steam, partially obscuring a rickety shelf of three racks stacked with big plastic jars of biscuits and sweetmeats. A low narrow bench placed perpendicular to the road provided a seating space for customers. Four men could sit here side-by-side as long as they didn't mind rubbing calves. Two calendars were stuck to the wall with glue. One was a painting of Radha and Krishna on a swing of flowers and twine; Radha was very dark and very thin and looked impossibly young, not even a teenager. The other was a photo of Muscle Beach in California; two tanned blondes with big breasts bursting from orange halter tops were lifting weights.

Bodhi walked over to the tea stall. "Ram, Ram, Pandey," he said. "If the tea is ready I'd like a cup."

"Arrey, Bodhi babu," said Pandey, "so early today?" Chaturanan Pandey was a small, wiry man of about thirty-five, with oily black hair parted in the middle and a strong and straight moustache. He had started this business a dozen years ago with nothing but a kerosene stove to make tea. The tarpaulin cover had been his first big addition. It was also the most important addition because it established his territorial jurisdiction. The shelf came next, followed by the bench. The drum oven had been the final improvement. It was an accepted fact on the street that this space was reserved for Pandey's tea stall. He paid the standard rental rate for such spaces—two thousand rupees a month shared between the local police and goons. Bodhi had been his customer from the very first days.

"What to do," said Bodhi, "you have to go when duty calls."

"Those are some true words, Bodhi babu," said Pandey, "true words indeed. Sit, sit. Your tea will be ready in two minutes."

Chaturanan Pandey, street entrepreneur and improviser, a permanent migrant who visited his village in Chhapra district but once a year, during Chhaat puja in the month of Kartik, with a wife he had married when she was fourteen and he seventeen, with two daughters in high school aiming for careers as government officers, had no idea that morning that his life was about to be turned upside down in a matter of days.

The tea came in a tiny clay cup. Bodhi slurped with satisfaction and stared at Raniganj Mansion in front of him.

~

At the time Raniganj Mansion was built, in the mid 1920s, the houses of prosperous Bengalis followed one of two layout formats, which in turn dictated the overall visual design. One layout could be called traditional, in the sense that the style predated the arrival of the British. Here, the locus of the plan was an inner courtyard and the building itself was a quadrangle around it; it was a gated community of a kind, with an inner private space reserved and secured for the women and children. The other layout was modern, in the sense that it followed the English design principle of a symmetric single alignment. The choice of design wasn't arbitrary. Wealthy Bengalis who worked with but chafed under colonial domination tended to use the traditional layout. It was a symbolic gesture of defiance. Wealthy Bengalis who were more aligned with their colonial masters tended to choose the single symmetric alignment for their houses. Raniganj Mansion was such a building.

It was a long two-storey hybrid structure, whose alignment, façade, proportions, and room sizes were British-inspired, but many of whose details, such as cornices and tiles, which were less visible or invisible from a distance, had distinct Islamic influences. Curlicues and crescent moons and silvery stardust patterns were common motifs, as were decorative interior columns with elaborate mouldings. The façade was white, or had been at some time; decades of indifferent maintenance had resulted in a blotchy grey panoply that was darkest at the walls adjoining the roof, and at the mouldings concealing the structural skeleton between the floors. The windows were large—a full-size mattress could easily be threaded through them—and were covered by thick, red wooden slats; old-fashioned Venetian blinds. There was a portico at the centre of the building. In the language of the time, it had been called a car-veranda. Five wide marble steps led from the portico to a peeling oaken main door with stained glass panels above it.

It was obvious that the building had been modified at different times. At both ends of the long side, which was parallel to the road, one could see remnants of colonnaded verandas. Some of these had been boxed in, obviously to add more usable office space, but the tapered Corinthian columns remained clearly visible. The additions were reasonably harmonious with the aesthetics of the original design. At first glance, the building projected an image of handsome stolidity, like the hero of an action film, laced with a shimmer of decline that was in keeping with the image of the city.

Bodhi knew the layout of Raniganj Mansion as well as he did his own flat. He had been coming here for years, and lately, after becoming a promoter, had begun paying attention to its details. The ground floor of the building was a utilitarian space. The tertiary functions of the Institute were housed here—accounts, supplies, canteen, kitchen—along with the offices of the junior scholars. The upper floor had the more interesting rooms. The Reading Room was the largest in the building. It looked much as it used to when the mansion was new. Next to it was the Rare Documents Room which was a repository of old manuscripts, scrolls, maps, out-of-print books, and artefacts like brochures, pamphlets, and banners. Most of the things in this room were older than Raniganj Mansion itself. It always smelled of a mixture of wet sawdust and dead cockroaches. Chhotomama's office was on this upper floor.

The most distinctive feature of the building was its size. In a city where an eight hundred square foot flat was considered spacious for a household of five (plus one full-time servant), Raniganj Mansion looked positively wasteful. The front third of the property was open. To the left and centre of this open space sat a marble cherub pouting at the sky, its fat, folded bottom resting on a pedestal that flowered into a lotus at ground level. This used to be a fountain at one time, but Bodhi had never seen it spout. The rest of the front yard was divided into a gravelled parking area and a small, overgrown garden. A few sparrows were hopping and pecking on the lawn. A line of bored crows, mercifully silent, were perched on the parapet.

Bodhi had been here many times, but never, as far as he could remember, this early in the day. He had never understood why his uncle was so obsessed with this building—this wasn't new, Chhotomama's passion for it—for Bodhi was increasingly unable to see the house itself because all his attention was focused on the land on which it stood. However, at that unexpectedly contemplative moment, he was reminded that at one time he too had known the reason why a man would go out of his way to protect such a building.

Raniganj Mansion looked like an ageing dancer holding court on a grand stage. She had been dishevelled by time, but the fine lines that had made her a beauty were still visible. Chhotomama could see the beauty of the dancer, her grace and her confidence. He could probably imagine the mujras that must have taken place here, and hear the alluring tinkle of ghungroo and the longing notes of esraj. Chhotomama the communist didn't approve of the atrocious men and the atrocities that had funded the baithaks and mujras, and the bacchanalias and debaucheries that followed. Bloodsucking bastards, he called them. But there was this discomfiting paradox. Without those atrocities it wouldn't have been possible to sustain those higher forms of music and dance. Without the support of moneyed men for the high arts—be they kings or landlords—all art is folk art, Chhotomama said, diverse but unrefined, earthy but raw. There are no unmixed blessings, he said, there are no single-edged saws. Several theorists in the Party had warned him about deviant thought of this sort. "Don't get confused, comrade," they told him, "don't mix up bourgeois cultural production with the structural forces of historical materialism."

Bodhi, the promoter, could only see the stage, the land. He could only think of how much the land had cost then, when Raniganj Mansion had been built, and how much it would sell for now. How many square feet he could build on it and how much he could charge per square foot. He felt shallow and callow for having these crass materialistic thoughts. He felt a moral itch to become a better person. This moral itch used to be a familiar feeling. Tales of courage and sacrifice in uplifting films and books used to be inspirational. Now that the films were all about sluts and thugs and he no longer had the time or patience to read anything other than the newspaper, that feeling was rare. Reality certainly didn't remind him of his moral failings.

Good, better, best. These are all relative terms. Good compared to what? Better than whom? In a village of blind people, a one-eyed man is king. In a society of cannibals, a simple meat-eater is an abstinent. Who were the abstinent one-eyed men today? Men who were that way by choice and temperament and not because they were old or weak and had no option but to accept subjugation? None that Bodhi had seen in public life or among people he knew. His was a society of blind cannibals. Eat or be eaten.

Bodhi knew from experience that this feeling of moral inadequacy was like a rainbow. It was beautifully inspiring, but only for a moment. It wouldn't last.

~

Chhotomama's fears were well-founded. It had been established that the Institute did not own Raniganj Mansion. The property had been a gift in 1945, made for the sole purpose of creating the Bengal International Culture and History Institute. The original benefactor was a man named Prafulla Kumar Roy. He had been dead for decades and no one working at the Institute now had seen him in the flesh. In spirit, however, he was ever present; his oil portrait loomed in the Reading Room dressed in full princely regalia—turban, sword, pearls, gold—sporting a satisfied smile underneath a thick waxed moustache that curved down, then up.

Mr Prafulla Kumar Roy had had a generous spirit, no doubt, but not a carefree one. "You don't become a tycoon without good lawyers," Chhotomama said. True enough, because his gift had come with a stringent condition: Raniganj Mansion *had to* remain the one and only location of the Bengal International Culture and History Institute.

If it ceased to be so, for whatever reason— if the Institute was shut down or divided or renamed or relocated— the building and land it was built upon would revert to Mr Prafulla Kumar Roy's heirs as identified in his final will and testament.

The Save Raniganj Mansion team briefly debated the reasons for this odd condition. "It's as if he didn't want to make the gift at all, but was forced to," said Bodhi. "No, no," said Chhotomama, "it was just a rich man's fancy, his way of telling the world that he could be as arbitrary as he wanted to be, and if you wanted his money, you'd just have to accept his capriciousness. That's how the rich behave. There's no reason for it." Events would soon prove Chhotomama wrong.

Whatever the reason for the odd condition attached to the donation, there was no getting around the steely fact that when the Institute moved to its new location, Raniganj Mansion would go to Mr Roy's heirs.

Who were they? Nobody knew.

Chhotomama talked about having seen the benefactor's son a few times, one Prashanta Kumar Roy, a big burly man with a booming voice and blustery presence. He used to maintain some relationship with the Institute, making well-announced and choreographed visits every two or three years, but he too had been dead for over a decade. After his death there had been no contact at all with the family. The Institute didn't invite the surviving Roys to its special occasions, partly because the present location of the surviving Roys was unknown, but no less because the Institute had no special occasions. It was hard to convince

Chhotomama that any occasion was special and worthy of recognition in a way that made it stand out from every ordinary day. He believed in equality in all dimensions. The surviving Roys, whoever they were, had never felt it necessary to inspect the condition of what once had been their family property.

The first phase, the Save Raniganj Mansion team decided, would be to get some facts, learn as much as possible about the current composition of the Roy family, and try to gauge how they would react to the news that a very valuable property, worth several crores, was about to fall into their collective lap. The second phase—everyone agreed that this might be tricky—would involve convincing them that they should give up on the crores to preserve Raniganj Mansion for posterity.

"But how can we get this information without telling them why we want it?" Neera asked.

They were in Chhotomama's office. He sat behind a government-issue grey steel desk covered with papers and files. The others sat across the desk on straight-backed wooden chairs. Neera was present in her professional capacity as the administrative assistant to the director of the Institute. She was taking notes. She wore a yellow cotton Tangail sari. A long string of tuberose was wrapped around her left wrist like a bangle. "How does she get the time to look so perfect so early on a Sunday morning" Bodhi wondered, "when Cookie can't even wake up to attend the meeting?" His mind began to turn into a gloopy melt as the sweet perfume of the tuberose shot directly into his nose like a guided missile and made the left corner of his mouth twitch spasmodically. He had begun to bend involuntarily in the direction of her wrist but her words jerked him back to an upright position.

"What do you mean by we?" he yelped, his voice rising in pitch as alarm shot up his spine. Neera had to be kept out of this. Inserting her into this sensitive situation would be like pouring liquid ammonia over a pile of unknown chemicals. An explosion was guaranteed. This was a man's job, and no woman, especially no woman like Neera, could possibly handle it. She could inaugurate an art exhibition. She could judge an elocution competition. She could even... if there wasn't any way to avoid it...run a three-legged race at a picnic. But she couldn't be allowed to come within miles of this affair. Not now. "Who specifically is going to do this?" he asked.

"That depends on what we do, doesn't it?" Neera smiled confidently. "If we need stealth and guile don't you think a woman can do a better job?"

"Don't forget that I am a promoter," Bodhi retorted. "If there's any group with more stealth and guile in this city I'd like to meet them. We wrote the book on stealth and guile. Haven't you heard about us?" Bodhi had more verbal dexterity and courage with Neera when there were other people around. It was the couple situations that left him speechless.

"Well then Bodhi (she never called him BB in front of others), what do you propose we should do?"

"What if I show up as myself? A promoter. I'll be interested in checking out their property...whatever it is... I'll be making inquiries about whether they'd be interested in selling? To do this I'll need to know all about the family and their relationships. I do this all the time, not at random houses, of course, because I start with some inside information, but still..."

"What if they are renters? How can we presume they are homeowners?" Bankoli's French-cut beard stiffened with scepticism.

"They must be," Chhotomama said. "A family that can afford to donate a mansion like this has to have enough money to own their home. When has that class of landed gentry sunk so low that they can't buy one measly house? Need I remind you people about the history of our people? The exploitations and rapaciousness of primitive capitalism. The ability of that class to thrive regardless of the conditions of the world system and the global economy. I'm willing to wager that we're going to find the Roys in the lap..."

Everyone in the room could sense the beginning of a lecture and looked for a polite way to pre-empt it. Bankoli and Neera hesitated. They were his subordinates. Their beseeching looks forced Bodhi to speak up. "In fact, if they aren't homeowners, really rich homeowners, you're finished, Chhotomama," he said. "There's no way they'll let you keep Raniganj Mansion. There's too much money in it."

"Even if we assume that they are not renters, they could be living in a flat, or it could be several flats. What if it's a large family spread all over the city? Or why this city, they could be anywhere in the world. Delhi, Bombay, England, America...anywhere." Bankoli remained sceptical and practical.

The room fell silent. This was a new kind of research problem for Chhotomama—how to get personal information about an unknown number of people in unknown locations without letting them know why he was seeking personal information about them? His large and organised brain—capable of holding page after page of dense and detailed information, imagining the minutiae of lives of people that had lived two hundred years ago, understanding theories of history and culture packed with words of many syllables—was stretched to its limit as he tried to think of a way to be deceitful without lying.

There was no way around it. This couldn't be done without some ethical gymnastics. The end mattered more than the means to achieve it. The greater good, which Chhotomama had no doubt was the preservation of Raniganj Mansion, had to triumph over the lesser evil of lying and deceiving to achieve the end.

Chhotomama had had an intuition about this all along. He had known things would get murky quickly. That's why he had asked Bodhi and Cookie for help. He wished Cookie had come to this meeting. He would have known what to do straightaway. But Bodhi would do. He wasn't as creative or practical as Cookie, but he had been a promoter long enough that he would do. Chhotomama wouldn't have to do any lying or deceiving personally because Bodhi would do it for him.

~

That's what promoters were good at. That's why there were few words that carried as much meaning or generated as much feeling in the city as promoter. It was a name for the lowest of the low. The land sellers, poor fellows, were virtuous; what choice did they have but to give in to temptation? If, despite no encouragement on your part, people started throwing gobs of money at you, what were you supposed to do? The apartment buyers were virtuous of course, for who didn't deserve to live comfortably? But, the middleman who made the transaction between buyer and seller possible, why was he nothing but a vulture? Middlemen were like mango chutney in a chicken sandwich, like rhinoplasty on Ma Durga—crude, inauthentic, unnecessary. Bloody *dalals* they were. Society would be much better off if all middlemen were eliminated.

"I am not like those promoters," Bodhi protested when he could, "you can't paint everyone with the same brush. I am a middle-class promoter."

He was right, but no one listened.

The city's promoters were stratified like its residents. At the top were the big players who worked with really big chunks of land. Abandoned factories and industrial estates. Acres and acres on the outskirts. These big players were too big to be called promoters; they were acknowledged as real estate developers and given their due respect. They built for the moneyed class: traders and shopwallas, technology and finance men, entertainers and non-resident jet-setters. They had artfully lit offices with tastefully arranged leather furniture on the good floors of plush buildings with glass frontage. Each of their projects had its own website. Their salesmen wore dark jackets. Their secretaries wore sleeveless blouses. They didn't bother with local hoodlums or Party apparatchiks to approve of their actions because they had the personal numbers of ministers on their mobile phones. They paid off these ministers directly, in crores, several crores if the project was big enough. They had no need to intimidate defenceless widows or murder inconvenient husbands or build six-storey buildings with four floors approved.

Promoters like Bodhi, on the other hand, were found in every lane and gulli in the city, and quite a few were men like him, educated boys from respectable families of moderate means, who had been unable to find well-paid work in air-conditioned offices, and who were now buying old houses from and selling new flats to other respectable families of moderate means. The flats they built were small and simple and located in unpretentious neighbourhoods. For the buyers they represented the culmination of a lifetime of scrimping and saving. They had never owned any property and would never own another.

These middle-class promoters had to deal with the local hoodlums and Party apparatchiks, of course, because they didn't have access to ministers and bigwigs. They had to set aside a portion of the project cost for *night soil* payments—six and a half per cent of the total cost of the projects Heavenly Homes Ltd. had done so far. Speed money, hush money, look-the-other-way money, don't-get-in-my-way money, I-know-you-have-expenses-too money, mehngai money, here's-a-gold-necklace-for-your-daughter's-wedding money, there's-a-roshogollah-that-grew-on-my-tree money, wealth-must-trickle-down money, honey money money. They had to lie and cheat constantly, but these were small lies and minor cheats—a little fudging of the square footage here, a little less cement in the mortar there, the cheaper tile, the leak-prone faucet, the commode with no warranty, the made-in-China door lock instead of Godrej—things like that. These were no more significant than the truth-adjustments everywhere, in every profession from banking to carpentry, in every product from fresh milk to basmati rice. Everything was adjustable, the truth more than anything else.

Yet, promoters had the worst reputation.

To be fair, it must be noted that along with notoriety, promoters had acquired the glamour and wisdom that used to be associated with doctors, and before there was professionalised healing, witch-doctors and ojhas. People sought promoters out at gatherings for advice on what to buy and where to buy and how much to pay. I have this pain, people used to say to doctors at social gatherings in the old days, right around here...Nowadays, at social gatherings, people told promoters—I'm looking at this property, it's right behind the hospital for the blind... Property acquisition was the biggest subject of discussion in the city. In every room that Bodhi went, people talked of property. And he was a shaman who had access to the dark arts of that mysterious subject.

Shamans have their powers and uses, doubtless, but they also have reputational problems. Access to the dark arts comes with whispers and mutterings about the practitioners of those arts. There was simply no getting away from the notoriety of promoters. Bodhi protested in vain that the profession was as fine and honourable as any but had been tarnished by the actions of a few men at the bottom of its barrel. They were hustlers from the unmentionable class who gave all promoters a bad name.

Everyone had heard these stories and seen these men. They were the leading characters of modern urban legends.

There was Bireshwar 'Peto' Mondol, whose nickname came from his expertise in making and using Petos, the homemade hand grenades used in local skirmishes. Peto Mondol had gotten his start as a promoter by intimidating homeowners into selling their properties in his neighbourhood stronghold in Kalighat; he made enough money from these projects to open a multi-specialty hospital (*Best Health Nursing Home—We Spatialize in Goll Bladder and Kidney*), and now was a minor celebrity, seen rubbing shoulders with TV stars and MLAs in the society pages of the city papers. One of the MLAs he had been photographed with frequently was Javed 'Vat 69' Khan, a career criminal from before he was a teenager, who had started as a trainee smuggler of foreign whisky and cigarettes in the years when there used to be import restrictions and heavy taxes on luxury goods. Vat 69 Khan later seduced a woman who owned two houses in New Alipur, garrotted her husband (with a plastic washing line, blue-green, the legend-makers whispered), assumed control of both properties, and rebooted to life as a promoter. His generosity to the Opposition Party was rewarded with a ticket to the legislative assembly, his victory was assured by his thugs, and now he was not only a legislator but also a producer of patriotic TV serials. The Javed Khan Media Arts Company had produced *Rani Rashmoni* and *Shaheed Khudiram*, two of the longest-running shows in Bangla TV history.

It irritated Bodhi no end to be clubbed together with these low-class lowlifes. Are all singers the same, he asked.

Don't people know the difference between Sonu Nigam from Bollywood and Sonu Kumar, the bandwalla in the zero-star multi-cuisine restaurant-bar near the docks? Are all writers the same? From Tolstoy and Tagore to the pink-jacket pornographers of Bot-tola Press? All cricketers? From Sachin and Saurav to the run machines in Vivekananda Park? Then why should all promoters be the same? Why did people refuse to understand? Why were they so self righteous? Bodhi could work himself into private fits of indignation over the obstinate moralising of people who looked down on his profession in general and him by association.

The hypocrisy of it all.

To desire power was fine, but to desire money was not. It made no sense. The focus was not, as it should be, on desire, and the kind of men who desired more than others, and were willing to do anything to attain their desires, but on the object of the desire. To want was not objectionable by itself. To do anything to get what one wanted was not objectionable either. All's fair in love and war. What mattered was what one wanted. To desire power was fine. Men who desired power were called leaders. *Netaji. Guruji. Panditji.* To desire sex was tolerable. Men are just overgrown boys, after all. But to desire money, oh no, no, no. That's just greed. Morally reprehensible greed.

People saw through binoculars, but with different orientations. The rats who desired money looked as big as crocodiles when the binocular was turned one way. The crocodiles who desired power looked as small as rats when the same binocular was turned the other way.

There was no reason why that should be, but that's just the way it was.

There was no escape from the taint of financial success in Bodhi's plodding middle-class world.

~

"Are you in, Bodhi?" Chhotomama asked. "Will you be able to do this for us?"

What could Bodhi say? Chhotomama's face glowed like a missionary's among his tribals. His path was so righteous that no good man could refuse him. Bodhi couldn't say no because he wanted to be...and felt deep down that he was...a good man. To say no would identify him as a member of the forces of badness. Chhotomama knew that no nephew of his, even if he was a promoter, could be fundamentally bad. Authentic badness ran in other families, not his.

Chhotomama also knew what everyone else knew, what Cookie called the first law of India—*family comes first.*

If your family didn't look after you, who would? Business families looked after each other (other than his own family, Cookie was careful to note the exception that proved the rule). Movie families and music families did the same. Politics was a family business. Criminality, to the extent that it could be separated from politics, was too. Cookie had spent many drunken hours raging against the injustice of Europeans and their descendants taking credit for figuring out the facts of genetics when it was obvious that Indians had known these facts for centuries. The entire Indian social system was based on genetics. If you were the son of a nobody, it was only to be expected that you too would be a nobody; it was your right and your duty. If, on the other hand, your father was a cricket commentator or quiz master, you too possessed the genes for cricket commentary or quiz-mastering. The job was yours by birthright.

"All you need to do is get us started, Bodhi," said Neera, "and we'll take over from there. It's not that difficult, is it?"

Neera's eyes were eager, her voice had a timbre of entreaty Bodhi had never heard before. She pulled at one of her frizzy strands of hair and twisted it around her left index finger. A few petals of tuberose fell from the bangle on her wrist. In slow motion they floated down to the folds of her yellow Tangail sari. Bodhi looked on mesmerised. Even if he could defy the first law of India, he couldn't deny its second law—goddesses must be obeyed or there would be hell to pay.

Neera's support for Chhotomama's project was heartfelt and total. Bodhi could sense it. She wanted this. It was not for him to question why she wanted it, just as it had never occurred to him to ask her—Why vegetarianism? Why Tibet? To be in love is to surrender self and doubt. Bodhi had learnt to want what Neera wanted. He would walk on burning coal to get her what she wanted. He would run over quicksand and swim through toxic waste. He would wrestle pythons and chase cheetahs. This was nothing.

# Part II
# The Investigation

In which Bodhi digs for facts and finds himself in a hole

# 1

"This family is cursed by Rahu," said Mrs Rajeshwari Roy. "That has been my lot in this life, to fight the Curse of Rahu and somehow keep this family alive." She brought her palms together and tapped her forehead thrice, mumbling something Bodhi couldn't make out. "All I can hope for is that Ma Kali will recognise my efforts and give me better luck in my next life." Three more taps of pressed palms on her forehead.

Bodhi was well-informed on the Curse of Rahu. His mother had been god-fearing and superstitious, and despite her husband's frowns and finger-wagging, had filled Bodhi's head with stories of gods and demons from her ancestral village. But by the time his voice broke, Bodhi had become dismissive of the old gods. The older he grew and more modern, the less he believed in mumbo jumbo. His office didn't have any sign of religiosity. No framed calendars of gods, no statues, no incense sticks, no prayer beads. Soon, he began to hear grumbles from his clients. "So Mr Banerjee," several said with obvious disapproval, "you don't seem to be a very religious man. And you aren't married either. Hmmm..." The implication was obvious. How could they believe in someone who didn't believe in the almighty? How could they entrust their lifetime savings to such a person, especially if he wasn't married (and therefore hadn't learned how to be responsible) and had as a business partner that belligerent godless Sikh, Cookie? At first, Bodhi had reacted with haughtiness and pride in his atheism. Later, he had professed to agnosticism and a shortage of time. But neither approach had appeased his clients.

The first crack in the edifice of rationality came with the adoption of Vaastu and Feng Shui. There were clients who swore by one or the other, or both. Vaastu would bring luck. Feng Shui would bring peace. Peace and luck, luck and peace; who could say no to these? "Someone prideful and obstinate," said Cookie. "Someone who thinks that he knows better than others and has no problem in imposing his belief on others. Someone stupid. Someone with no business sense who's been kept solvent by his business partner. Someone who can't smell his own bullshit."

Bodhi had given in. Heavenly Homes Ltd. started hiring Vaastu and Feng Shui consultants to bless their creations. The consultants weren't picky about what they blessed; almost anything that paid them the requisite fees were blessed, so there was hardly any need to actually modify designs or change angles and orientations. Bodhi soon forgot that he used to object to Vaastu and Feng Shui on principle.

Within months, the crack in the edifice became a doorway to a new reality. After much soul searching, and relentless prodding from Cookie, Bodhi had installed two plaster-cast idols in his office. Saraswati and Laxmi. Alabaster pale and golden tan. Beatific vacant smiles. Serenity. He had many moments of self recrimination in the months immediately after doing the deed (for betraying his father and Chhotomama and his own beliefs) but not many lately. He had gotten used to the presence of the well-lit ladies ensconced on a shelf next to the AC. He had begun to appreciate the honeymoon suite smell in the office from the fresh garlands draped on the goddesses by one of the office bearers every morning. He hadn't evolved so far as to be seen praying publicly. But lately, after meeting Neera, he had found himself in conversation with the placid figurines more than once—not so much in prayer as in deal-making. He had offered to give up smoking, or the profits from his biggest project, or one inch in height, even an inch and a half, in order to possess her love.

His clients had turned him into an idol-worshipper. Neera was turning him into a believer.

~

They talked about curses for a while.

"Did you know that a Curse of Rahu lasts for at least eighteen years? At least eighteen years, sometimes more than that," said Maya. Her full name was Mahamaya, but everyone called her Maya. She was nine or ten years old, a pigtailed sprite, narrow as a flute and enthusiastic as a puppy. She had returned from school only a few minutes before Bodhi had shown up at their door, unannounced, and was still wearing her uniform of white blouse and navy blue skirt. She was following their conversation sitting next to her grandmother, cross-legged, one sharp elbow on rickety knee, pointed chin on upturned palm.

Bodhi scribbled on a notepad. He had brought one to look authentic, like a journalist. That's what the Save Raniganj Mansion team had decided—that Bodhi would approach the Roy family pretending to be a journalist interested in the family's history, especially its philanthropy, for a magazine article. The goal would be to enter like a needle and leave like a tractor, hauling loads of information on all claimants to Raniganj Mansion and, to the extent possible, their individual views on its preservation.

*Rajeshwari Roy = Mother boss = Widow of Prashanta Kumar Roy*, he wrote.

*Mahamaya Roy (??) = Maya = Granddaughter (whose child?)*, he added.

"Is that so?" Bodhi said in an overly bright voice.

"Yes. And you don't even know when a curse will begin or end."

Grandmother and granddaughter were deadly serious about the curse. They gave him a detailed account. A CURSE OF RAHU (in Maya's telling, every letter was capitalised) could be identified by two elements—surprise and longevity. First, it was unpredictable, like an ambush, or a pregnancy of triplets. It could come from nowhere, when you were least expecting it. Even supremely capable astrologers frequently failed to predict the arrival of an honest-to-goodness genuine Curse of Rahu. Grandmother Roy knew this well because she had consulted the best in the city. What was worse, a genuine Curse of Rahu could go on forever, longer than a fanatic's faith or a movie star's youth. A year or two were nothing. One needed to think of Aurangzeb's reign, or Stalin's, or Amitabh Bachchan's career, or the communists in the state. One needed to think in decades, not mere years.

They told him about the story behind the curse. Like most good stories, it was about revenge. They discussed the dangers posed by the curse. Bodhi happily made a list. They identified nine major points:

1 There may be danger from thieves, powerful persons, poisons, and weapons.
2 One may face insult and defame from lowly people such as shit-cleaners and corpse-handlers. Not only that, one may have to earn a living by doing a lowly job or business such as cleaning other people's shit.
3 One may suffer due to weakness, venereal diseases, cough, asthma, and urinary ailments. One's piss may turn red.
4 Good food may not be available. One may have to eat food cooked by shit-cleaners or corpse-handlers.
5 One's spouse and son may behave wickedly.
6 One's mother may suffer pain.
7 Enmity with relatives and cheating by friends is possible. (Is it necessary to have a Curse of Rahu for this? Bodhi wondered as he wrote his notes.)
8 There may be loss of wealth or fall from a vehicle. Elephants and camels are to be avoided.
9 Problems due to immovable assets and anxiety related to house and land are possible.

~

"My father-in-law was a great man," Grandmother Roy eventually got to the point. "A giant among pygmies."

"Yes, please tell me about him," Bodhi said. "It's his generosity that got me curious. He was obviously a wealthy and powerful man to be able to give so much away. But our generation knows so little about him. No one seems to have heard of him."

"Youngsters today," Grandmother Roy sighed, "what do they know about the past? They are all so caught up in the present. This granddaughter of mine though," she patted Maya's head, "she's not going to be like them. Yes, my sweet chomchom. You're going to bring back this family's name and honour, aren't you baby?"

Maya reached up and pinched her grandmother's sunken cheeks with both hands. The tiny old woman melted with happiness. Her thin bony arms and tufts of short white hair made her look like a bird in winter, shorn of feathers and almost weightless. She wore a hearing aid in one ear and bifocal glasses with a crack in the left lens that Bodhi could see from where he was sitting, five feet away. There was no jewellery visible anywhere on her body and her sari was a simple white sheet with a thin blue border.

Bodhi allowed this scene of domestic bliss play out for a moment. Don't hurry the client party, said the unwritten code of his business, unless you have to.

"My great grandfather was a zamindar," said Maya. "Tell him na Thamma." Bodhi wanted to kiss the little girl in gratitude. She was going to be an asset in this investigation.

"Yes, dear. I was coming to that." Grandmother Roy brought her bifocals close to her mouth, spat once on each lens, and rubbed them clean, squeak, squeak, with the pallu of her sari. "Maya is right. My husband's family were zamindars in Comilla district, near the town of Leishara."

Of course, they were. What else would they be? Bodhi had assumed this all along. Who else would have had enough money in those days to build a house as big as Raniganj Mansion, and not only build it, but give it away? Bodhi's assumption wasn't based on extensive knowledge on zamindars. Truth be told, he was better informed about people and things far away in time and space than from his own, local past. He knew more about the French revolution than about the Sepoy rebellion and songs favoured by American hippies than protesting sharecroppers in Medinipur. Chhotomama and Baba took pains to point out this gaping hole in Bodhi's intellectual fabric, but couldn't really blame him for it. "We are a self-lobotomised race," they told each other frequently over whisky, with solemn expressions and slow nods. "We are congenitally unable to remember our own past."

So, what Bodhi knew about zamindars was what everyone knew, what was common knowledge, and it came from old black and white films, when they still used to make films about zamindars and peasants. Like most characters from the past—from kings and priests to baijis and devadasis—Bodhi's imagination had been captured by images in movies. All Bodhi had at his disposal were fragments of an unrecoverable world in which zamindars were rich and lazy and wasteful rural landlords and dedicated tax collectors for the British. Most of them were also greedy and rapacious men whose selfishness and cruelty created untold misery for the peasants. This was common knowledge.

In Grandmother Roy's mind, that was the golden age. The Roy family used to lord over three thousand acres of land. They used to maintain a stable of horses and a private militia. Ustad Paigambar Khan, father of the legendary Ustad Bismillah Khan, had played shehnai at the wedding of her father-in-law in 1929. The morning after the wedding feast, they had fed one thousand and one indigents, including one hundred and one poor and deserving Brahmans. Three servants had been assigned solely to the task of keeping count of the indigent being fed to ensure that the auspicious number of one thousand and one had been reached but not exceeded.

Not only was Grandmother Roy's father-in-law a zamindar, he was a gentleman, she said. He treated his subjects with kindness and dignity. He helped them financially and spiritually when they faced hardship. Unlike other members of the zamindar fraternity, her father-in-law didn't gamble or whore around. Not one of the women of easy virtue in Sonagachhi or Kalighat knew his name. Not one bookie at the racecourse could recognise him by sight. Little Maya nodded her head wisely, as if she understood what was being said and approved of it too.

"But," Bodhi said, "there's one thing I don't understand. There were so many zamindars in those days, hundreds, maybe thousands...I don't know. They weren't going about donating their properties. What made Mr Prafulla Kumar Roy so special?"

"Yes, Thamma, tell him." Maya clearly was well-informed about these stories of Roy power.

"This is what I was coming to," Grandmother Roy said with a touch of sharpness to indicate her displeasure at being hurried in her storytelling. This was a rare day for her.

No one had asked her about the glories of the past in a long time, and she wanted to extract the sweet juice of those prideful memories as slowly as possible. "You're right Mr Banerjee. There were many, many zamindars, and many, many others, little bamboo shoots, claiming to be zamindars. You add all their land together, it's larger than Russia. Ha, ha, ha. You know what I'm saying, right. Liars! The whole lot. My father-in-law was a real zamindar, but he was much more than that. He was an industrialist. One of the first in the country. A rare Bengali."

"What industry? Jute? Leather?" Bodhi asked.

"No. Coal." Grandmother Roy said. "We were owners of the Patherdihi coal mines." Bodhi had never heard of it. Seeing his blank expression, she added, "It's near the Bihar border, close to Raniganj."

"Ah, that's why the house is called Raniganj Mansion. I didn't know."

"Yes, yes. But please understand, his motive was not to become rich. Money he already had plenty of. He wanted to show the sahibs that brown people like us could also become industrialists. That we too could run industries and factories. He meant this to be a slap in the face of the white man. You see, my father-in-law was a nationalist."

She paused and wiped her glasses again.

"I was married in 1957, Mr Banerjee. I was just seventeen years old. A lot had changed by then. Our country had become independent. The zamindari system had been banned. Not that it would have mattered to this family. Our lands were now in East Pakistan. No, all that was gone by the time I came to this family."

"So, would you say the fortunes of the Roys had already declined by then?" Bodhi took a step toward acknowledging what was obvious.

~

It was difficult to associate the nameless house he was sitting in and the drab neighbourhood the house was located in with a zamindari of three thousand acres. It was a squat, unpainted, two-storey structure, not tiny, but utterly nondescript and indistinguishable from the dozens of similar mounds of brick and mortar that littered the locality like the unsupervised droppings of the cows and mongrel dogs that wandered its streets. The house was secured with black iron grills and gates on every possible entrance, though there wasn't much to steal. Some of the furniture inside the house was impressive, surely remnants of the salad days of zamindari, but everything else was ordinary, tacky. Whitewashed walls with large damp patches, tatty curtains, plastic covers, naked light-bulbs.

It had taken the staff of the Institute a couple of days to find the last known address of the Roy family matriarch. Bodhi knew the area, a lower middle-class neighbourhood called Pratapgarh that showed up inside the south-eastern quarter of the metropolis in maps, but judging by appearance, could well have been a village. Pratapgarh and its surrounding communities were built on haphazardly filled-in wetland marshes. The built environment of houses and roads was nestled within a patchwork of fisheries and ponds, the latter so overgrown with hyacinth and moss that one could see water, green as a lawn, only where the ghats came down, where all day long the residents of these neighbourhoods brushed, bathed, washed clothes, and gossiped.

The main roads in Pratapgarh were lined with ramshackle shops and stores, all erected within a foot or two of the edge of the paved surface, like plaque accumulating inside arteries. The side roads were narrower still, barely wide enough for two pregnant cows to pass side-by-side. The houses here weren't necessarily small, but they were almost uniformly squalid, like this one. The people who lived here were not the high fliers of the city. In fact, they weren't fliers of any sort; they were centipedes, like these Roys, hundreds of legs crawling nowhere. As soon as he got the address from Chhotomama, Bodhi knew that the Roy family was in serious decline, and if that was true, Chhotomama wouldn't see his wish come true. A jumble of unsorted thoughts raced through his head. Was this good for him or not? *Yes, no, no, yes, no, yes.* All depended on how things turned out. How he played his cards. Bodhi couldn't help thinking that the Roys' economic decline wasn't a bad outcome for him. He could try to save Raniganj Mansion and win Neera's hand and Chhotomama's gratitude by doing so, but he would fail, because failure was inevitable, and when he failed to save Raniganj Mansion he would become the promoter that he really was and destroy it and become a very rich man.

Bodhi could be good and do right and win at the same time.

~

Grandmother Roy appeared not to have heard Bodhi's question, or perhaps she hadn't liked its tone, so he repeated it, with gentility. "I was curious...were the Roys already living here when you got married?" Bodhi knew the answer but had to ask the question. Pratapgarh hadn't existed when Grandmother Roy got married. Nothing in this locality had existed fifty years ago.

"Oh no," said Grandmother Roy. "Not at all. After my marriage I moved into Bliss Cottage. That's where the Roys lived then."

The Bliss Cottage she described was a pleasure palace in Bhabanipur, in the genteel southern heart of the city, not far from Raniganj Mansion. The fifteen-room, three-storey house had been immaculately maintained by a platoon of cheerful servants. There were two full-time gardeners to tend the inner courtyard and its rose and sunflower bushes and perfectly even lawn (that, in winter, served as a badminton court for Grandmother Roy's children). The backyard had an outhouse where the servants lived, and a mango tree, a guava tree, and a jackfruit tree, each of which produced buckets of succulent fruit year after year. Inside the house worked a head cook and his assistant, two ayahs (one for each child), and two cleaning women who did the washing and dusting and sweeping with such zeal that every surface sparkled like polished brass.

"And Raniganj Mansion?" Bodhi asked.

"That was gone long ago. My father-in-law had given it away in a fit of nationalism." Bodhi began to see a different side of Grandmother Roy. The lady was superstitious and ritualistic no doubt and probably bigoted and gullible too. She had married as a teenager and Bodhi was sure that she had never gone to college. Maybe she hadn't even finished high school. Women like her rarely did. She could add and subtract but would be completely useless at long division. She could read Bangla—the newspaper, of course, and ghost stories and melodramas—but not much more than that. Yet, underneath the sparse feathers of a fragile and doddering winter bird there were hints of a fanciful and determined mind. This was a woman who had been used to ordering people about. It was a habit, like heroin addiction, that was expensive to acquire and hard to break.

"You don't sound happy about it," Bodhi said.

"Oh, I had nothing to do with it. This was well before my time. My husband (may his soul rest in peace) was a young boy when it happened." Grandmother Roy shook her head. "I don't want to give the impression that I am unhappy about it. No, no. We...this family...we're very proud that it happened. What a wonderful spirit my father-in-law possessed."

"But..."

"But it's the cause he gave it for that brings sadness. Sometimes. He gave his mansion to the nation, and the nation later took everything from us. There's no justice in this world. No gratefulness. That's all. We would give that mansion away again." Bodhi's ears pricked up at this. He made a note. "It's from sacrifices like this that a nation becomes great. The nation in return should be expected to honour these sacrifices. But not this nation. No, not ours." Grandmother Roy sighed with a faraway look in her eyes.

Then she told Bodhi about the first Curse of Rahu to visit the Roy family.

~

*Pethni*, Grandmother Roy called her. Demon witch. The high priestess of Rahu.

She couldn't bring herself to call her by name—Srimati Indira Gandhi, Prime Minister of India, daughter of Sri Jawaharlal Nehru, also Prime Minister of India, mother of Sri Rajiv Gandhi, yet another Prime Minister of India. Grandmother Roy had nothing against Jawaharlal personally. She considered him a decent and honourable man. And handsome too, in a spindly, spidery way. She only wished that he had been impotent (literally, not metaphorically) or his wife infertile, so that the family line had ended with him, and the pethni had never been born. Alternatively, Jawaharlal's wife could have been super-fertile, like Gandhari, and produced many children who would have hacked each other to death, like the royal children of old used to, in their desire to be the only ruler of the land.

Just one child, especially this one, had been a terrible idea.

Bodhi wasn't sure that Grandmother Roy knew about Mrs Gandhi's well-documented bad behaviour, such as suspending the constitution, throwing her political opposition in jail, mollycoddling her murderous younger son, turning serious leaders into sycophantic buffoons, turning sycophantic buffoons into serious leaders, and generally corrupting the moral fibre of the young nation. She may have been aware of all this in a jumbled and inchoate way, but it wouldn't have mattered to her. She had never been interested in politics and like all wealthy women of her time had been an unquestioning Congress voter.

Also, she was a big believer in family values. When Jawaharlal died and his place was taken by all kinds of undesirables, first an uncouth peasant in ill-fitting clothes from the cow belt, then a Madrasi as dark as a buffalo, she disapproved. When Mrs Gandhi finally manipulated her way into succeeding her father as the supreme leader, Grandmother Roy had been happy that the right family was back in charge, and the undesirables who had been masquerading as leaders in the interim had been put in their place, a few rows behind people of good breeding.

No, Grandmother Roy's hatred was created by a single act of Mrs Gandhi. Beginning in 1972 and before the middle of 1974, the demon witch nationalised the coal industry of the country. The government took control of all the hundreds of big and little private mines, the Roy family's among them, citing all kinds of reasons.

"They were ridiculous," Grandmother Roy said. "They said the mines were dangerous, that we didn't have safety standards. That the miners were unhappy and exploited and poorly paid. Complete rubbish. And just like that they took my husband's mine away. One lakh tonnes of coal we used to produce every year. Not a joke, no? My poor husband, he had dedicated his life to the well-being of the workers, he never recovered from the shock."

Bodhi and Maya listened quietly.

"The pethni wore white cotton saris and covered her head like a good Hindu woman, she visited temples wearing big tilaks on her forehead and prayer-beads around her neck, but underneath that make-believe piety was the real person—a ruthless witch who would destroy any number of people just to get more for herself. Her husband couldn't stand her. Her own aunt was scared of her. Can you imagine? What could my poor husband do to resist this devil woman? Nothing. Nothing. Nobody could do anything. The pethni struck like a thunderous storm from a clear blue sky, and after that this family was never the same again."

Grandmother Roy worked herself into an emotional blubber. She sighed and snorted and cried big round teardrops. Maya started crying too. It's hard not to when someone else is. Bodhi waited with an uncomfortable look on his face, as if he had stumbled into a private fight of a married couple and couldn't escape. Emotional displays by elderly women had a tendency to trigger his flight instinct, a result of long conditioning by his mother.

It took a few minutes for Grandmother Roy to gain composure. Little Maya stood behind her grandmother and wrapped her thin arms around her bony neck and wiped away her tears.

"You know that the pethni's son, the younger one, the goonda, he died in a plane crash," Grandmother Roy said. "This was maybe six or seven years after she ruined us. The wheels of justice, sometimes, just sometimes, they turn in the wind, and when they do they grind the evil-doers into dust. I cannot explain to you how happy I felt that day. At my age I couldn't dance in the street. What would people say? But I gave a special Kali puja. I sacrificed a pair of goats, just like in the old days. Rarely have I felt so close to Ma Kali in my life."

Bodhi fidgeted and began to think about leaving. Should she be saying these things to a stranger?

"Then, three or four years later the pethni herself got killed. By her own bodyguards. Like I said, nobody could stand that woman, least of all the people who were close to her. This time I didn't have enough money to do the goat sacrifice again, so for twenty one days in a row I went to Kalighat, and each day...each and every day, come rain come shine...I laid a garland of one hundred and one marigolds at the feet of the mother. The pujari was so touched. He thought I was praying for the pethni's soul. Ha ha. Ha ha ha." She laughed so hard that she had to tilt her head back to draw more oxygen.

What did Maya think about the last part of her grandmother's tale? She had probably heard this before, Bodhi concluded, and worried for a moment about the little girl's upbringing. He was relieved when she was sent to her room to study for some test coming soon. "There's always a test coming soon," she grumbled but left. Grandmother Roy also excused herself to say her evening prayers. "Please wait," she said, "I'll be back in fifteen minutes."

~

*Dhong! Dhong! Dhong!* Bodhi heard Grandmother Roy have a go at a metal hammer and tong to scare away the evil spirits that were always around in her mind, especially during prayers. He began to speculate whether she was completely unhinged or just had a blind spot on the Indira Gandhi issue. Should he leave now and come back later and speak to someone else? The problem was—as entertaining as Grandmother Roy's story had been, it hadn't been very informative. He still didn't know much about her children, who lived where, who did what, and so on. He still didn't know how the Roy fortune had come down from Bliss Cottage to this dump. The nationalisation of their coal mine was a problem, yes, but surely they got paid for it. What happened to that money? And she had mentioned that this was the first Curse of Rahu. Did that mean there was a second, and a third? Maybe there was an infinite series of curses he would have to sit through.

Bodhi paced about the room. He walked to a framed black and white photo hanging on a wall next to the dining table. The place looked like Kashmir but could have been Himachal. In the far background there were snow-covered mountain peaks and in the near background there were deodar trees like elongated pyramids. Grandmother Roy and a big man (surely her husband) were seated on simple wooden chairs on a gently sloping grass field. He was wearing a dark three-piece suit and had crossed his left leg over his right. Grandmother Roy was leaning toward him and her right palm was gently draped over his left arm. There were two children, both boys. The older one seemed to be twelve or thirteen years old. He was wearing dark glasses, looking debonair. The other boy was a few years younger, probably in kindergarten or class one. His face was in profile, peeking from behind his ayah's sari.

It was a picture of complete contentment.

Later, on reconstructing the scene in his mind, Bodhi believed that this was the moment when he heard a sharp but oddly melodious shriek followed by series of small thumps. He turned around and saw a woman at the door, semi-crouched, like a kung fu warrior, pointing a short, closed, red umbrella at him, its tip drawing irregular arcs in the air because the hand holding it was trembling like a leaf under rain. Scattered on the floor around the woman were two small plastic bags and a number of onions that had rolled out of one of them.

"Don't move or I'll scream again," the crouching woman said. Bodhi put his hands in the air in the universal gesture of surrender. "Who are you and what are you doing inside my house?"

Bodhi gulped and was about to stammer something when Maya came skipping from her room and shouted, "It's all right Ma, it's all right," and then collapsed on the sofa in a jiggle of laughter. The hubbub subsided, introductions followed, and the onions were put back in the bag.

The crouching woman was Shilpi Roy, Maya's mother, Grandmother Roy's daughter-in-law. She was in her mid-thirties, older than Bodhi by four or five years. Her complexion was very dark, Santhal dark, and her eyes were very bright and quite inconsolable. They seemed to be brimming with tears, as if one loud word from anyone would send the drops tumbling down her cheeks. She wasn't tall, maybe an inch above five feet, and neither was she thin, carrying maybe five kilos more than she would like, but the extra material was distributed evenly over her face and limbs and torso. Plump but proportionate, Bodhi made a mental note. Her shoulder-length straight hair was parted in the middle. There was no trace of sindoor in it. She wore a magenta-coloured synthetic sari with white tiger paws the size of two-rupee coins block-printed on it. There was something familiar about that sari. Bodhi had seen it before.

"I have seen you somewhere," Shilpi Roy said.

"That sari..."

"It's my uniform."

"Of course. Barrackpore Farms. Do you work at the store near Dhakuria?"

"Yes. I'm the assistant manager there."

"I shop there regularly. It's very close to where I live. Your broiler chicken is excellent."

They conversed easily. Bodhi gave her the fiction about his interest in the Roy family for an article. She would be happy to talk to him, but not today, it had been a long day. Perhaps this weekend? Maybe Sunday afternoon? They exchanged mobile numbers.

Bodhi walked to his car which was parked around the corner to avoid being seen by the Roys. He found himself whistling 'Jeena Yahan, Marna Yahan.'

# 2

That night Bodhi had the Kali dream again. The black and bloody goddess after whom the city was named had been the source of some of his most spectacular nightmares. He used to have them as a child, when he hated Kali puja and Diwali and the double and triple-decker cracker bombs that made his heart go *jhannn* and sent him scurrying under the bed. The nightmares went away for years, but over the last few months they had returned.

Kali came into his dreams wanting to cut off his penis—why, given its unthreatening stature, he could never figure out—and chased him with a swinging cutlass up and down an unfamiliar house and out into an unfamiliar street thronging with staring strangers, slurping her big red tongue and rattling her necklace of severed heads, topless, with big bouncing breasts, wearing a single item of clothing, a Polynesian grass skirt. Somewhere in the background, invisible men played a brisk bongo beat with castanets. *Chhaka chhaka chhaka chhaka*. Bodhi was naked too, without even the filigree of a grass skirt to cover his stringy thin thighs and disappearing balls. He ran and ran and ran until he woke up trembling.

He tried to get back to sleep but couldn't. His mind raced with rambling thoughts of Neera. She was the first thought in his head when he woke and the last thought he was conscious of before he slept. What game was she playing? What did she want? Did her special friend really exist? Now that she had promised to show the special friend in the flesh, should he believe her, or should he withhold belief till there was physical confirmation? What if the special friend did show up, what then? Was he supposed to back off and become a good friend, a well-wisher? What if he didn't show up? Would that prove Neera was a liar or a lunatic or both and that he should run from her as fast as he could? Could he run from her even if he was sure that she was a liar or a lunatic or both? Was there anything she could do that would make him want her less? That raised the biggest question of all: Was Bodhi even sure that he knew what he wanted? Was it possible to know what one wants? Could one want opposites at the same time: integrity and wealth, fame and anonymity, Neera and Un-Neera? Neera, but without the extreme Neera-ness?

He forced himself to think of something else. He remembered the bizarre story he had heard that day, the birdlike woman who had narrated it, and her adoring little granddaughter. What a strange household, and he had met only a fraction of it. The most pleasant memory of the day, he found, was the plump dark face of Mrs Shilpi Roy and her bright doomed eyes.

He gave up on sleep and walked to the balcony adjoining the drawing room. It was a small space. His mother's flower pots occupied most of it. The flowers were gone and the plants were dead brown stalks, but his father wouldn't allow Bodhi to get rid of the pots. Bodhi went to his corner—his smoking spot—where he had cleared a few square feet of standing space. He lit his first cigarette of the day.

Two mongrels were cruising the street below, nuzzling each other, looking alert every now and then with jumpy ears and tails as if to remind themselves of their self-appointed roles as guard dogs. Bodhi recognised the leading mongrel, a pinched and scarred warrior who believed in territorial integrity and dutifully chased anyone who dared to be on foot on their street after midnight. Mustaque, the dhobi who had set up shop across the street from his flat long before it had been built, and Mustaque's brother-in-law Ansari, from whose makeshift stall Bodhi bought cigarettes at the intersection leading to the main road, were sleeping on Mustaque's ironing table—side-by-side, head-to-toe, like copulating earthworms. The table was wide enough to iron saris but barely wide enough to hold them both. Underneath the awning where he did his business, Mustaque's clay oven, the one that warmed his iron, still had a slowly dying fire. A thin ribbon of smoke, hardly more substantial than the heavy haze left behind by the day's outpouring of diesel and petrol fumes, curled from the oven up to the new flats on the other side of the street, where one room on the fourth floor of the building had a light on, probably for the scrawny, pimply boy preparing for his higher secondary exams. Even though the light was on, the boy was surely asleep, as was everyone else in the neighbourhood.

~

Bodhi had a busy day. The morning started with a site visit in Behala, where Heavenly Homes Ltd. was putting up a G+4 building with eight flats. This was a standard project in the city. The ground floor was a parking area (wherein came the G) with a four-storey structure built above it (providing the +4). Each flat in this particular project had two bedrooms and two bathrooms plus a kitchen and drawing-dining hall packed into about 700 square feet of plinth area. The buyers were paying for more—the common and open areas too—a total of 870 square feet of super built up area per flat. Thank goodness for the super built up area. It was the difference between profit and loss for promoters.

Heavenly Homes Ltd. was charging Rs. 2,600 per square foot of super built up area and another lakh for the parking space. Two of the eight flats were for the original owners of the land. Bodhi was hopeful that Heavenly Homes Ltd. would clear at least fifteen percent on the project after the remaining six flats were sold (all but one had already been sold), and all the bills had been paid and all the receipts received. His take, if all went well, would be somewhere around ten lakh rupees—more than six times what his father had received from his provident fund after thirty three years of teaching.

Bodhi listened patiently to the usual complaints from the site supervisor. There were two boxes with broken tiles that had to be returned for exchange; a night guard had been drinking, more than what was expected and tolerable in that job, and would have to be fired; a local goonda from the Opposition Party was demanding a hefty donation for a cultural extravaganza he was organising in the neighbourhood and would have to be paid off. Bodhi said what needed to be said without making any more commitments than needed to be made.

Back in his office he had a meeting with his informant Bablu Das who had news of a ten katha property in the far south of the city that could come on the market. It was very preliminary, but Bablu Das felt that Bodhi sir should visit the owners soon. Bodhi sir knew how to convince people. He had a way with them. Bablu Das wore a black-and-red checked shirt with an upturned collar and yellow piping. The top third of the shirt was unbuttoned. The opening glistened with two golden chains snaking like mountain brooks under an afternoon sun through the dense forest of his chest hair. Is that real gold, Bodhi wondered as he half-listened to the man, and if it is, how did this unemployed and ignorant thug make enough money to acquire this much gold? He was afraid to look too hard for an answer and afraid of the barely suppressed menace in the man's eyes. Those eyes were ingratiating at the moment, but Bodhi knew that they could change in an instant, like a traffic signal, into something quite threatening.

Between the time Bablu Das left and Bodhi's next appointment, a potential client, arrived, he daydreamed about Neera.

~

Back home, Bodhi prepared for another evening out.

He made a final inspection of his face in a small decorative mirror hanging behind the front door and had just tried out a wry and enigmatic practice smile when his father spoke from where he was sitting, on a rocking chair in the drawing section of the drawing-cum-dining hall.

The hall was a twelve-by-thirty rectangle, easily the largest space in the flat, and the first room one encountered on coming through the front door. One half of that rectangle, the half that was closer to the front door, was the drawing room. There was a folding-door exit to a small veranda, six-feet by three, on the wall facing the front door. An entertainment centre was placed against the wall between the front door and the veranda. It had a TV and a stereo system and framed photographs of Bodhi's mother and sister and her children. There was one long sofa with a reddish-brown corduroy cover placed against another wall, a centre table with a glass top, two wicker stools with padded seats, and the rocking chair on which Bodhi's father was sitting.

The room looked sort of new because it was only about six years old, but smelled like a geriatric ward, suffused with a sweet but sharp aroma whose ingredients included coconut oil, overripe bananas, cough syrup, and coriander chutney.

Baba's eyes were on the TV. "Late tonight?" he asked.

Bodhi hadn't noticed him. His mind was on other things. Evening had fallen and it was quite dark outside, but the light in the drawing room hadn't been switched on. The TV was on, but it almost always was in the flat. It didn't mean anyone was watching.

"Maybe," Bodhi said. "I don't know. Probably."

"Where are you going?"

"Someone's house, you don't know him," Bodhi said. He could sense that his father was in a questioning mood. The more data he was fed the more questions there would be.

"With friends? Something going on?"

"No. Not really. Just like that." Bodhi decided that he had told Baba as much as he needed to know. In the last couple of years Bodhi had started withholding information from his father, unfortunately at the same time that his father had become more inquisitive than ever. He hardly left the flat these days other than for a daily morning walk, and the less often he left it the more curious he became about things happening outside. Bodhi had concluded that the less Baba knew about everything the better it was for everyone, especially him. It kept Baba from venturing into areas where his inputs were unlikely to be helpful and Bodhi from having to invent plausible half-truths.

"Meeting your girlfriend?" Baba asked.

"What! What girlfriend? What are you talking about?" Bodhi asked, trying to keep the shock out of his voice.

"You know who I mean. Don't be coy with me, Bodhi, and don't think that I don't know what's going on."

"Baba! Please!" Bodhi said, with what he hoped was an indignant expression. He was alarmed that Baba knew about the existence of a girlfriend.

"Don't *Baba Please* me," Baba said. "Talk to your sister. She phoned today. She wants to advertise."

"What for?"

"A wife for you, what else? We don't know what's happening with this Neera person. Your sister doesn't think it's going anywhere."

Bodhi was dumbfounded. Not only did his father know about a girlfriend, he even knew her name. Had Chhotomama been telling tales? Bodhi scratched his beard. But how could Chhotomama know? Bodhi hadn't told him anything either. Was he that transparent?

He didn't want anyone in the family to know about Neera because he didn't know what she felt about him. It was a classic conundrum—he wouldn't say anything till he was sure the answer would be positive, but he would never know the answer unless he said something first. He was violating a law older than Manu's: the man has to apply for the position of lover, the woman decides whether or not to accept the application. These roles couldn't be reversed, because if they were, the woman would be branded a loose character, a hussy. This was as simple a proposition as there could be—water is wet, night follows day, beggars can't be choosers—but too much for Bodhi. He was too meek to ask. This diffidence came on top of Bodhi's natural reticence and general secretiveness. He didn't want to expose his desire and open himself to ridicule or pity if that desire remained unfulfilled. Bodhi had a deep fear of ridicule. He couldn't laugh at himself when others laughed at him and neither could he manufacture snappy retorts. He spent many hours plotting revenge on people who had ridiculed him.

"Your sister can't believe that a girl like Neera would marry into a family like ours, and neither can I," Baba went on. "We're like oil and water, Bodhi. Different layers."

"*Uff.* Will you people please stop bothering me? Who on earth is talking of marriage? Give me a little peace, please."

"Is your sister wrong? Can you imagine that Neera would move into this household and this house?"

"I'm leaving now. Don't wait up for me."

"You don't tell us anything Bodhi."

"There's nothing to tell. You'll be the first to know when there's something to tell." Bodhi thought of slamming the door on his way out, but didn't.

~

Chandan, Bodhi's driver, chose a route through Gariahat. Bodhi was nervous—he had never been to Neera's house or met her father—and didn't notice until it was too late to choose a less congested path.

Gariahat intersection was the centre of shopping in the city's southern half—or used to be before the malls started to spring up. Each corner was a well-known meeting point. Shops lined every inch of the space beyond the pavement which, in turn, was taken over by street merchants of brand name rejects and knock-offs and an assortment of everyday items from underwear and dinnerware to international and domestic porn. Most of the buses ferrying office workers from the south to the government square and commercial hubs in the central part of the city had to go through here. A flyover had been constructed a few years ago to alleviate the congestion, but traffic remained dense at all hours.

The road from Gariahat to Neera's house was a transect through the last 200 years of the city's archaeology.

Traces of the segregated city the British had created were still visible. The colonial city had had three divisions. There were white enclaves where the British lived in long, cool, high-ceilinged bungalows set on broad tree-lined avenues, serviced by legions of native servants—guards, gardeners, maids, cooks, and nannies—who lived in designated servants' outhouses or in other nooks and crevices of the vast spaces the British occupied. At the other end of the city clustered the black ghettoes, where thousands upon thousands of natives were crammed into an unplanned, unregulated mishmash of lean-to's and brick houses, many of which later became unapproachable by cars because of the narrowness of the streets. Sandwiched between the two were the odds-and-ends settlements, where lived the outcasts of both societies; the traders—the Armenians and Jews and Pathans who came to the cosmopolitan city where there was a market for everything, from camel-hair coats to tiger-milk biscuits; and the mixed-ups—the products of Anglo-Indian couplings and Christian converts. These neighbourhoods were neither stately nor miserable, but pleasant, liveable areas of tolerance and commerce. This was the heart of the city today. Theatre Road was one of the main passages through this heart.

Neera lived with her father on Theatre Road.

~

She opened the door wearing a homebody look. Baggy white T-shirt over loose green pajamas. Unkempt frizzy hair. Four brass earrings. Behind her trailed her two smiling beagles—Pomo and Poco—scratching their nails, squeech, squeech, on the marble floor.

They marched through a generous foyer into the living room, a large space lit only by floor and table lamps. No glaring fluorescents here. In that ambiguous light Bodhi could sense but not really see the details of the antique mahogany furniture and original oil paintings on the walls. He could also sense that some things were missing from the room, things that he expected to see in any middle-class living room. Later, he realised what they were—a TV and a dinner table. They were somewhere in the flat, they had to be, but in other rooms. The flat had plenty of other rooms. Bodhi tried to guess its size. He did this at every flat he saw for the first time. Professional curiosity. But here he couldn't. Was it three thousand square feet or four? There was no way to tell. There was too much he couldn't see.

Mr Barua was tall and pale, like his daughter, with ruddy cheeks. He was defiantly bald and had sad eyes that drooped down toward his ears, like a dachshund. Chhotomama was already there, dressed in his communist intellectual uniform of kurta and pajama and scowl. Bankoli and Cookie hadn't been invited to this gathering.

They waited for the chief guest of the evening, a senior bureaucrat in the ministry of housing and an acquaintance of Mr Barua. He was expected to provide good information on the preservation of heritage buildings.

The men sipped Scotch and talked about success.

Mr Barua admired self-made men. Where would the world be without drive and initiative, without self-made men? Mr Barua himself was one, having been born in a market town in Tejpur district in Assam and risen to become the chief executive of an advertising agency. Now he owned one. Chhotomama was another self-made man, a child of refugees from East Bengal who had to live in a slum for several years after their escape from the homeland, and risen to the highest rung of intellectual achievement.

Chhotomama looked pleased and uncomfortable at the same time. Mr Barua expressed admiration for Bodhi too, for having the sense and guts to grab one of the few business opportunities left in the city.

"So how did you do it, young man?" Mr Barua asked. "How did you manage to get a break in the housing business?"

"Umm," said Bodhi and looked at Chhotomama pleadingly. His uncle's eyes were hard to read. Was that glint a sign of enjoyment at Bodhi's discomfort or was it pity? Neera sat next to daddy and stroked Poco and Pomo on her lap. Her eyes were on Bodhi and she seemed to be curious about the answer. She had never asked this question in the months she had known her awkward suitor.

"Getting a break…that's the most important thing," said Mr Barua, who had asked the question because he knew the answer. "Nobody will give a break to us middle-class strivers. We have to make our own breaks. No doctor saab?"

"Indeed," said Chhotomama, "nobody will give a break to anybody, least of all to the poor and the peasants."

"Spoken like a saccha Marxist," said Mr Barua, "ha ha. But doctor saab, what will the peasants do even if they get a break? It's not like they know anything or have any skills." He had forgotten his question to Bodhi and was now eager to engage the communist intellectual in light arm-wrestling. Like most self-made men he thought that all politician-communists were power-hungry hypocrites and all intellectual-communists were well-meaning morons. But he couldn't say this aloud because his daughter, though too well-bred to become a card-carrying communist, was sympathetic to all kinds of lost causes—Adivasi rights, animal rights, gay rights, vegetarianism, organic food, spiritualism, homeopathy, Ayurveda, the Dalai Lama, Medha Patkar, Binayak Sen—maybe this bumbling young man she had brought into the house, who had already overturned a coffee table on the way in, was one of those lost causes—and had chosen to work for a research institute when she could have worked at her father's firm or, for that matter, anywhere, because he, Mr Barua, knew everyone worth knowing in the city.

Bodhi didn't find out till later, but Mr Barua was getting increasingly worried about his daughter. He had hoped that Neera's interests were just fads, silly things young people believed in because they weren't old enough to know better. He had hoped that she hadn't inherited her mother's flightiness, the whimsicality that had made her leave him twenty years ago for a photographer who used to work under him, then leave that man a few years later for a forest conservationist fifteen years older than her, and take up residence with him in a hill village somewhere near Kaziranga. She had never staked a claim on Neera and hadn't had another child. She communicated with her daughter fitfully, and over the years began to act more like an older, distant friend than a mother.

Neera was approaching thirty but her attraction to marginal things remained undiminished. She had expressed no interest in getting married, or in taking over his business, or, according to her father, in anything substantial and worthwhile that required diligence and dedication. If you're interested in research, Mr Barua had told her, then get a proper degree and do it properly. She appeared to have ignored his suggestion.

The conversation darted around amiably, punctuated by an occasional hard-edged remark. Mr Barua was too self-assured to get into a serious argument and Chhotomama knew he was a supplicant that day.

"Mr Barua," he said at one point, "I have to ask you one thing? What'll happen to your company when you retire? Who's going to run it?"

"That's a good question, sir, and the answer is obvious" Mr Barua said. "I will never retire. Ha, ha, ha." Everyone laughed at this hilarious joke. "If I do retire (ha, ha) I hope that this little daughter of mine will take over." He patted Neera's head. She looked at him with a Saraswati smile—fixed and inscrutable.

Bodhi was familiar with that expression. "But..." he began.

"Yes, I know she's working at your institute now, but that's for her to get experience outside the firm. Surely you don't expect her to be there forever. She's there to learn to take orders. Be a team player. Learn to take criticism. If she starts at the top she'll never know what it feels like to be at the bottom. Isn't that correct, *sweetie*?" The look of puzzled exasperation in Mr Barua's eyes led Bodhi to think that this was a serious question; Mr Barua really didn't know the answer.

"I think we should get some stories planted in the media about the legacy of Raniganj Mansion and the need to preserve it," Neera said as if she was taking part in a different conversation.

Bodhi was puzzled. What about the special friend in America? Was he invisible to Neera's father too? Didn't he know that the special friend was coming to the city, possibly to pluck his daughter out of the country for good using some pretence like a master's degree in something or the other? He resolved to ask Neera directly about her plans with the special friend. He wasn't sure however that this resolve would remain as resolute when he saw her again.

~

The bureaucrat arrived an hour late. Traffic, he said. He wasn't very knowledgeable about architectural preservation but that didn't stop him from having strong opinions on it. He asked a few questions about Raniganj Mansion—How old was it? How big was it? Did anyone famous ever live in it? Did anything famous ever happen in it?—and told them that he would look into the issue and put them in touch with the person who actually knew something about the subject. But generally he wasn't in favour of things like architectural preservation and environmental conservation. They were playthings of the rich, he said, and poor societies like ours would be foolish to pay much attention to these distractions. He and Chhotomama exchanged some sharp words, but the hostilities remained civilised.

The tightly clustered discussion began to break up. Neera beckoned Bodhi to a side, close to the entertainment centre. She was in a good mood today, she said. She didn't offer a reason for it and Bodhi knew better than to ask for one. She inserted a CD in the player. To Bodhi's surprise it was a song from fifty years ago.

This is the place,
under this tree shade,
in this sweet dreamland,
where we will laugh and play,
just the two of us,
for the remaining days of our lives.
This forest of honey and shadows,
these trees with bees that dance and murmur,
this is the place
where we will be together,
with brilliant colour and music forever,
for the remaining days of our lives.

Neera never mentioned the special friend (maybe they had had a fight). She never touched him, no little brush of a shoulder or pat on an arm. She smiled beatifically and swayed her head to the lilting melody and Bodhi's kidneys lurched with her every move. He was more confused than ever and thought about her all the way home and into bed and an hour of tossing and turning.

# 3

Bodhi wanted to talk to Mrs Shilpi Roy soon. Sunday was too far away, he told himself, to renew his investigation of the Roys. He needed to get this thing moving.

The Barrackpore Farms store where Shilpi Roy worked was a ten minute walk from Bodhi's flat. He followed a young man to the back of the store where the staff had their offices. The young man knocked on a brown plywood door and shouted, "Shilpi *di*, there's someone to see you." Without waiting for a response the young man pushed the door open.

The office was an oblong of about seventy square feet, jammed with furniture, cabinets, and random loose objects. The narrow back wall had a small window with dark brown drapes covering the top half and an aged white AC sputtering below the drapes, dripping water into a red plastic canister on the floor. Shilpi Roy sat behind an all-purpose table that held a computer monitor, piles of mauve and baby blue folders, several loose sheets of printed paper held down by small statues of Ganesh in many poses—standing, squatting, pirouetting, reclining, playing guitar—a few pens, one scissor, and two paper cups.

"*Arrey* Mr Banerjee, come in, come in," she smiled.

"I'm sorry to barge in like this..." "No, no, Madan, get a cup of tea for the gentleman..." "Please excuse this mess..."

"I was in the neighbourhood and..." "My boss is on leave and..." "If you have a few minutes..." "Certainly...Madan, are you getting the tea?..." "If this is a bad time..." "I'm always behind at work anyway..."

Bodhi waited for the tea to be delivered before he began his questions.

"Your mother-in-law mentioned a three thousand acre zamindari in Comilla."

"Is that what she said? Hmmm. What else did she say?"

"We talked about the coal mine..."

"And the nationalisation and horrible Mrs Gandhi, right?" She chewed nervously on her left pinkie. "Mr Banerjee, I'm not sure how to say this, but my mother-in-law tends to live in her own universe." Bodhi nodded. "That universe is similar to ours most of the time, but as far as the past is concerned...her memories don't always match up with reality."

"Yes. I got a sense of that. That's why...could you explain...I mean if you don't mind."

"About the zamindari, for instance. The family had some land to start with, but you could hardly call the man a serious zamindar. I mean my mother-in-law's father-in-law. What does that make him? My grandfather-in-law? That's funny." A faint smile danced across her face. "A moneylender, that's what he was. That's how he made his money. I don't think he ever had more than two or three hundred acres."

"Oh." Bodhi's knowledge on moneylenders was as shallow as on zamindars and came from the same source—old movies. Both were evil types of men, zamindars in bullying ways, moneylenders in creepy ways. Moneylenders were played by drooling, oily, old men who were either extremely fat or extremely thin. They were always counting money with their extremely fat or extremely thin fingers or behaving lecherously toward the innocent bahu-betis of the village. Not like zamindars, who may have been just as villainous on the subjects of greed and lust, but were fair-skinned and well-dressed and had dignified wives and luscious, altruistic daughters.

When Bodhi reported this conversation to Chhotomama, he set the record straight. Except in a few cases, there was no real difference between zamindars and moneylenders, he said. Usually they were one and the same. *Zamindar = Moneylender*. In those bad old days, much like the good ones now, the peasants always lived on the edge of disaster. The zamindars took three-fourths of their crop in taxes, Chhotomama explained, and, as a matter of course, the peasants were left with almost nothing. Whenever there was a big expense, like a marriage or death or an important puja or sacrifice or some other ritual, these peasants had to borrow money. Those same landlords that had taken their crops then became moneylenders, at back-breaking rates, using the peasant's thimbleful of land as collateral. Zip. Fast forward. Land gone to moneylender. By the beginning of the twentieth century, a large fraction of the zamindars of Bengal were ruthless men who had started out as moneylenders. *Moneylender = Zamindar*. The circle of life.

"Okay," Bodhi said to Shilpi Roy, "but what about the colliery then? Your family did own one, didn't they?"

"Oh yes, there's no doubt about that."

"So, the family money had three sources. Zamindari and money lending, and the colliery on top, right? Do I have this part correct?"

"Well...yes and no. I don't know whether I should tell you all this." Shilpi Roy chewed on her pen. She wanted to spill some family secrets but didn't want to look too enthusiastic doing it.

"Please Mrs Roy, I understand your hesitation completely. But the truth is the truth, isn't it." Even as he said this Bodhi had doubts about his statement. "You wouldn't want untruths to be published."

"But...this truth is quite unpleasant, Mr Banerjee. In fact, I'm not even certain that it is the truth. It is...how shall I say...a Roy family fable. My brother-in-law, who lives upstairs from us, he knows a lot more. He's the one who told me. My mother-in-law denies it completely. She won't even talk about it. Becomes very angry."

Bodhi waited.

"I presume you'll find out anyway. I believe there were newspaper stories about it at the time. In any case...there were rumours that my grandfather-in-law was a hoarder and a black marketer. During the famine of 1943."

Oh no! Not the famine of 1943! This was the one subject from his collective past that Bodhi had good information on. He had been instructed on the famine of 1943 by the family elders till he began to feel guilty that he hadn't suffered through it himself, as if that made him insufficiently Bengali and somehow unpatriotic. Chhotomama hadn't lived through the famine either but it was his single most favourite subject of conversation. When the mood took him, he could divert any topic—from waterlogging in the city streets to the minimalism of Japanese art—to the famine of 1943.

"When you have a war between imperialist-capitalists for control of the world's resources," Chhotomama would lecture, "and you combine that with a colonial government that exists to feed and supply and nurture the war, and add in local collaborators, our fellow natives, who responded to only two things—their imperialist masters and their own bottomless greed—then you get tragedy on the scale of our famine of 1943." His eyes would get misty. The large saucers behind the gloomy lenses would fill with water. "Do you know that we don't even know how many people died? Certainly thirty lakhs, maybe even fifty. Things got so bad that people used to rummage through cow dung to find undigested grains. They literally ate shit. Hundreds of thousands of families left their villages and came to this city to find something to eat. They became beggars. Proud, self-sufficient farmers became beggars in the city. They used to beg for rotten food and the leftover water from boiled rice. Oh, it was a terrible time. I've heard stories from my elders in the Party that you can't believe."

"If you want to know why I became a communist, why so many of us became communists," Chhotomama had told Bodhi several times, "then you have to know about the Bengal famine of 1943."

~

"Yes, my grandfather-in-law was a hoarder," Shilpi Roy said. "He had some rice mills and godowns and he held on to whatever passed through his hands. Didn't put it on the market so that he could make a killing when the prices went up. Oh, he made a killing. It wasn't the source of his fortune, of course, but added a lot to it. Even by his standards, this was abominable. Then again, the men in that family are something special." Shilpi Roy took a small bite at the pen she had been chewing off and on.

Bodhi was completely nonplussed now, not only by the fundamentally different versions of Mr Prafulla Kumar Roy offered by two women in his family, but also by the timing of events. Raniganj Mansion happened to be donated in 1945 by a moneylender who happened to have made a killing from hoarding and black-marketing rice in 1943 and 1944. It didn't make sense. Why be so generous when you're so greedy? Why give away the very thing you've worked so hard, even killed, to acquire?

"Thank you for this information, Mrs Roy," Bodhi said. "This is very helpful. If you have a couple of minutes more I'd like to ask one more thing that I wasn't clear about." Shilpi Roy nodded. "Please don't answer if you don't want to. This is embarrassing even to ask...but what happened to the Roy fortune? I mean the government must have paid something when they nationalised the mines. They couldn't just take it and pay nothing, could they?"

"Of course," she says, "the government paid, but not for the land, which wouldn't have been much anyway, but for the coal production. Twenty-five paisa per ton of coal they used to produce every year."

"Only twenty-five paisa!" Bodhi said. A good king-size cigarette cost ten rupees now. Twenty paisa could get you...

what? Three beedis? A couple of lozenges? Even beggars would refuse this amount.

"It wasn't too bad. If you do the calculations it comes to over Rs 25,000 a year. In those days that was quite a bit of money. Easily fifty times more than now, maybe even a hundred times more." Bodhi admired Shilpi Roy's confident knowledge of the facts and her cool-headed analysis. She was right. In his business, prices had moved at about that pace. In the right neighbourhoods, a flat bought for fifty thousand rupees thirty years ago could be sold for a hundred times that price now.

"So, if the money wasn't so bad, what happened? Why are you living like this? In a place like Pratapgarh? What happened to the money?"

"My mother-in-law didn't tell you?"

"We didn't get to that point. She went to do her puja, then you came and dropped the onions." Bodhi smiled. How easily he could speak with this woman. How difficult it was to speak with Neera. And here he was not even being himself. He was pretending to be someone he wasn't. Maybe that was the trick. Maybe he needed a disguise to come into his own with Neera. Maybe he should wear a mask when he met her—an imperious and disdainful one with cold eyes and a sneer—so that she couldn't see the hangdog expression on his face.

"Should I tell you everything in one day?" Shilpi Roy smiled back. "Shouldn't we leave something for the next day?"

"There will be a next day, Mrs Roy, I'm sure of that." She didn't know what Bodhi knew and he wasn't about to tell her. "Looks like I'll be writing a long article. Your family is much more interesting than I thought."

"Are you going to be writing all this? I thought you were going to write about Raniganj Mansion."

"Yes, that's correct, but..." Bodhi fumbled for an exit. He wished he had done some research on deception strategies used by journalists. "...but I have to have good knowledge of the deep background." That sounded believable.

"Actually, I don't care whether you write this or not. Those men were obnoxious. Plus, they are dead. They were shameless when alive, and I'm sure their ghosts haven't suddenly turned into saints."

"Heh, heh. Exactly."

"There are two things my mother-in-law will never tell you about her husband." Shilpi Roy had more secrets to share. "First, that he was a swindler. He swindled money from his partner, a man who was co-owner of the mine. This man...some Mr Laha...had a financial stake in the mine but wasn't involved in its day to day operations. He was what they used to call a sleeping partner in those days. Anyway, for years my father-in-law had paid this sleeping partner less than his fair share. I don't know the details of how the swindle worked. There was some business involving crooked accountants and fake balance sheets. There was a white book and a black book. In any case, when the mine was nationalised, my father-in-law got greedy, which wasn't unexpected from him, and claimed compensation based on the real accounts. That wasn't very clever because then all the scamming and scheming came into the open and the sleeping partner found out what had been going on. He took my father-in-law to court, and after many years of lawyer's fees and this and that, he won back his money, plus damages, plus I don't know what."

"A lot?"

"Yes, a lot. Not enough to put them on the street, but they had to sell their house."

"Bliss Cottage?"

"Yes. So you've been told about it. That one."

"Is that when they moved to Pratapgarh, where you are now?"

"No, that's much more recent. My in-laws sold Bliss Cottage and bought a nice house near Ballygunj, nothing fancy like Bliss Cottage, but nice. That's where I moved in when I got married. Don't forget, Mr Banerjee, there is a second thing my mother-in-law won't tell you."

"Yes, you said two things."

"This one you'll like. It turns out that my father-in-law had another sleeping partner. A mistress." She gave a tight smile that didn't make the journey from her lips to her eyes. "He had been maintaining another household for years. Apparently everyone knew, except my mother-in-law. He and the mistress used to appear together in public. They used to go to theatres and restaurants together. He used to spend many nights in her house. He used to tell my mother-in-law that he was studying with a tantric master."

Bodhi stared at her and swivelled his head from side-to-side in astonishment.

"The rogue didn't have a job and didn't have an income other than the colliery settlement. He was running two establishments, one of them with a mistress with expensive tastes, the other with a wife who thought she was still queen of a colliery, and he was buried to his forehead in debt. Guess what? You have to settle your debts sooner or later. His were settled after he died and the family understood the full extent of his...his...debauchery. That's when we moved to the house you have seen, after we were forced to sell the place in Ballygunj. This was the year after I got married. I like to think of the house in Pratapgarh as my wedding gift."

Bodhi kept staring at Shilpi Roy. She seemed to be enjoying herself. The smile on her face suggested an intimate knowledge of and calm contempt for the foolishness of mankind.

"And there's more. You might as well know as long as you don't use this information. They had a son. My father-in-law and his mistress. I believe he's about the same age as me."

That makes three sons, two legitimate and one bastard, Bodhi added up with admiration. All from virile Bengali sperm. They didn't make men like that anymore. A man even Cookie could look up to.

And how many houses? Raniganj Mansion of course, which was gifted away. Then Bliss Cottage—sold to pay off the colliery business partner. Then a modest house in Ballygunj—sold to pay off debts incurred by maintaining a mistress and a colliery queen. And finally the squalid nameless house Bodhi had visited in Pratapgarh.

Was this a story of how the mighty fall—because of greed and self-indulgence? Or was this a story of how the mighty rise—through greed and self-indulgence? Was the difference simply a matter of competence? A greedy but competent crook amasses a fortune and is followed by a greedy but incompetent crook who squanders it. What about the first law of India—family comes first, because genes are supreme? Was criminality inheritable, but competence not? Or did nature have a way of balancing out its distribution of genes for criminality and competence so that one family didn't have an endless supply of one type? What goes up, must come down. Here today, gone tomorrow. The circle of life. What about decency, then? Was that inheritable too? And what did decent people inherit other than their genes? Did they inherit the earth, but only after it had been turned into a wasteland by vileness?

"I have to digest all this, Mrs Roy," Bodhi said, thinking that he should share this information with the Save Raniganj Mansion team before he went any further. He hoped that he would be able to tell this story cogently. There were so many twists and turns. "And I must let you return to your work. But I'd like to follow up, if I may. Maybe this Sunday, like we planned earlier. Perhaps I'll get a chance to talk with your husband also."

"This Sunday is fine. We'll be home. But it'll be just the three of us—my mother-in-law, Maya, and me. My husband is not with us. We'll see you then."

Bodhi walked into a blazing day outside. His glasses misted over instantly. He blinked and rubbed them dry and thought about the ambiguity of the parting statement. "My husband is not with us." What did it mean? Was her husband dead? Were they divorced or separated? Why then was she living with her mother-in-law? The bigger question was—Who were these people? Did they breathe the same air and drink the same water as he? Was he the only normal person left in the universe?

# 4

Bodhi had breakfast with Baba the next day. This was unusual. Normally his father woke two hours before he did, and by the time he was up Baba had already had breakfast, taken a morning walk with the regulars, updated each other on the conditions of their respective aches, oozes, and bowel movements, returned and finished reading the paper. But today Baba had waited for Bodhi. He wanted to talk.

"How tall are you?" Baba asked after finishing his bowl of corn flakes.

"Five eleven," Bodhi said. "I thought you knew."

"We'll round it up to six," Baba said. "And your weight?"

"I don't know. Around 62 kilos. I haven't checked in a while. But why do you…"

"How much are you earning these days? White and black together."

"Baba! What kind of a question is that! What's going on?"

"You don't have to shout."

"I'm not shouting," Bodhi said. "Maybe you should turn the TV down."

"The TV's not loud."

"Baba, they can hear it in Bombay."

"Don't exaggerate like your mother (may her soul rest in peace). Hear it in Bombay indeed!"

"At least wear your hearing aid."

"You know I can't do that. I've told you a hundred crore times. That static sounds like a waterfall inside my head."

"Oh yes. I have to take it to the shop. Probably a loose connection."

"You said the same thing last week."

"I know. I'm sorry I forgot."

"And the week before that."

"I'll definitely do it this week. Promise."

They had lost the thread of the conversation by now so Baba tried to reel it back. "I was asking how much you earn these days. A round estimate will do."

"And I asked why you need to know this?"

"Don't I have a right to know…as your father?"

"And my height and weight too. Are you going to sell me by the kilo?"

"Something like that," Baba smiled. "Your sister needs this information to put into the Internet. She said everyone's doing arranged marriages on the Internet these days and she's going to get you started."

"And you can tell Didi to mind her own business. I'm not getting married now and I'm not getting married on the internet."

"If it's that girl Neera…"

"Why do you keep bringing her up? Have I ever mentioned her to you?"

"No, you haven't."

Bodhi raised both shoulders and both eyebrows simultaneously, to ask—why then do you keep bothering me with this.

"You haven't, but your Chhotomama has," Baba said. "He told me that you used to go to his office once every rathayatra, but nowadays it's every week and sometimes more than that. He knows that you haven't developed a taste for history or the plight of the poor all of a sudden. We'd both be happy if you did that. No, he thinks…he's pretty sure that you're very interested in this girl."

Bodhi had no response. So his public posture of nonchalance around Neera wasn't being very effective in covering his true feelings. Others could see that he was behaving like a goat.

"Your Chhotomama also says that this girl is out of your reach," Baba said. "She's from a really well-to-do family and you can do all the promotery you want but you'll never reach her class."

Trust Chhotomama to think that. Class surmounts everything, including love. Haven't communists ever been in love, Bodhi wondered, or has it always been with class-appropriate and elder-approved persons? Like arranged marriages.

"Remember where you come from, Bodhi, remember how you began," Baba said. "Remember that your financial success today wouldn't have been possible without the sacrifices made by your mother and me. We gave you the best education we could, but that wasn't enough. I don't blame you for that because I know you didn't create the system in which your education isn't valued. Then we gave you the only little capital we had. That, and nothing else, is the foundation of where you are today. I don't want to say more about this because it will sound prideful on my part and I know that you don't want to be reminded that you should be grateful."

Baba had reminded Bodhi...again...that the flat they were sitting in was owned by Baba. Not only that, the building in which their flat was one of eight identical flats was standing on land that used to be owned by Baba, land on which Baba had owned a house that he had bought with all his savings and some borrowings in 1979. He had reminded Bodhi that the building they were sitting in was the very first one constructed by Bodhi and Cookie. This was the start in their career as promoters.

Bodhi's father's house was the original Heavenly Home.

~

Bodhi could have corrected a few errors in Baba's claims, but didn't. The historical record would show that his father hadn't at all been in favour of turning his house into a flat building so that Bodhi could become a promoter. "I haven't struggled all my life to be honourable and respectable so that my son can become a lousy *dalal*," he had said. Bodhi's mother had been the one who made it happen—after months of unrelenting pressure from Bodhi. She too had been hesitant at first, but blind love eventually won out. She was bedridden by then and her wishes, which had largely been ignored by her husband when she was healthy, had become dying wishes.

"What if he throws us out of the flat once he has it?" her husband had asked.

"He won't. He's a good boy, he has a good heart," she had said. "But you should keep the flat in our name in any case, just to be sure."

"What if we lose the house and then he bungles the business?" her husband had asked. "He hasn't been particularly good at anything till now."

To be fair to Bodhi, this was an unduly harsh judgment. He had always been a studious boy; not good enough in all subjects, unfortunately, to become a doctor or engineer, which is why he had to follow a different career. But he wrote poetry and read the classics. Not everyone could be strong in math, could they? Being weak in algebra and calculus wasn't the end of the world, was it? Does the ability to solve differential equations make a person ethically superior? What does good conduct have to do with being good at algebra? But this was the aforementioned system, captured in a poem that all children were taught as soon as they could speak—

Boys who focus on their reading and writing courses
can spend their lives riding on elephants and horses
Boys who don't study and boys who bunk class
are destined to be run over by a corporation bus

"That Cookie is a clever boy," Bodhi's mother had said. "He'll make sure that our boy doesn't get into trouble."

"What are you talking about?" her husband had said. "Cookie's own father has thrown him out of the family business. How clever can he be?"

"You know these sardars are crazy," she had said. "Wearing those turbans in this heat...anyone would be driven to madness. Cookie's not like them. That he's cut his hair off is the best sign that he's normal, like us."

Logic prevailed. Or emotion. It wasn't easy to differentiate between these categories of explanation as far as Bodhi's mother was concerned. It took several months, but Bodhi's mother was eventually able to convince her husband to do this one thing, this one last thing for their only son.

Bodhi was grateful, or thought he was, at least as much as he needed to be, but he wished that the subject of his need to be grateful wasn't brought up as frequently as it was, like a compulsory question on a trigonometry exam; if sine theta and cos theta do a huge favour for tan theta, at what angle should tan theta prostrate itself to show its gratitude? What happens when cos theta is removed from the equation? Does the angle of tan theta's prostration to sine theta increase, decrease, or stay the same?

~

It's hard to be a capitalist without capital.

The money needed to demolish Baba's house and replace it with the flat building had been provided by Cookie's chacha*ji*, his father's younger brother, who owned a popular Mughlai restaurant near Park Circus and had also cut his hair against his family's wishes. When Cookie's father had punished Cookie for cutting his hair, this chacha*ji* had stood by him. There was community of commiseration between cut-surds, an unspoken brotherhood similar to that of short men married to taller women. They recognised each other instantly, these cut-surds and short husbands, even if they had never met before, and nodded empathetically, little nods and curtsies visible only to their fellow sufferers, that said—we have something in common, a pain that no one outside our fraternity understands. Take this money puttar, his uncle had told Cookie, and return it when you can.

Cookie and Bodhi never talked about which of them came up with the idea of promoting Baba's property. It was a touchy subject. But someone had to be first, someone always is. Even identical twins have a birth order. Bodhi had a clear memory of that first conversation. He and Cookie were upstairs at Shahenshah restaurant, next to New Market, having egg-mutton rolls and beer.

"I hate my job," Cookie said.

"Not as much as I hate mine," Bodhi said.

"I think I'll divorce Pinky and go back to snack daddy," Cookie said. "I can't stand travelling by bus every day."

"You're such a precious gem. Kohinoor of India."

"No, seriously," Cookie said, "have you smelled a minibus at six o'clock on a Friday evening? It's like the landfill at Dhapa. Have you seen the size of the sweat patches on those underarms? It's bigger than their heads. Terrifying, like a blob from outer space, growing out of control in front of your eyes."

"Welcome to the real world, you spoilt brat. I've been travelling by bus all my life." Bodhi said, feeling morally superior in his lifelong tenure as a commoner.

"And you've never smelled those underarms?"

"Never."

"And you're supposed to be a sensitive man. A poet, no less."

"I'm sensitive to the pain of others, you idiot, not their body odour."

"You don't say."

"Trust me."

"I know," Cookie said. "Let's become promoters." Just like that. Out of the blue.

"Ha ha," Bodhi said. "With what? We don't have money and we don't have land and we don't know anything about the business."

Then they sang *All You Need is Love* for a minute. After the singing stopped, Cookie said, "Your father owns your house, doesn't he?"

That's how Bodhi remembered the conversation. He had never asked Cookie about how he remembered it. They agreed that it was a brilliant idea. Both had recognised that this was the one business they could get into that had a large payoff but required relatively little skill. All the skilled work was done by others. Licensed architects made the designs, which were virtually identical boxes anyway. Experienced masons did the early dhalai work with steel and concrete and later finished off the plaster and tiles. Electricians did the wiring, plumbers did the piping, and they did much the same work in all buildings. The rest was *jugaad*. Manage this and manage that. Patao this guy, chillao at that guy. Sometimes one alternately cajoled and shouted at the same guy. Their division of labour had always been clear—Bodhi was the cajoler, Cookie specialised in shouting.

No, what they had really needed was capital, not skill or experience. Bodhi's parents had provided one crucial element, the land; Cookie's chacha*ji* had provided the other crucial element, the cash, twenty lakhs for working capital. After that first project, Bodhi and Cookie had worked on fourteen other buildings in six years, the largest of them a sixteen-flat project in Garia. They had two projects going right now and a third was about to begin. There was no doubt that their business was a success. Success has many fathers but this one seemed to be a bastard, because neither of them had shown much enthusiasm for carrying the burden of eternal gratitude all on his shoulders.

Was there a less useful emotion than gratitude? It was far better to owe money, Bodhi felt, than a favour to be grateful for. Money could be paid back, but a favour, a one-of-a-kind favour, could never be returned. One remained forever in debt and that didn't create a good feeling inside. The expectation of gratitude was corrosive, like an acid eating away the soft tissue of civility till it exposed the raw nerves of resentment underneath.

~

"Bodhi, my son," Baba said, "I'm afraid you're going to get hurt if you keep pursuing this girl. You must know your limits. That's the only way for people like us to survive in this world. If you try to rise beyond your limits, people who are already at those higher levels, people with less morality and humanity than you, are going to chop your head off with less concern than they would have in tossing a banana peel on a footpath."

This is the same old predictable middle-class moralising, Bodhi thought but didn't say, that has kept you people where you are, in the middle. These so-called morals are based on nothing but fear, nothing but a whimpering instinct for self-preservation. Protect yourself above all else and decorate your defensive behaviour with high ethical language.

"Look around you, Baba," Bodhi said. "It's a new world out there. Not your world. Not Chhotomama's world. Not even the world I grew up in. I have to find my limit in this world, na Baba, not a world that has vanished?"

# 5

The following Sunday dawned hot and humid. Bodhi woke up late and, to his surprise, in a cheerful mood. He took his father along for a shopping expedition to the vegetable and fish market. "It's too late," Baba grumbled, "all the good stuff is gone." But he changed into clean and ironed clothes and happily joined his son on a rickshaw to the bazaar. They spent an hour bargaining and ferreting out quality in its smelly lanes and slippery alleys and ended up buying much more than they needed. More work for the cook and more complaints from her that would go in one ear and out the other.

Bodhi and Baba had an overstuffed lunch and updated each other about the juicy goings-on of their relatives, far and near. Bodhi talked about one of his cousins living in Delhi who was in an affair with a co-worker and had been caught by his wife during one of her periodic snoops through his mobile phone while he was asleep. The rumour was, the tell-tale text from the co-worker said, 'I pine for your willow inside my sticky wicket my Yuvraj Singh.' Baba couldn't understand one of his cousins' explanations for delaying his daughter's wedding date announcement, especially when almost fifteen months had passed after the engagement ceremony. This one's going nowhere, agreed father and son; sad—marriages breaking up even before they happen. *Kalyug!* Both had heard of one of Bodhi's nephews in Bombay who was threatening suicide if he wasn't allowed to marry his lover within the month; he was 19 and she was 18 and neither had earned a rupee in their lives.

Nothing of consequence or of a personal nature was brought up by father or son.

~

After lunch Bodhi drove himself over to Pratapgarh. He was a confident enough driver to handle Sunday afternoon traffic. He parked around the corner again, to avoid being seen driving a nice car. He was going to act like a journalist now, not a promoter. His cheerful mood from the morning hadn't abated and he whistled 'Hum Dil De Chuke Sanam' on his jaunt to the Roy residence.

Inside he found a reception party waiting for him. Grandmother Roy and Shilpi Roy he already knew. But instead of little Maya, there was a middle-aged couple. The man was close to fifty, thin, with a healthy head of salt and pepper hair, and steel-frame glasses. He had patches of mottled white skin on his face and arms from vitiligo. He looked like a man who wanted to be someone else. The woman was fair and stout and wore a printed cotton sari. A thick line of sindoor marked the middle parting in her hair which was tied into a pugnacious knot on the nape of her neck. Both new people looked tense. The man had a constipated expression and the woman looked like she would like to roll a few chapattis using human flesh as dough.

The man was Pankaj Kamal Roy, the older son of Grandmother Roy. He worked, Bodhi found out later, as a salesman in a toy and gift store in Gariahat. The woman was his wife, Anjali Roy, and she didn't work outside the house. "Ah, good," thought Bodhi, "now I'm getting to know the full family."

That was his last positive till the night he was jailed.

"So Mr Banerjee, if that's your real name," Mr Pankaj Kamal Roy said, before Bodhi had a chance to sit down, "will you kindly tell us who you are and what your intentions are before we call the police?"

"Oh shit," thought Bodhi, "oh shit, oh shit, oh shit." He hadn't prepared a contingency plan for this situation.

"I…I," he stammered, "I really am Bodhichitto Banerjee. Please believe me."

"Bodhichitto!" snorted Mrs Anjali Roy.

"Yes, Dada," Shilpi Roy said in a flat tone to her brother-in-law, "like I told you, that's his real name. But he's not a reporter. He's a promoter."

Bodhi's overeager visit to Shilpi Roy's office earlier in the week had given him away. After he left, Shilpi Roy had been approached by the office bearer, Madan, who had served them tea. Madan had inquired whether Shilpi-di was in the market to buy a flat, because if she was, he, Madan, had access to higher-class promoters than the man that had just visited her. How did Madan know that her visitor was a promoter, Shilpi Roy had asked. Everyone knew, she was told, this was a man from the neighbourhood and there were no secrets here.

Bodhi evaluated his options. He could (A) tell the truth, or as much of the truth as needed to defuse the crisis, and deal with these people later, in a non-crisis setting, or (B) delay for now, and talk to Chhotomama, and let him handle the problem, at least for now. His first instinct was to go for plan B till his practical mind discovered a hitch in it. What if he wasn't allowed to delay? What if the Roys had arranged for some local goons to hang around and beat him up if he provided unsatisfactory answers? He knew this type well, these Roys of Pratapgarh. If they weren't already homeowners, they could have been his clients. This type wouldn't go to the police for anything, because they suspected, justifiably, that Bodhi could pull strings or bribe people and get away unscathed. Bodhi's type always did and the Roys' type knew that. No, they must have arranged for some local toughs to rough him up. Law and order were best left to the local goon squad. That lady, the older daughter-in-law, looked like she herself could have been a goon in her youth. Those paan-stained teeth and that look in her eyes. She reminded Bodhi of his informant Bablu Das.

Bodhi abhorred violence, especially the possibility of its application to his body. He chose plan A with the hope that the conversation would flow in a direction that would give him an opportunity to shift to plan B.

He began by telling them that he had no interest in their property and no evil motives and that he wasn't even operating on his own behalf, but making inquiries as a representative of a respected professor, a man they must have seen on TV, his Chhotomama.

"Making inquiries for what?" asked Mrs Anjali Roy, clearly a woman with a habit of demanding answers.

This was the moment of decision. Should Bodhi tell them directly, or let Chhotomama do it? His natural inclination was to indirectness and reticence, but as the shock of being discovered wore off, as he began to think with his head rather than through panicky instinct, he remembered his original prognosis of the situation, a prognosis confirmed by Cookie, that the Roys simply couldn't refuse the gaajar ka halwa of Raniganj Mansion.

There was too much money in it and the Roys obviously didn't have much. Bodhi and Cookie could turn this situation around—so from not having much the Roys would go to having too much money—and make very large sums themselves in the process. This was an opportunity for Bodhi and Cookie to make money like they never had before.

~

How much was Raniganj Mansion worth? Soon after Cookie came to know of the plan to Save Raniganj Mansion, he had sat Bodhi down to figure it out explicitly. "Listen, partner," he said, "I know Chhotomama is your beloved uncle and all that, and I respect him too and blah blah blah, but have you thought about how much money is in that property?"

Bodhi assured him that he had given it some thought.

"What if the owners decide to sell?" Cookie asked. "Who in their right minds wouldn't, unless they were like Goenka or Birla? Even they'd probably sell, bhosadike. And we know there aren't any Bengalis with that kind of money. Ha ha."

Bodhi told him that this idea had crossed his mind also.

"So if Raniganj Mansion is going to be sold, why shouldn't we be the promoters?" Cookie warmed up. "For once we have the inside track on a really nice property. What am I saying? It's far beyond really nice. It's fabulous. We've never come within shouting distance of a property like this. This is in a different planet from the garbage we deal with in Garia and Behala. This could be our career, 'Chaudvin Ka Chand', this could take us over the hump. We could become players."

Bodhi stated that this possibility too hadn't escaped his attention. How could it? There was no doubt that this would be the biggest project of their career. By a large margin. It would move them two steps higher in the hierarchy of promoters in the city. No longer would their clients come solely from the upper crust of the lower middle-class; Heavenly Homes Ltd. would be able to make a breakthrough to the upper crust of the upper middle-class. Bodhi imagined that if he lived modestly for the rest of his life, which he could because his needs were modest even if his desires weren't, he could retire with the profits from this single project.

They got down to some calculations. In their exercise, the building itself was worth nothing. If they couldn't replace Raniganj Mansion with something much bigger, the project would be pointless. Therefore, the building was worth less than nothing. All three hundred tonnes of bricks and mortar were worth less than nothing. It would actually cost some money to bring it down. They would need to hire a gang of demolition men that would use hammers and chisels and bare hands to take the building down brick by aged brick.

All the value was in the land. Neither Bodhi nor Cookie knew the exact dimensions of Raniganj Mansion, but they were experienced promoters, and like butchers know goats and beauty contest judges know vital-stats, they had a good rough estimate. Somewhere around twenty-five thousand square feet. A little over half an acre.

"How much can we build on? How high do we go? Six floors? Seven floors?" asked Cookie, deferring to Bodhi's expertise in this domain.

"I don't think so," said Bodhi.

The municipal building code limited how much plinth area could be created based on the width of the road in front of a property, which determined the magic number—the floor-area-ratio, known as FAR in the business. The wider the road, the higher the FAR, something between 1.25 and 3.0. The smallest FARs applied to the alleys and byways in the most congested parts of the city, not neighbourhoods like Elgin Road, where Raniganj Mansion was located.

"Let's assume that it's our project and let's make conservative assumptions, shall we?" Bodhi continued. "Let's assume that the FAR will be two. It could be higher, but let's assume it won't. That means we can build about fifty thousand saleable square feet. Let's also assume that we'll build ten thousand square feet per floor. That's going to allow us to design the flats with lots of verandas and windows, you know...the high-end buyers like that...and leave some nice open space where we can put in a playground and maybe a garden. I think we can go up to five floors."

The number of floors they could build didn't really matter much at the margin. The basic calculation had two variables: the total square footage to be sold and the price per square foot.

"Let's be conservative again," Bodhi said, "and assume that the price to the buyer will be six thousand rupees per square foot. I think we could go for more in that neighbourhood, but let's say we don't. Six thousand times fifty thousand. That makes a project of thirty crores." He smiled like philosopher who had finally figured out that the building blocks of the universe were sugar and chocolate.

"*Aha,*" said Cookie.

"*Oho,*" said Bodhi.

They giggled like children chasing butterflies. Nothing else needed to be said because the rest of the calculations followed with familiarity, like a nursery rhyme. It would cost seven crores to build the house. Bodhi and Cookie would keep twenty percent of the sales; that would be three crores for each. The rest, seventeen crores, would go the landowner. The final numbers would change, but not for less.

"Seventeen gulabi crores for the Roys," said Cookie, "and very likely even more than that. From Charminar to Qutub Minar. Saaley! I'd run over my grandmother with one of my father's buses for that kind of money."

"I'd run over your grandmother too," said Bodhi, "for that kind of money." They laughed giddily for another minute.

"Does Chhotomama seriously think that the Roys are going to say no to this?" Cookie said. "Is he crazy?"

What could Bodhi say? Was there any doubt that his uncle was crazy? Who else but a lunatic could be a communist these days? Who else but a lunatic could believe in the betterment of human nature?

"Are you any less crazy, Bodhi?" asked Cookie. "You're going along with Chhotomama's make-believe world."

"What can I do, Cookie? I can't betray him after promising support. You were there. You promised to help too."

"What about the three crore rupees? *Ching ching ching.* You want your share to go to someone else? Because hear you me, confused beanpole, someone *is* going to break Raniganj Mansion down and make serious money from it. Regardless of what you do, it's going to happen. When it happens, and if it's not us, then I'm personally going to make batata fry with your balls and serve it to the office staff."

"It's impossible, Cookie. I can't do it. My family will disown me. No one will talk to me again. And Neera... she...I'll have no chance with her if I do this. She's fully behind Chhotomama. This is exactly the kind of thing she likes to do."

Family or fortune? The girl or the money? Bodhi had had an intimation of the dilemma to come when he had first seen the Roy house in Pratapgarh and fully understood their financial condition, but he had pushed that thought away as premature and dangerous. He didn't want to think about it until he had to, because thought could lead to action and the possibility of action petrified him. Now here was Cookie, in his face as usual, being pushy and demanding that he think those thoughts. Bodhi was reminded about the similarities between himself and the elder Pandava brother Yudhisthir, whom he had earlier seen as a weak man but now saw as a good man, deeply conflicted only because he was a good man. Had he not been a good man, there wouldn't have been any conflict inside his head. Only good men worry about doing bad things. Bad men don't bother.

How to do good and be right and win at the same time?

"What do you see in that girl, Bodhi?" For months Cookie had been itching to say something about Neera and now that Bodhi had brought up the subject himself, he had the opening he needed. He had maintained an unexpectedly diplomatic silence and held his tongue in the hope that Bodhi's fascination with Neera would go away; but it hadn't and could now get in the way of a big payday.

In Cookie's direct understanding of the world, a man would do anything to win the woman he loved, including forsake family and fortune. He, Cookie, materialistic and nonsense-free Cookie, who pooh-poohed sentimentality and mawkishness, had done the same, much to his own amazement. He had married Pinky, his Bengali and Hindu wife, with the near-certain knowledge that his father, his conservative and traditional Sikh father who cared more for the approval of his community than his son's happiness, would disinherit him if he did so. Sure, Cookie was all of twenty-three when he did this, an immature and reckless mustang; but he had a feeling that he would have done the same thing at any age, even now. The motivations would be more complicated. The need to defy his father would always be part of it. But after clearing away all the underbrush of complexity and multitude there would remain one true tree—his love for his woman.

Cookie was sure that Bodhi would betray Chhotomama with far less hesitation than he would Neera. But whereas Cookie had sacrificed a thriving business for true love, Bodhi was showing every sign of sacrificing a fortune for an infatuation. Neera, clearly, was the bigger problem.

"She's doesn't seem to be your type at all, yaar," Cookie said. "Looks too hi-fi for people like us. You know...like she doesn't even shit."

"What's my type then, since you seem to know everything?" Bodhi was aware that Neera and Cookie wouldn't and didn't get along. She had told him after first meeting Cookie, "your friend is a little Punjabi type, isn't he? So crude. I'm surprised he's your best friend." Bodhi had defended Cookie, first as a real Punjabi, not a Punjabi type, and then as not really very Punjabi because of his Bengali wife and steadfast refusal to Bhangra. Cookie is an easily misunderstood man, he had said, underneath that rough exterior is a heart of gold.

Cookie hadn't heard his defence, of course, and even if he had, it wouldn't have changed his mind. "You need someone more gharelu but intellectual," he said. "Someone who owns jeans and looks good in them but prefers churidars. Someone who doesn't wear more than two earrings at a time. You can watch art movies together and recite love poems to each other. And have studious children who'll become doctors."

"You're asking me to commit suicide, Cookie," Bodhi said. "If I follow your idea, there's no question that I'll lose Neera. Are you a friend or what? Is this how friends behave?"

"Let me ask you something," Cookie said. "Neera is about our age? Right? Why isn't she married?"

"How would I know? I've never asked her. Are you nuts? I couldn't ask that."

"But aren't you curious?"

"Maybe she's never met the right guy."

"Or maybe there is no right guy for her. Maybe she doesn't know how to love anyone other than herself. Maybe she's so comfortable in her own cocoon that she's never let any man get through."

Bodhi had thought of all this and a lot more. Cookie didn't know everything. Bodhi hadn't told him about the special friend in America for fear of this very conversation they were having. Cookie would be apoplectic if he knew Bodhi had an invisible rival who could swoosh down at any moment and whisk away his lady love on an international flight.

"Since when did you become a psychologist?" Bodhi said.

"You don't have to be a psychologist to recognise a tease," Cookie said. "I'm telling you Albert Pinto, step away from this woman right now. Run as far as you can. She's never going to be yours. She'll go out with you and laugh at your jokes and maybe even sleep with you. It's not that important to her. Only you are hung up about it. But she's never going to marry you. I can give this in writing."

"I can't, Cookie. I love her."

"No you don't. You may be in love with her—which I doubt very much because I think it's just an obsession—but it's not the same thing as loving her. I've done both. I know." To be in love, he explained with more seriousness than Bodhi had seen from his friend in years, is a selfish act; to love is to sacrifice.

"I'm ready to sacrifice," Bodhi said. "Three crores isn't enough? I'm ready to give it up to save Raniganj Mansion. Isn't that what's really bothering you?"

"That's not a sacrifice, joru ka ghulam, that's just stupid. First of all, you're forgetting about my three crores. Your sacrifice," Cookie made air quotes with his pinkies, "includes my share. What am I going to get in return? Second of all, you can't save Raniganj Mansion any more than you can be king of England. Where's your head, Bodhi? Can't you see the most obvious thing? Nobody can save Raniganj Mansion. I'm not saying that you go directly to the Roys and tell them everything. But when the opportunity presents itself, as it will, trust you me, let them know who you are and what you can do to help them make some serious cash from this."

# 6

The moment prophesied by Cookie had arrived. The Roys now knew that Bodhi was a promoter. They also knew something was up, but had no idea what it was. So Bodhi tried to tell them. He apologised for coming to them using a false identity. It was the delicateness of the situation, he said, that forced him to behave in a way that he never would have under normal circumstances.

"Yes, yes," said Mrs Anjali Roy, "enough with the delicateness. *Jottoshob nyakamo*. Now get on with it."

"You know, of course, that your grandfather donated Raniganj Mansion to the Bengal International Culture and History Institute," Bodhi said looking directly at Pankaj Kamal Roy. This, he assumed, was going to be discussion between worldly men.

"Yes, a landmark in this family's proud history," said Grandmother Roy from her sofa seat.

Maybe a different choice of words from Grandmother Roy would have sent the conversation in a different direction, maybe if she hadn't said anything at all the path of history would have veered elsewhere, but these words instantly magnified Mrs Anjali Roy's agitation. She had been prickly from the beginning, and now she exploded. "Donated, my foot," she said, her nostrils flaring alarmingly wide, like the head of a king cobra about to strike. "What nonsense."

"I'm sorry," said Bodhi, "I don't understand, Mr Roy. Wasn't Raniganj Mansion a donation from your grandfather Mr Prafulla Kumar Roy?"

"Tell him," said Mrs Anjali Roy to her husband with one crisp twist of her head. "Tell this man about the so-called donation."

"Ah, Anjali," her husband said, "why are you getting so upset."

"How many times do I have to tell you? Are you deaf? Why am I getting upset? You don't know why I'm getting upset! You don't know what's made me upset for all these years! I've heard just about enough about the greatness of you goddam Roys of Comilla. The great Prafulla Kumar Roy and his son the great Prashanta Kumar Roy and the stables full of horses and elephants and the mansions full of servants and slaves. From horses and elephants to rats and roaches in this shithole. What a glorious family. And the queen of this shithole, your mother, acts like it's the Diwan-i-Khas at the Red Fort. Isn't that right, Shilpi?" she asked her sister-in-law. Shilpi Roy blinked rapidly. Her inconsolable eyes were sadder than Bodhi had seen them yet. "Isn't it time someone spoke up and told that old woman the truth?"

Bodhi didn't dare say a word. He understood that his sudden appearance had provided fresh ammunition to a long running feud in the family and nothing he said would make any difference to this dynamic—except make it worse. He had seen enough family disputes to fill a matinee show. They were the biggest obstacles in his business—properties that should be sold but couldn't because the primary potential beneficiaries hated each other so much that they were willing to keep warring for ever rather than see their enemy make money and move away. These hatreds were often the deepest and most meaningful relationships in their lives.

"If you won't speak, I will," Mrs Anjali Roy said to her husband.

Grandmother Roy's face was as dark as a power cut in Kalighat.

"What my wife means," said Pankaj Kamal Roy, "is that my grandfather made the donation, but maybe...we've heard rumours...that maybe it wasn't entirely of his free will."

"For heaven's sake, Pankaj, for once tell it like it is," his wife interjected. "It wasn't a donation at all. It was to save the old creep from jail. Shilpi has told you, hasn't she, that my husband's grandfather was a hoarder and black marketer during the famine of 1943?" Bodhi nodded. "Didn't you wonder why a harami like him would donate anything at all, let alone a palace in the heart of the city?" Bodhi nodded again. The elder Roy bahu was not only aggressive, she was smart. This was the very question he had been pondering. "You needn't wonder any more. My husband's grandfather got caught, his name came in the papers as one of the leading hoarders, and the police were going to arrest him. But the slippery eel made a deal with some Congress netas. Donate your property, they said, and we'll keep you out of jail. And the public will think you're a nationalist hero. Hypocrites. *Kuttas*."

A high-decibel discussion followed. Accusations and abuses flew back and forth like a shuttlecock at a badminton match. Liar. Shameless liar. Fraud. Ingrate. Low-class ingrate. Bitch. Hussy. Grandmother Roy cried. Mrs Anjali Roy screamed. Pankaj Kamal Roy manfully tried to bring peace between his wife and his mother. Shilpi Roy looked from one face to another but couldn't find words to speak. But no shouting match can go on forever. Storms pass, earthquakes stop, and all things end. This one stopped when Mrs Anjali Roy collapsed in a sobbing heap.

~

Bodhi began to understand what Prafulla Kumar Roy had done. Slippery eel, indeed. He had been forced to give up his mansion to stay out of jail, but when the politicians who had strong-armed him weren't looking—and why, given the tumult of the time (with independence coming and Hindu-Muslim riots brewing) should they pay too much attention to one miserable hoarder—he had pulled a fast one. His lawyers must have written up a bequest that would revert the property to the family at the first opportunity. No one was looking hard, so it must have been quite easy to do. He must have hoped that this reversal would happen in his own lifetime, but it didn't matter because it was about to happen now.

Bodhi also reassessed his strategy while the Roys were tearing each other apart. This wouldn't be a good time to break good news. The environment was saturated with emotion and irrationality. Even good news was likely to be interpreted in unexpected and undesirable ways. He might get beaten up by both parties—mother and daughter-in-law. He had seen it happen often enough, a good samaritan who tries to break up a domestic dispute and turns into the object of focused fury from both sides.

"May I suggest that we start again," he said when finally there was a kind of silence, punctuated by sniffles from all three Mrs Roys. "Properly. It would be best if my Chhotomama was present. He is the man in charge of the Institute. He is the one who sent me here. I suggest that we meet tomorrow at Raniganj Mansion. At ten." Bodhi made an executive decision. "I will inform Chhotomama and confirm before this evening."

"Can't you tell us a little bit about what this is about?" an exhausted Pankaj Kamal Roy found enough energy to ask a question. His contrived manhood at the beginning of the meeting had been crushed like a stalk of sugarcane in the teeth of a juice-extractor. The only thing left was distressed pulp. "Maybe not the details, but just a précis."

"If I could make a précis of this I would Mr Roy, believe me," Bodhi said. "I really think it would be best if everyone hears about the situation with a cool head, from the person who is in the best position to explain everything."

Pankaj Kamal Roy nodded. Whatever it was, it wouldn't be good news because he hadn't gotten good news in over three decades. And bad news could always wait another day.

"Mrs Roy," Bodhi said to Shilpi Roy, "it would be very helpful to have your husband around tomorrow."

"Well," she said, "he won't be available."

Was he paraplegic, Bodhi thought, was he stashed away in some room in this house, drooling without a care while his family played out this sentimental drama? Was he soft in the head or manic, that he had to be hidden from the public?

"If it is possible at all...I mean if you need help to get him to Raniganj Mansion..." Bodhi hesitated.

Like a shooting ember from a dying fire Mrs Anjali Roy spoke again. "Tell him, Shilpi. This man has heard everything. Why pretend." When Shilpi Roy remained silent, Anjali Roy said, "her husband, my dear brother-in-law, won't be able to attend because he doesn't live in this house. He has abandoned his wife and his daughter and is probably shacked up with some rundi somewhere."

~

The man's name was Pijush Kanta Roy. He was the younger son of Grandmother Roy, the little boy peeking from behind his ayah's sari in the photograph hanging next to the dinner table. He used to work for Eastern Railways as a booking clerk. Five years ago, when Pijush Kanta Roy was thirty-seven years old, on an ordinary Wednesday morning in August, he had left the house to go to the local bazaar with the usual two polyester bags to buy the usual fish and usual vegetables for the day; the fish and vegetables couldn't mix in the same bag because Grandmother Roy was an observant Hindu widow. He had never returned. The police had been informed, the family had put notices in the newspapers, but Pijush Kanta Roy had never been seen or heard from again. His daughter, Maya, had been four years old at the time.

"It's all Rahu's doing," sobbed Grandmother Roy, holding her head with both hands. "It's Rahu's curse on this family." This, then, must have been curse number two, or was it three.

"Mother believes that my brother has taken sanyas," Pankaj Kamal Roy said. "She believes he left the family for a higher spiritual calling."

"More cow dung," said his wife, appearing to be gaining strength for another round of family sports. "If he had taken sanyas, why would Shilpi's jewellery disappear the same time? What was left of her dowry...what that sodden drunkard hadn't sold already...six gold bangles, one gold necklace, and two pairs of earrings. We remember everything, don't we Shilpi? No, no, of course he didn't take sanyas. He is no tyagi; the man is a number one *bhogi*. The creep just ran away. He's a scoundrel and a fraud, just like his father and grandfather."

Shilpi Roy looked at Bodhi with unreadable eyes. See, she seemed to say, you're not the only one with secrets.

Bodhi gave them his visiting card, the real one, and left. As he walked to his car he wondered about Shilpi Roy. Why did she stay in this house of lies and pain? Why did she let her daughter be subjected to its daily corrosions? Was it to protect Grandmother Roy from her ferocious elder daughter-in-law? She did look kind enough to do a silly thing like that. Or was it because she was no longer welcome at her parents' house? Maybe her parents were dead and her siblings simply didn't want her back. Most likely it was about money. Shilpi Roy didn't earn enough to survive on her own. She had probably never worked before her husband absconded, and now she was stuck. It was a good decision, because it was about to pay off to an extent that none of these Roys could imagine.

# 7

Chhotomama was distraught when Bodhi came to his flat and explained the situation. The Roys had found out who Bodhi was and they had to be told the truth. Right now. The Roys were a bickering, squabbling, quarrelsome lot, like taxi drivers at Howrah station, and carried ancient hatreds, like...well...any two groups that could be motivated into a fight using real or imagined ancient hatreds. They may have had a lot of money at some time, but had very little now, and the younger generation had seen almost none of the old money. It would take a miracle on the order of Krishna's preservation of Draupadi's honour in evil Duryodhan's court, Bodhi told his uncle, to preserve Raniganj Mansion from their clutches.

Chhotomama's flat was a government quarter he had lived in for over twenty years. The location was convenient—near the rail lines to the east of Ballygunj—and allowed easy movement in all directions. The neighbourhood always smelled of a combination of mould and smoke, like an opium den after a night of heavy consumption. The flat was unpretentious and minimalist. There were few art objects other than faded prints of Jamini Roy and Abanindranath Tagore paintings. There were none of the hanging and tinkling curios that the house of a cultured man like him could be expected to display.

Chhotomama had never married. If asked why, he would habitually say that he was married to the Party. Perhaps, a woman in his life could have brought beautiful and useless objects into his house.

They sat in the only bedroom in the flat, a corner room with windows on two walls. A large window with three panels ran along the long wall and a smaller one with two panels was on the short wall. A single bed was placed beneath the large window. It had a thick cotton bedcover with a block-printed design of purple roses intertwined with magenta stems on a dark blue base. Chhotomama hadn't bought this bedcover. He didn't like buying things and delegated these tasks to whoever was handy. There was a metal-blue steel almirah along the short wall. Between the almirah and the bed there was a wooden writing table. A chair was tucked underneath it. Its seat was made of thin plastic strips interwoven like a wicker basket. Many of the strips were frayed, some were torn, and when Bodhi pulled the chair out and sat on it, the seat sagged like a cobweb under a bee. Chhotomama sat on the bed.

There were books everywhere, on every flat surface, from tables and almirah tops to the commode cover and microwave. On Chhotomama's bedside table there was a glass of water covered with a round plastic mat and a pile of three books. On top was a long-used and well-thumbed volume—*Italian Road to Socialism: An Interview* by Eric Hobsbawm.

"What am I going to do, Bodhi?" asked Chhotomama with a helplessness that Bodhi had never seen.

"I don't know, Chhotomama. I don't think there's anything you can do."

"What if we decide not to move the Institute? This is what I've been thinking about. What if the Institute remains in Raniganj Mansion? Then the Roys are out of the picture, no? They won't have any claim on the house then."

"Can you do that? Is this your decision to make? What about all the space the government has allotted to you?"

~

Chhotomama phoned Bankoli. Even in that agitated state he couldn't think of pulling back on years of planning without the support of his successor. Bodhi heard only Chhotomama's side of the conversation.

"Hello, Dr Bankoli, I had an idea that I wanted to run by you. I was thinking that maybe we should re-evaluate our idea of moving the Institute out of Raniganj Mansion...

"Yes, I know this is part of the strategic plan...

"Thank you for the kind words. It didn't take a lot of vision to see that the Institute's growth was being cramped by the space...

"Yes, I know the primary mission of the Institute is research...

"Thank you for reminding me...

"I'm sorry that you feel that our goal of trying to preserve Raniganj Mansion has become a personal mission....

"Did you say a foolhardy mission? No, I must have misheard you then because it sure seemed like you said foolhardy...

"Oh, you said *jandardi* mission, a public-spirited mission...

"Thank you, thank you...

"I wasn't aware that you have been in touch with senior Party members...

"Yes, I understand that you take your orders from them, not me. I know how it works...I've been there myself, heh, heh...but I thought you'd discuss with me before...

"I might have been opposed to the idea. Maybe, maybe, but...

"I'm aware that the government doesn't have an unlimited budget...

"So there's no money for architectural preservation? You know this for a fact...

"Oh, you have spoken to the general secretary of the Party too. You've been busy, haven't you...

"So you haven't spoken to him directly but have been told about his feelings...

"Yes, I have heard that myself. Like you, not from his mouth but from others. Yes, the general secretary wouldn't mind seeing all the zamindar houses turn to rubble. I can understand that position. I agree that they were the scourges of Bengal. In fact, when I was younger, I too was of the view...

"Of course, the housing sector is important. I'm not denying that...

"How is this a wrong signal to the housing sector? What difference does one house on half an acre make to the housing sector? Don't you think this is going a bit too...

"Yes, I should have thought of this earlier. My mistake. Obviously my strategic vision isn't as good as you say it is...

"No, no, I'm not being sarcastic...

"I should look for a private benefactor? They said that? And whose suggestion was this if I may ask...

"So, the Todi's and the Khaitan's have both expressed some interest in putting money into preservation. They should, don't you think, considering how much they make from the housing business...

"Do I sound angry? If I do, maybe I am angry...

"I understand. I understand very clearly. The state has abdicated its responsibility, so I need to find a rich man to save Raniganj Mansion from the greed of the middle-class...

"You're not the first person to tell me that I see class in everything. Isn't that what we communists are supposed to do? What can I do, Dr Bankoli, this old dog just can't learn new tricks..."

~

It wasn't hard for Bodhi to follow the conversation though he could hear only one side of it because he had a good sense of what Bankoli was saying. Chhotomama's designated successor had visited the office of Heavenly Homes Ltd. a couple of days ago and told Bodhi and Cookie similar things. He had told them that his feeling was that Raniganj Mansion would be sold, and that it was a regrettable but inevitable outcome, one that nonetheless was endorsed by seniors in the Party. Chhotomama had no supporters. He was isolated. What Bankoli didn't say openly, but left hanging in the air were hints that he wouldn't be averse to being part of a deal that advantaged Heavenly Homes Ltd. in future financial and market transactions involving Raniganj Mansion. "Chuhe ka aulad," said Cookie, after Bankoli left, "the first rat to desert a sinking ship."

Chhotomama would have slammed the phone down had it been an old ITI clunker. But it wasn't. It was a sleek cordless handset with a backlit digital keypad. He pressed the off button with as much venom as he could muster. His eyes were orbs of anger. He took several deep breaths before speaking.

"Did you hear that, Bodhi? This man...he's supposed to be my replacement and he's already behaving as if I'm dead and cremated at Keoratala. I was the person who hired him and he's turned on me even before I'm gone."

"There's no gratefulness in this world," said Bodhi, who had suffered long from the expectation of gratefulness. "You shouldn't except anyone to be grateful. In fact, as Vidyasagar said, you should expect retribution from exactly those whom you've done any favour."

"Bankoli called himself a soldier."

"For which army?"

"The Party, I guess. The forces of good? The forces of greed? I don't know."

Uncle and nephew looked at each for a moment.

"So, this is what it's come to," Chhotomama said.

"This is how it's been for years now, Chhotomama, that's what I've been trying to tell you, but you never listen."

"What, that money speaks?"

"Yes, it speaks louder than anything and everyone listens to it. I do."

"What's so new about that? You think that we don't know about the power of money? You think I'm an irrational old fool who doesn't understand how the world works? No, no, don't pretend, you know that I know what you think about me. I'll tell you what's different now, I'll tell you what's new? Not that money speaks, or that it speaks loudly, but that nothing else speaks and nobody else has a voice. Only money does and the people who have money do. You know what happens when that happens. Everything is for sale. Today I'm trying to protect an old building. Tomorrow the poor and the old will have their organs harvested. Who'll protect them? Young women will sell their ovaries. Who'll save them and their unborn children? The children that will be born will be sold into servitude. There is so much money now, so much more than before, and so much poverty, as much as ever, that nothing can be saved from people with money."

Bodhi didn't respond. He could have said that this was much too dramatic, out of character for a careful man like Chhotomama. That everything Chhotomama was afraid would happen was already happening and had been happening for a long, long time. That Chhotomama was wrong, as usual, because there was nothing new under the sun, just the same old things, more of some, less of others.

# 8

The largest room in Raniganj Mansion, the only one that had also retained its grandeur, was the Reading Room on the upper floor. This had originally been the baithak-khana, the room where the lord of the house used to meet men of equivalent or superior social status. Supplicants and underlings used to meet in a separate, smaller room on the ground floor, which now served as a supply room for the Institute. Each new director of the Institute—Chhotomama was the sixth—had played around with other rooms and spaces, but had left this one alone. It looked more or less like it used to three-quarters of a century ago, like the smoking room of a gentleman explorer's club.

Hunting was the room's motif. An assortment of animal heads were mounted on the walls—three deer (two Chital, one Sambhar), two black bears, and a Royal Bengal tiger with its skin attached. Aside from a dominating oil portrait of Mr Prafulla Kumar Roy with a resplendent moustache, there were paintings of elephants and rhinos and a falcon in flight. There was an empty gun rack and other antiques. Two victrolas were placed in diagonal corners. Both had the lids up and a 78 RPM record on the turntable. They were only for show because no one knew whether the machines worked. Old records by Gauhar Jan and Heera Bai were arranged decoratively. These hadn't been part of Prafulla

Kumar Roy's donation but acquisitions by the Institute. Four round tables of teak were placed close to the corners of the room, and each had two matching chairs. The room had a door on each wall. One led to the stairs, one to a balcony, one to an anteroom to Chhotomama's office, and one to the Rare Documents Room.

The centre of the Reading Room was occupied by a long oval table of knotty, polished pine. Ten chairs surrounded it, four on each long side, and one at each narrow end. All but one chair was occupied. Chhotomama sat at one head. To his left sat the nominal members of the Save Raniganj Mansion team. It was a rump unit because Bankoli, today in a brown safari suit, was a known defector. Neera sat in the middle. She wore five earrings.

Grandmother Roy sat at the other end. With her were the remaining adult Roys—Pankaj Kamal, Anjali, and Shilpi—and a man, about fifty years old, whom Bodhi hadn't seen before and hadn't been introduced to. Bodhi tried to imagine that this was the Roys' lawyer but couldn't, because these Roys simply weren't sophisticated enough to come to a property meeting with a lawyer. The man was more likely a general do-gooder from the neighbourhood, a sort-of friend of Pankaj Kamal Roy, the kind of man who lives in every neighbourhood, who appears to be well-informed on every issue and leads public events like pujas and funeral processions. He was probably a Party member. Or he could be an Opposition Party member.

The room had been cleared of outsiders. From a partially open window a beam of sunlight had thrust into it like a sneaky visitor and a Brownian motion of dust particles cavorted lazily in its shaft. The reading room didn't have air-conditioners. This sacrifice had been necessary to retain its ambience of a time lost. Three ancient fans hung from long poles attached to the fifteen feet high ceiling and stirred the air more than agitating it. There was agitation enough in the minds of the sweating humans sitting around the table.

~

Chhotomama covered his distress with professionalism. He took out a set of index cards from his drooping shoulder bag, cleared his throat, and began a treatise on ruins.

"My dear Roy family. Welcome to Raniganj Mansion, a house that was built by your ancestors. Please don't mind if I begin with some background information before we get to the business at hand. You're the descendants of zamindars, and you are, in ways that most people don't realise, the creators of Bengal's architectural traditions. I won't pretend that I'm fond of zamindars as a group, and I believe there's no need for an explanation. But I must give credit where it is due. They built things that have lasted. The only things that have lasted through the rigours of our unforgiving climate are things that were made with materials that could last. Our poor, who have always been numerous, built with mud and baked mud and more mud. They built their houses with mud and their temples and shrines with mud. Sometimes they used leaves and fronds and bamboo to reinforce or cover the mud. But sooner or later all mud washes away. What remains is what rich men build with stone and brick and mortar. Before the

British came, the rich men of Bengal were the nawabs and jagirdars and mansabdars who ruled this land under the protection of the Mughals. Today, even their palaces are in virtual ruins. Shame on us. Have any of you ever visited Murshidabad? Have any of you seen the palaces of the last nawabs of Bengal. No, I know you haven't. I don't blame you. Almost nobody has, because there's not much left to see. The British aren't my favourite people either, but one must again give credit where it is due. At least they built to last. Most of the beautiful buildings in this city were built by them. Let me correct myself. Not most, but all the beautiful buildings in this city were built by them or during their time. The really big ones—the Writers Buildings and GPOs—will stay for decades, thank goodness. But what will happen to the smaller buildings built by them? What will happen to the grand houses built by the zamindars? Many are in ruins already. They are in ruins in Bangladesh, in Pabna and Khulna districts, and they are in ruins in the districts of Bengal, in Howrah and Birbhum and Bardhhaman, and they are in ruins in this city. Go to the north part of the city, where most of the zamindars built their homes, and see for yourself what ruins look like. See for yourself what happens to man's grand creations when nature returns with a vengeance. See the trees growing out of walls, see the roofs collapsed by one relentless monsoon after another. We don't seem to have the money or the energy or the desire to preserve any of it. Here, in the south, there were few zamindar houses to begin with. The few that were there are being turned into cubicled monstrosities by our housing industry. Sorry,

Bodhi, but it's necessary to call an object by its true name. A cubicled monstrosity is a cubicled monstrosity; there's no kind word for it. Can any of you name a single building within five miles of here that's on anyone's must-see list? Can you identify a single building whose name you know or that you've been inside that's more than sixty years old? You can't because there aren't any, other than some houses of industrial magnates in Alipur, hidden away from public eyes behind high walls and big trees. What's left is Raniganj Mansion and maybe half a dozen buildings like it. They're still around because some zamindars, for whatever reasons, turned them into public institutions. They'll be gone too. It won't take long. And our children and grandchildren will ask, doesn't our city have a history? Where's that history except in textbooks and photos? Where's that history that we can see with our own eyes? What answer do we have for the generations to come?"

~

While Chhotomama was speaking, a bearer had served tea. Chhotomama made the mistake of pausing at this point to take a sip from his cup, as a result of which the remainder of his speech will forever remain unknown.

Mrs Anjali Roy jumped into the breach. "Why are you lecturing us all this?" she said. "Do you need a donation from us?"

"If that's what you're after," said her husband, Mr Pankaj Kamal Roy, "you should be ashamed of yourselves. It's not enough that we donate the house. Now you demand more from us."

"What cheek!" said his wife.

"You can't get blood out of stone," said her husband.

"Even a worm will turn at last," said she.

"No, no," Bankoli stepped in, "you're misunderstanding us. That's not what we're talking about at all. Please allow me," with a quick look at Chhotomama, "to come to the point. Mr Roy, your grandfather donated Raniganj Mansion to the Institute, right?"

Bodhi worried that Mrs Anjali Roy would have something to say on the subject of "donation" again.

"Yes, of course," said Pankaj Kamal Roy quickly, just as worried about the same possibility.

"If I may ask, who was your grandfather's heir?" asked Bankoli. "Who inherited his property?"

"My father," said Pankaj Kamal Roy. "He was my grandfather's only child. At least the only one who survived to adulthood. There was a sister who died very young. Isn't that right, mother?" Grandmother Roy nodded.

"Did your grandfather leave a proper and legal will?"

"Yes," said Grandmother Roy. "Pankaj doesn't know, ask me. He was just a little boy then. 1965 it was. Right before the war with Pakistan. Yes, we have the will."

"And if I may be discourteous, madam, may I ask when did your husband leave for his heavenly abode?" asked Bankoli. Why is he tempting fate, thought Bodhi. Each one of these questions is a hand grenade for Anjali Roy. She would like nothing better than to pull the pin with teeth stained by decades of chewing paan stuffed with head-spinning zarda and toss the grenade into this mob.

"October 20th it was, in 1996," Grandmother Roy said. It had been an auspicious day on the Hindu calendar. Mahasthami during Durga Puja, and a Sunday too. Her husband had dropped dead from a heart attack in the middle of an enormous lunch of luchi, pulao, goat curry, and fried eggplant.

"Did your husband leave a will, Rajeshwari Devi?" asked Chhotomama, worried now that Bankoli had taken the lead and would be seen by the Roys as the more powerful person at the Institute. "Who were his inheritors?"

"We are the inheritors," said Grandmother Roy. "Myself and my two sons. We were designated as equal inheritors of my husband's property."

"Debts, you mean," Anjali Roy burst in. "Debts. That's what we inherited from my father-in-law. No properties but a mountain of debts."

Bodhi had earlier updated the Save Raniganj Mansion team about the nosedive of the Roy estate under the stewardship of Mr Prashanta Kumar Roy. He had told them about the colliery fraud and its settlement. He had told them about the mistress and the illegitimate son with the mistress. He had described the Roy family's journey from Raniganj Mansion to Bliss Cottage to an unnamed house in Ballygunj to their current resting place in Pratapgarh. Each new house, he had guessed, was half the size of the previous one, and because it was further away from the centre of the city, one-quarter in value. The Roys were like a retreating army, he had said, taking on casualties even running backward.

~

The truth couldn't be avoided any longer. Chhotomama told the Roys about the impending move of the Institute out of Raniganj Mansion.

"What difference does that make to us?" demanded Mrs Anjali Roy, leaving no doubt about the identity of the real leader of the family. "We aren't being invited to live here, are we?"

"In a manner of speaking, yes, you are," said Chhotomama. He explained the provisions in Prafulla Kumar Roy's donation of Raniganj Mansion to the Institute. When the Institute moved out, he explained, the Roys would be back as owners of the property.

One by one, the Roys understood what they were being told. Judging by the expressions on their faces, Shilpi Roy was the first to comprehend the new reality. Her eyes widened as she covered her open mouth with her hand.

Mrs Anjali Roy shrieked. "Oh my goodness. The old man had been planning this all along. What an evil genius. These Roy men are something else, aren't they Shilpi? Except this good for nothing okra I married." Her smile, the first Bodhi had seen from her, was like a new moon on its third night. It wiped away a dozen years from her baleful face and turned it into something unexpectedly tender, like a contract killer snuggling an infant.

The okra, her husband, sat speechless with a stunned expression while tears rolled down his cheeks.

"If this is so straightforward, why have you gone through all this song and dance to tell us," asked Grandmother Roy sternly. She had expressed neither surprise nor joy at receiving the news. Perhaps she had known about this provision all along. "You could have come to our house like proper gentlemen and told us properly."

"I apologise sincerely for the way we have done things, Rajeshwari Devi," said Chhotomama with an earnest scowl, "but the truth is we didn't know who you were or how to approach you. Because the bigger truth also is that we would like to preserve Raniganj Mansion as it is and we weren't sure that you would go along. There, I've said it. We would like to preserve Raniganj Mansion as it is, as one of the few surviving zamindar houses in this city. We desparately need your generosity."

"But why shouldn't Raniganj Mansion remain the way it is?" said Grandmother Roy. "It looks perfectly fine to me."

Pankaj Kamal Roy and his wife exchanged alarmed looks. Their worldly minds had been whirring with the ignorant calculations of lottery winners at the moment of knowledge—How much will I really get? How much will be gone in taxes? How much will be left? How much is that flat I've always wanted? How big a car can I buy? How much is a ticket to London? A kilo of gold?

"Don't you understand anything, mother-in-law," said Mrs Anjali Roy, her voice like a whiplash. "Why do you think these people have been playing hide and seek with us? Why do you think they sent a promoter to speak to us?"

"Of course I do, Anjali," said Grandmother Roy with cold condescension. "Don't forget that I am the wife of an industrialist, not a clerk. I understand that this land is worth some money now. How much is it, Mr Banerjee?" She looked at Bodhi with authority.

"I'm not sure..." Bodhi lied. "I don't have the property dimensions and...but several crores I'd say."

"How many is several? Two or five?" asked Grandmother Roy.

"More, I think," said Bodhi, not wanting to appear overenthusiastic to either the Roys or Chhotomama and Neera.

"Ten?" asked Pankaj Kamal Roy with a tremor in his voice.

"Quite possibly," said Bodhi, uncomfortable now and unwilling to part with his privileged information, his one true skill in the real estate game, a calculation of the actual market value of a property. "Look, this is not a trivial matter, figuring out the price of a property. I can do it for you of course, but not here and not like this. But if you want a real number to play with, it's not a bad idea to keep ten crores as the minimum. It could be higher than that, but not lower."

"*Joy Ma Kali,*" said Mrs Anjali Roy. Her husband fainted and fell from his chair.

It took a few minutes to revive him. Their anonymous companion sprinkled droplets of water on his face while his wife fanned it vigorously with the pallu of her sari. Together they propped him back on his chair.

"This is the greatest day of my life," were the first words from him. "Praise Lord Vishnu, praise Ma Kali, without whose blessings all our suffering would have been in vain. I cannot believe that finally...after all these years...the divine power has raised her face and looked at us. It's a miracle. Praise Lord Vishnu. *Joy Ma Kali.*"

"I take it that you're not in favour of preserving Raniganj Mansion," Chhotomama said.

"Isn't it obvious?" said Mrs Anjali Roy. "Isn't that why you have been trying to hide this information from us? Of course, we'll sell this piece of junk. It's not pretty and we have no use for it."

Chhotomama made a face like a disappointed duck. His lips turned down at the corners and his nose rose in the air. He was expecting to hear this, of course, but a little finesse would have been nice.

"Wait one minute," said Grandmother Roy. "Just hold it for one minute. I don't think you and your husband can decide this by yourselves, Anjali. According to my husband's will I am as much an owner of Raniganj Mansion as you, and I have absolutely no intention of selling it."

Almost no one in the room was expecting to hear this, with the exception of Mrs Anjali Roy. She was prepared. "You crazy witch," she screamed, "you pompous little... selfish little witch. I knew...I just knew that you were waiting to stick it to us. You miserable, unhappy witch, you can't bear to see us get one day of happiness, can you? Can't stand it? One moment of happiness for us is too much for you, isn't it you dry twig?"

"Anjali, please, there are people here," her husband said, his ashen face suggesting that this might have been a better moment to faint.

"What do I care about these people? Are they going to feed me or clothe me that I have to be polite to them? They can fry in hell. They don't want us to sell this house either, you understand that, don't you. All of this coy bullshit is to deprive us of what is rightfully ours. They are all in this together. That old man with that mouth full of speech, that promoter they sent to our house to say sweet things... all lies, your mother...all of them...and all of them can go to jahannam."

What followed was what Bodhi expected. Mrs Anjali Roy threw a bilious fit. Grandmother Roy matched her word for word, with more determination and less profanity. Pankaj Kamal and Shilpi Roy and the unnamed do-gooder from the neighbourhood tried to calm them down. Chhotomama and the other non-Roys were embarrassed at having to witness such wanton dysfunction and their inability to do anything about it. Neera appeared to be the most shocked, as if she had never seen anything like this outside the city's fish-markets, which she hadn't seen anyway, only heard about, because women like her never went there. It was all very tedious.

~

Grandmother Roy's position was simple. She didn't articulate it clearly—beyond stating that Raniganj Mansion had been a gift and well-bred people didn't take back what they had gifted—but Bodhi had a rudimentary understanding of what she meant. Later, when he got to know her better, he would fully understand why she took the position she did.

Raniganj Mansion was the Roy family's only hope of attaining immortality…or something that approximated immortality. Her children were what they were—one a sneaky absconder, the other a spineless whiner—and nothing great, or even above average, would ever be achieved by either of them. If Raniganj Mansion disappeared, as it inevitably would to fill the Roy pockets with crores, the last visible achievement of the glorious Roys of Comilla would be gone. Nothing that had marked their power and prestige would be left on earth.

Bodhi had already understood that the material desires of the younger Roys didn't particularly concern Grandmother Roy. She herself was close to the end of her life, and if the remaining years were to be spent in squalid Pratapgarh instead of splendid Raniganj Mansion, so be it. She didn't hanker for physical comforts. She didn't wear gold or silk and probably hadn't for years. It was obvious that she didn't eat meat or drink alcohol. She wouldn't be throwing parties to show off her wealth. A glitzy wedding for her granddaughter Maya would be nice, but she didn't expect to be alive when that happened. She wouldn't be travelling to London or New York because she had no desire to come in close contact with the *goras* and their impure barbaric practices. Benares was good enough for her, and women like her, and that she could surely manage with what she already had. At most she may have wanted an AC in her room, and Bodhi doubted even that, because he knew of a rumour circulating through the bhajan mandals of the city that many elderly women were dying from pneumonia from the newly installed ACs in their houses. Malicious people said that this was the revenge of the daughter-in-law. Killing their mothers-in-law with kindness.

Added to this basic motivation, surely, was the mouth-watering spice of spite. After talking to different sources in the Roy household and collating other pieces of random evidence, Bodhi was later able to splice together a brief resume of Grandmother Roy's elder daughter-in-law. She had been a pouty-mouthed and fair-skinned maiden when she had married into the Roy family. The Roys may have been fallen zamindars by then, but they still had enough cachet to acquire the plumpety-plump pinkety-pink virgins, the juicy roshogollahs on the marriage market, especially if they were from families with less money than aspiration.

But Anjali Roy never had children. She and her husband had tried all the totems and magic stones and baba*jis* that their family and friends had recommended, but had never gotten to the point of examining, as she regularly claimed, whether her husband's sperm count was to blame. That barrenness, and the years of further fall, and the daily drudgery with her severely domesticated husband, his spreading vitiligo and lack of vigour, had turned her into a bitter and unforgiving person. The last two-three years had been the worst, perhaps because of the hormonal onslaughts of menopause, and now she was a terror in the house, a virago whose temper was always on the edge of lost and language was straight from the gutters of her neighbourhood.

Her furies frequently focused on her mother-in-law... for so many reasons—that she still commanded respect and obedience from her son, that she still had a big say in family financial matters, that she looked down upon the daughter-in-law's common origins, that she constantly boasted about the glory days of the Roys, and above all, that she completely denied the essential vileness of the men in the Roy lineage. Mrs Anjali Roy saw herself as a very moral person, more and more so as the years passed, and couldn't tolerate her mother-in-law's continuing satisfaction with the past. Her mother-in-law, in turn, saw the naked desire in the daughter-in-law's eyes when the Raniganj Mansion crores came up for discussion, and in refusing to go along with her son and his wife, must have derived some vengeful pleasure.

~

"Mrs Roy," Neera said to Shilpi when the shouting was over, "we haven't heard from you yet. What's your position on the future of Raniganj Mansion?"

Shilpi Roy smiled. "It's very nice of you to ask, but I don't think my position matters at all. I'm not an inheritor of my father-in-law's property. My husband is, and as Mr Banerjee must have told you," (Bodhi had), "he's not here to tell us what he thinks. I could tell you what he would say, but that doesn't count, does it?"

Pijush Kanta Roy, Shilpi's husband, was technically a 'missing person.' His body had never been found, so he couldn't be declared dead, at least not until seven years had passed from the day he had gone missing. There were two years and three months to go till that seven year limit would be reached. Shilpi Roy explained all this with the quiet confidence Bodhi had come to expect from her. She had asked around and been assured that this was the law of the land. She could appeal to a court for divorce in absentia, if there was any urgency to get a divorce—if, for instance, she wanted to marry again and quickly—but other than that it was best simply to wait out the seven years.

The Roys left separately. Bodhi offered the services of his car and driver to all of them. Grandmother Roy and Shilpi accepted. Pankaj Kamal and Anjali Roy refused, as did the unnamed do-gooder. A public bus had been good enough to bring them here, they said, it was good enough to take them back.

The battle lines were drawn.

# Part III
# The Strike

In which Bodhi is left with no choice but to do something

# 1

The river Ganga ambles in from Bihar, and after less than fifty miles inside Bengal, it goes over the hiccup at the Farakka dam and slides into Bangladesh, where it merges with the sorrowful Brahmaputra boomeranging its way through hilly states too numerous to mention, and splurges its way to the Bay of Bengal as the Padma of fishermen's dreams and nightmares. Its main distributary in Bengal is the Hooghly, a dignified and quiet river that flows through the metropolis without fuss. Bengali Hindus, aghast at the idea that the real Ganga flows among Bengali Muslims who have no use for it other than fishing and transportation—practical, soulless relations—call the Hooghly their Ganga. The Hooghly is a quiet river but a mighty one. Its banks are far enough apart that it took twenty years for a bridge to be built across it, so far apart that the uninformed may well believe that this is the real Ganga.

Bodhi and Neera sat in a restaurant on the top deck of a large boat moored permanently on the left bank of the Hooghly. The restaurant was almost empty. There were more waiters than customers. Few people, it seemed, were willing to pay the restaurant's high prices for a midweek lunch during a broiling day in late-May. No one was in any hurry, neither the customers to place their orders, nor the waiters to take them.

The river was alive with crossings and commerce. Double-decker launches ferried passengers between the banks—back and forth between the government square on one side and the central train station on the other. Putt-putts powered by raucous outboard motors carried people and things up and down its length, the other axis of the river. Elongated dinghies with solitary oarsmen drifted on the muddy brown wavelets, seemingly without purpose. On the bank by the boat-restaurant, trains chuffed by at intervals, running on the circular commuter line. Between the rail line and the moored restaurant there was a large sandlot in which children played on slides and swings. Their squeals of joy were loud enough, at times, to be heard above the thrum and sputter of the motors on the different river-craft.

Two days had passed after the all-party summit meeting at Raniganj Mansion. Nothing had changed in that time; at least no communication had come from the Roys. Cookie had berated Bodhi for screwing up, for getting on the wrong side of those very Roys that would eventually sell the property. Bodhi's dithering had cut them out of the action. Cookie was furious. There's no right side with these Roys, Bodhi had tried to assure Cookie, don't worry and don't hurry. It'll turn out all right. Bodhi said these words but had no confidence in them. He was afraid to admit that by trying to be all things to all people he had blown his chance.

He still didn't know how he could achieve both ends—please Neera and Chhotomama at the same time that he became rich from Raniganj Mansion—but he felt that it would be better to have an option, and the only way to have an option was to delay action. Wait, he told Cookie, don't rush into this. It's too complicated.

If Raniganj Mansion was fated for destruction, which meant that Neera and Chhotomama couldn't be satisfied, then Bodhi surely wanted to be the agent in charge of Raniganj Mansion's conversion to a high-class apartment building. In a perfect world, Raniganj Mansion would be beyond saving, but not because Bodhi didn't try to save it, and then, when its destruction was inevitable, he would be the one to destroy it. That would be perfect. Everyone would have done the right thing and nature would have taken its course. Wait, he pleaded with Cookie, let nature take its course.

~

Neera had called Bodhi the night before. She wanted to talk. Bodhi's heart had leapt with hope. He had suggested as a meeting place what he thought was the most romantic spot in the city—close to nature, but expensive enough to be exclusive. After that he had spent more than an hour dreaming about rainbows and waterfalls and Machu Picchu and Angkor Wat before he asked himself the essential question. What did Neera want to talk about? About them, or Raniganj Mansion?

The latter, as it turned out.

"What's going to happen, BB?" Neera asked. She wore a white blouse with a deep green ankle-length skirt printed with mystifying brown circles looping in and out of each other. Her sunshades were on top of her head. Her eyes were cloudy and despondent.

"Maybe nothing in the short term," Bodhi said. "If Grandmother Roy sticks to her guns and her son and daughter-in-law do the same, nothing's going to change immediately. They're deadlocked. I've seen this many times. Lawyers may get involved and the whole thing might get tied into legal knots. So, maybe nothing will happen right now."

"But in the long term…?"

"In the long term Grandmother Roy is going to die and there'll be no one to stop her son and bahu from doing what they please. And we know what they want to do, don't we? It may take five years, or it may take ten, but Raniganj Mansion will come down. It can't be stopped. I'll bet that it won't take that long. It's going to happen sooner than that." Bodhi saw no harm in preparing the ground for what was inevitable.

Neera's face scrunched and her slanted eyes crinkled as if she was in physical discomfort, as if she had a leg cramp or migraine. These were the moments that melted Bodhi into a goo of molasses. His ordinary interactions with Neera were about inconsequential things like where to go and what to eat, and his most common emotion was anxiety. He wanted to please her and not make a fool of himself while doing so. But these little shooting stars of vulnerability from Neera were as unplanned as they were gut-wrenching. He wanted to do more than please her. He wanted to protect her. He wanted to be the man who made the pain go away. He wanted to be the *man*.

These moments were added to the dossier of oddities that Bodhi was building on Neera. For instance, she drank her hot coffee cold. She held her cup like a talisman for as long as it took for the coffee to cool. It took her an hour to drink one cup. Why? Why not have cold coffee instead? Bodhi had no idea. But he adored her for it. There was nothing inherently adorable about this idiosyncrasy. It wasn't hard to imagine a husband getting irritated by this very feature in a wife of twenty five years. "We're going to miss the flight unless you finish that coffee right now." "You're going to have to choose between finishing that coffee and watching your daughter get married." But till that happened, till people fell out of love into tolerance or something worse, like indifference or loathing, there it was.

The mystery of taste. The enigma of preference.

Bodhi loved that Neera drank her hot coffee cold. One could look for deep meaning in this, and one could, as a result, find a lot of meaning, so much that it became meaningless. The search for meaning itself was troubling. It meant that everything had meaning, everything had to have meaning. Nothing could be beyond explanation. Nothing could be meaningless.

Bodhi cherished Neera's scrunched face of pain at the thought that Raniganj Mansion was destined for destruction. He didn't enjoy the fact that she was pained, but that she could feel pain over something so pointless. That she could care enough about a thing, an inanimate object, to feel pained at the imagination of its loss. It was a fleeting emotion, no doubt, like most emotions. Sanchari bhava. Like a child's tears. Like the heartbreak of a newlywed bride leaving her parents' home for her husband's. It would go away. Neera would forget that pain during the routines of her life, when she was working, or traveling, or choosing between earrings or fruit juices. To be in pain all the time, if it became a sthayi bhava, was an impossible condition—depressive, manic, suicidal. It couldn't possibly be healthy or lead to rational decisions.

But to not have the ability to feel that pain, which was Bodhi's condition now, was dehumanising. He had become apathetic and insensitive, Bodhi worried, and didn't know how to become the person he remembered having once been. He worried even more that he didn't want to be exactly that same person again, naïve and gullible and quite unfit to compete with the sharks and barracudas ruling the waters he swam in now, the Bodhi that had been destined for a grumpy, skimpy, brat-infested lifetime of lower middle-class inconsequence.

Maybe Neera was his salvation. Maybe she would lead him to that place where he was an achiever, and, at the same time, aware of and responsive to the aches and oozes and pains all around him. Maybe she was a goddess, sent to earth to give him special powers. Maybe he could become that one of a kind creature—a sensitive promoter, a poet promoter. Maybe he could be good and do right and win at the same time.

~

"Can't we do something?" Neera asked. "Can't we take some action that'll stop those awful Roys? I must tell you, BB, I really wanted to slap that woman."

"What can we do? It's going to be their property and they'll have every right to do what they wish with their property. That's how it works. Someone will have to pay them if they want to save Raniganj Mansion. Who'll pay and not expect anything in return?"

"The government. Isn't it the government's job to protect and preserve?"

"But ten crores plus, Neera. That's a lot of money. And the real price is actually even more than that. It's the salary of more than a thousand ordinary workers for a year. Why would our government spend so much money on this one house? The government is close to bankrupt anyway, but even if it wasn't, don't you think that they have other, more deserving projects to put the money into? Like roads and hospitals and things like that?"

"What about public opinion?" Neera tried a different approach. "Isn't it possible to create public support for preservation?"

This charming innocence was exactly what Bodhi had lost. He appreciated that Neera possessed it, but couldn't imagine that he could ever go back to it. "What public and what opinion?" he said. "Our public tolerates everything. What don't we tolerate? Hours and hours of traffic jams. Piles and piles of stinking garbage on the streets. Strikes, bandhs, hartals, gheraos, rasta rokos, rail rokos, power cuts, traffic accidents, pollution, goondagardi, hospitals that are death traps, schools that are money traps...everything. Our public has the hide of a rhinoceros. You want this public to rise up and demand architectural preservation? I don't know what to say." Bodhi had never spoken this directly to Neera. He had never contradicted her to her face. Quietly, he congratulated himself. Maybe he was getting to the point where he could become assertive about his rights as a potential lover, and a full-fledged man to boot, with all kinds of manly rights.

"You're so cynical. I didn't know you were so cynical."

"I'm realistic. I'm pragmatic." Better that Neera should know these things. Better that she should be aware that underneath that soft exterior of a poet lurked a tough no-nonsense promoter.

"What you call pragmatism is just an acceptance of things the way they are. Nothing will ever change if everyone has this attitude. If you say change isn't possible, then change becomes impossible. By believing it you make it true. This isn't pragmatism, this is defeatism."

Without awareness there can't be action! Without action there can't be change! Chhotomama's words. Siege the city with village power! Revolution is not a dinner party! The people united can never be defeated! Chhotomama had a slogan for every occasion.

Bodhi leaned back in his chair. Had his uncle been indoctrinating his assistant? Bodhi already knew that there were several Neeras. There was a Neera that dangled him like a puppet with coquetry and half-truths, a Neera that was a treasure trove of trivial information on stars and starlets and their trinket lives, and a Neera that had strong views on the rights of marginal peoples and minorities. She had the ability to change from one Neera to another in an instant and Bodhi was never sure which one he was facing from moment to moment. Did she have multiple-personality disorder? Would she suddenly growl in a man's voice one of these days and spit and belch like Cookie at a construction site? What a frightening thought.

"So, what's the alternative?" Bodhi said. "Do you have any ideas?"

She did. She wanted to use the media to publicise the plight of Raniganj Mansion. She had friends in the media and she was sure she could get a story or two planted in the papers. Bodhi tried to dissuade her. Going to the media was like going into a dark alley in an unknown city in the middle of the night. The alley could lead to an abyss, or you could get mugged, or it could open on to a plaza with beautiful people dancing under twinkling lights. The most likely outcome was nothing. The alley would most likely be boring and uneventful and simply lead to another alley that was just as boring and uneventful. The story would sink like a handful of sand in a kathasagar of endless stories, most of them about sex or violence or scandal. This one would probably sink without making a sound. But if there was a reaction, if it did make a sound, it would become something you couldn't control. It would acquire a life of its own. Opportunists and crazies would emerge like scorpions from under rocks. They would hijack the story. They would become the story.

Bodhi felt like shaking Neera out of this clueless blundering but was afraid to, not so much because it would hurt the fragile and delicate woman of his imagination, but because if hurt, the wilful Neera could emerge and torture him endlessly. He swore at himself for his timidity. How could he ever get a girl like her if he had so little confidence? What happened to the man who moments ago had been congratulating himself on his assertiveness? Bodhi wished he had an alter ego or stand-in, a prompter from the wings, who would tell Neera what needed to be told. "This is not how the world works, sweetie pie. Let me show you how things really happen." Cookie could do this in his sleep.

"Please make sure that Chhotomama approves of your plan," Bodhi said in resignation.

"We've already talked about it."

"And he approves?"

"Not fully yet, but he will," Neera said with a smile.

By the time they were ready to leave, the tide had ebbed and the boat-restaurant had sunk to a level several feet below the jetty. The gangway to the bank rose at a forbiddingly steep angle. Should Bodhi offer his hand to help Neera walk the plank? His mind went through a thousand calculations in a micro-second. What if she refused? What if she didn't refuse? What if she was offended? What if she took his hand and never let go? The calculations didn't yield an unambiguous result and instinct took over. When Bodhi offered his hand Neera took it without hesitation. Hand-in-hand they climbed up. All the blood in his body rushed to this one hand. All the nerve endings bunched into this one palm. He retained his walking reflex, like a zombie, but lost speech.

Those were the most memorable fifty feet in Bodhi's life. The final ten came after they had reached the top and Neera no longer needed his support. She didn't disengage her hand and may have held on for longer, maybe forever, but Bodhi removed his hand—later he thought that he may have snatched it away—and instantly cursed himself. What was wrong with him? Didn't he know what he wanted? Wasn't this exactly what he wanted more than anything else...to walk hand-in-hand with Neera...along the river and into a gorgeous sunset...till time stood still and music filled the air? Was it or not?

# 2

A few days later, in the same day's paper, the *Daily Wire* carried two items on Raniganj Mansion, but only one of them mentioned it by name. This was an article written by Neera's journalist friend. It was a simple story about architectural preservation in the *CityBeat* section of the paper titled, 'Endangered Heritage'. A big colour photo of Raniganj Mansion took up most of the column inches. It was accompanied by a brief description of about 250 words. The writer didn't name names, didn't quote people (other than 'sources'), and took a narrative arc of blaming the government for its indifference to the city's heritage buildings.

The second item appeared in the Classified section. It had a photo of a round-cheeked man in his mid-thirties, with a thin, trimmed moustache, a prominent widow's peak and surprised eyebrows. Underneath his picture were these words:

> Pijush Kanta Roy, dearest husband, father, son, and brother, please come back home. We love you and beg your forgiveness. Your wife and daughter are heartbroken without you. Your mother and brother miss you every day. The house that your grandfather donated is back with the family. We need you to

take care of this big responsibility. Rajeshwari, Pankaj Kamal, Anjali, Shilpi, and Mahamaya Roy of Pratapgarh.

The two items in the paper were like two slow-burning fuses leading to the same bomb. One fuse or the other would surely set off an explosion. But for the first few days it appeared that both fuses may have been duds, because there was no reaction from anywhere. It appeared that Bodhi had been right, that this was another handful of sand in an ocean-full of stories. But he wasn't. Had he been, he wouldn't have ended up in jail.

The first sign that things were about to change came with a phone call from Shilpi Roy. She wanted an appointment with Bodhi. It was urgent, but she couldn't tell him why over the phone. Could she make an appointment for tomorrow? At 10 o'clock?

Bodhi asked Cookie to stay around. He didn't know what was coming and he needed a witness and backup for whatever it was. Cookie was more than eager to help. His impatience with the lack of action was boiling over and he was hoping that someone, anyone, would make a move. Bodhi had had to use all his powers of dissuasion to keep Cookie from approaching the Roys by himself.

Shilpi Roy looked worn out. There were dark circles underneath her eyes, darker than her dark skin. She wore her Barrackpore Farms uniform, a magenta sari printed with white tiger paws. She was going to work after this meeting.

"Thank you for agreeing to see me Mr Banerjee," she said, wiping her perspiring face with a big pink handkerchief.

"I was afraid that our recent exchanges would have put you off completely."

"No, no, not at all," Bodhi said. "Everything that happened was my fault. I did everything the wrong way. I'm very happy that you're still talking with us."

"So, Mrs Roy," Cookie said, eager to get things going, "I assume that this is not a social visit."

"That's correct. This is not a social visit. In fact, I'm not sure why I'm here or that I should be here at all, but I simply don't know what to do."

Bodhi and Cookie waited.

"Let me tell you the important news first. As it turns out, I'm not a widow after all." She said with a small smile.

"You have heard from your husband?" asked Bodhi.

"Better than that. He showed up four days ago. No phone call or anything. Straight to the house. My mother-in-law opened the door and almost died of shock."

"You must be very happy. And Maya too, she must be overjoyed."

Shilpi Roy smiled again, a pasted thing, a thin and wavering line that could easily crumble into sobs. "Maya is happy to see what her father looks like. She had forgotten completely. You see, she was just four when he disappeared."

Where had he been all these years? Mr Pijush Kanta Roy claimed that he had been swept up in the whirlwind of history, an innocent victim of a vast criminal enterprise. The morning he had disappeared after having left home to buy the fish and vegetables for the day, there had been a small, unreported incident in the local market. It was a skirmish, not large enough to make the news but significant enough to have changed his life forever. A vendor of religious consumables (incense sticks, brittle sweets, jasmine garlands, gangajal) had caught a boy of twelve or so trying to steal his brittle sweets. When Pijush Kanta Roy came upon the scene, the vendor had been beating the little thief mercilessly, *thwack! thwack!*, at the centre of a small crowd that was providing encouragement and sneaking in a slap or two. Pijush Kanta Roy had been appalled by this injustice and some inner voice had compelled him to intervene. One thing led to another, and the next thing he knew he was at Kanpur railway station with bruises all over his body, a red towel on his shoulder and a white bundle on his head to carry heavy loads. He was a coolie. He had no memory of how he got to Kanpur station nor what his life had been before that day. Slowly, he realised that he had been beaten and drugged into unconsciousness and then abducted by some associates of the vendor that had been thrashing the little thief of brittle sweets. Pijush Kanta Roy, upstanding member of the middle-class and scion of the zamindars of Comilla, had been sold into bonded labour. It was, he said, a regular racket.

He began to remember his past life only in the last year or so, but not everything, just some fragments. He couldn't remember where he had lived or what his telephone number used to be. He remembered that he had a wife and a daughter and a mother. He remembered their faces but not their names. He knew he had another life to get back to, but had no way of getting back. He was distraught and desperate and poor and miserable.

Fortunately, he kept up with news from the city. He had read the paper and the appeal from his family. In a flash, he had remembered everything. The names of his wife and daughter, his address, everything. He had gotten on the first train he could—the Kalka Mail if you wanted to know—and here he was.

"What about the gold and jewellery that went missing with him?" asked Bodhi.

"No one's brought it up yet," said Shilpi Roy. "We've been discussing other issues."

"Do you believe any of this?" asked Cookie.

"Well…no. Stranger things have happened in the world, sure, but this is my husband we're talking about, a born liar. A son and grandson of cheaters and swindlers. So…no."

Shilpi Roy believed that wherever her husband had been living, it must have been outside Bengal, somewhere in north India, because he was throwing in fancy words with *z's* in them that sounded like Urdu, words like *budtameez* and *bezubaan* and *zabardast* and *zaalim* that he probably hadn't even known earlier. He had lost some weight and some hair but looked stronger and fitter than ever. He could have been working as a coolie, as he claimed, or hitting the gym on a regular basis. He remained as uninterested in his wife and daughter as he had had been before his disappearance.

Pijush Kanta Roy wanted to sell Raniganj Mansion. He was looking for a reliable and honest promoter because he knew that the whole business was full of crooks and cheats.

"Is that why you've come to us?" asked Cookie, "because you want us to help him sell the house."

"No, not exactly."

Bodhi and Cookie waited again.

"Mr Banerjee," Shilpi Roy said, "we have no secrets left from you. You know what we're like. You have seen us at our worst. And you too came to our house pretending to be someone you aren't. So, in a way, we too have seen you at your worst. But for some reason I can't explain, I feel I can trust you."

Cookie looked at Bodhi with a twinkle in his eye. Bodhi was impassive. He didn't unfurl his sad and empathetic smile, neither did he do his insincere act of self-deprecation. Compliment number nineteen, quietly went the counter inside his head. He would have to remember to add this to his list.

"My husband is not a good man, Mr Singh," Shilpi Roy said to Cookie. "He was not a good man before he abandoned us. He may have been a reasonable man at some point in his life, maybe as a child, and perhaps in the first couple of years after our marriage when I did see sparks of decency in him. But those were rare, and by the time he abandoned us, they had vanished."

Pijush Kanta Roy was an alcoholic. Unlike Cookie, who was one too, he couldn't hide his alcoholism and, what was worse, he was a violent drunk. He used to beat his wife on a regular basis. Slaps, kicks, and even bare-fisted punches. Once he had tried to push her down the stairs. Another time, he had thrown Maya from the bed because she had cuddled up to him for some affection when he was hungover. His daughter had been hardly two years old then.

"It's a miracle that Maya didn't suffer any serious damage. She could have died. That brute! You said that

I must be happy that he's back. Nothing could be further from the truth. I'm very unhappy and very afraid. I had really hoped that he was gone forever, that he was dead."

She used to dream, she said, that the police would come to their house asking her to identify a corpse and that she would go to the morgue with them and see his blue and bloated body lying on a metal gurney. He would have drowned to death or been run over by a bus or dismembered by a train. The method of dying wouldn't matter as long as he was dead. She would identify him with suppressed glee and, like her mother-in-law used to celebrate the death of her enemies, she would mark the occasion with a generous offering at Kalighat, not because she was a Kali devotee, but because she knew of no better way to celebrate the death of an evil man.

"I'm so sorry, Mrs Roy," said Bodhi. "I had no idea. Have you talked to the police?"

"I'm not afraid for my safety, Mr Banerjee. Pijush is a violent man, but he doesn't scare me. I've seen what he can do. Maybe he can do worse now. He does look meaner and more violent than before. Maybe he'll kill me, but that will just end the suffering. I don't fear death." Cookie looked at Bodhi and rolled his eyes.

Shilpi Roy believed in fate and destiny, she said, but unlike her mother-in-law she didn't think that it was possible to invite divine intervention in her favour by being prayerful and ritualistic. She was modern in an old-fashioned way. Her destiny—which therefore was her responsibility—was to raise her daughter to be a moral and educated woman and protect her mother-in-law from tyrants like her older daughter-in-law and her younger son.

These burdens of samsara would be over in a few years—Maya would get married and her mother-in-law would pass away—and Shilpi Roy looked forward to the day when she could devote her entire energy to active social service.

Her husband's reappearance had created a dilemma. If Raniganj Mansion was sold, her husband would make crores and she was sure that that he would abscond again, as soon as he had physical possession of the crores. But if he did stay, even for a few years, she would live a life of material luxury with an abusive and unloving husband. The thought made her skin crawl. If, on the other hand, Raniganj Mansion wasn't sold, her husband could disappear as quickly as he had reappeared, but more likely he would stay as long as it took to reach a final conclusion that the mansion couldn't be sold. That could take years, decades. It could become his life's mission. There was one thing Shilpi Roy wanted more than anything else. To make her husband disappear again. She was looking for a magician who could make that happen and send her back to the life she had till last week, with a daughter she was devoted to and a grateful (albeit cantankerous) mother-in-law.

"I'm not afraid for myself, but for my mother-in-law. I'm worried that if she doesn't change her mind about selling Raniganj Mansion, she may be in danger."

"What do you mean? What danger?"

"You can't believe what's going on in our house now. There's shouting from morning to night. My sister-in-law and my husband, of course, shouting at my mother-in-law. She must change her mind. She has to change her mind. She must agree to sell Raniganj Mansion. The more they shout the more stubborn she gets. Not only will she not agree to sell, she's talking about donating her share of the house to some philanthropic organisation, maybe the Ramakrishna Mission, so that it can never be sold. She wants to ensure that her share can never be sold, so Raniganj Mansion can never be sold."

"Oh my," said Bodhi, "that would upset your sister-in-law quite a bit." Not to mention him and Cookie too. This wasn't a positive development.

"Yes, but her bark is much worse than her bite. I don't think she'll actually do this. My husband, on the other hand, is something else. He seems to be even more callous and indifferent...and violent...than he was before. He's threatening to have his mother declared insane. He's going to put her in an asylum, he says, and then she won't be able to take any decision on anything. She won't be able to donate her property and she won't be able to fight the sale of the mansion. Because, you see, she'll be declared incompetent to take such decisions." Shilpi Roy's eyes swelled with tears. She blew her nose into her large pink hanky.

"What about her older son?" asked Bodhi. "Doesn't he have some responsibility here?"

"You've seen him, Mr Banerjee," Shilpi Roy said. "He's a weak man. He's not bad at heart, but he simply can't stand up to his wife or his brother. Now I'm not even sure that he wants to stand up to them. So many crores of rupees can change everything, no?"

"You mother-in-law isn't really insane, is she?" asked Cookie. "Her stories about the past are pretty wild, don't you think?"

"Of course she's not insane. Sure, she has some strange ideas, but who doesn't? My brother-in-law buys fifteen lottery tickets every week and he's never won a thing. Not even a radio. My sister-in-law believes in reincarnation and thinks that she was Rani Padmini of Chittor in a previous life. Talk to her for ten minutes and she'll tell you about how she protected her honour from Alauddin Khilji. If my mother-in-law is crazy, so are they. And my husband? Is that a believable story he's telling us? If he expects anyone to believe it, he must be crazy. They are all crazy. Not just my mother-in-law. The whole family is insane."

~

"So, what does she expect you to do?" asked Chhotomama.

"And why does she expect you to do anything?" asked Neera. "Doesn't she have anyone else to help her?"

"It wasn't clear what she wanted from us," said Bodhi.

"Bodhi is being too kind," said Cookie. "She dropped enough hints that she thinks that we can neutralise her husband's threats with our own."

"What do you mean?" asked Chhotomama.

"She thinks that we're in close contact with the underbelly of the city, all the goondas and mafias. We're promoters, see, so we must know these people. She seems to think that we can send some of these worthies to her house to scare her husband into behaving. Do a godfather shakedown, so to speak."

"Can you?" asked Neera, looking with narrowed, suspicious eyes at Bodhi. "Is this true? Do you know these sorts of people?"

"No, no, of course not," Bodhi said with a pained expression. How could you even think that?

But before he could finish, Cookie said, "Of course we do. You can't be in our business without knowing some shady people. Ha ha."

Bodhi glared at Cookie. "We don't really *know* these people Cookie, we're merely acquainted with some of them. There's a big difference."

"That's true, Neera," said Cookie. "Bodhi doesn't know these goondas at a personal level, but I do. Pretty fine people they are too, most of them, once you get to know them. Very god-fearing and quite devoted to their mothers."

Neera made a face that was midway between a smile and a grimace. Her lips went wide, but the left corner turned down. It was an expression of dismissal. Cookie grinned from ear to ear, refusing to be dismissed.

Bodhi wished he could disappear from the room, like Pijush Kanta Roy from his unsatisfying life. He wished that he could be more consistent in his tastes, so that he wouldn't at the same time love a man like Cookie and a woman like Neera. They were opposites of each other, not because they wanted to be, but because they couldn't help themselves. And he loved them both. He liked Cookie's boldness, his ability to always be himself regardless of how others would prefer him, and his authentic lack of seriousness on all matters other than money. At the same time, Bodhi liked Neera's earnestness, her ability to float above everything mundane as if the real world wasn't real at all but a construction by people who decided for you what was real and what wasn't, and her belief that one could change that constructed world with will or imagination.

He knew what Cookie would say—"Abey dhool ka phool, you don't have to think about money if you have plenty of it, and when you have plenty, you start thinking that it doesn't matter." He could guess what Neera would say: "Happiness has nothing to do with money. For some people, yes, maybe, but for most people, not at all. Do you know what makes you happy, Bodhi? Have you found your inner fountain of joy?" Bodhi agreed with both of them and felt that they were in a battle for his soul.

"Uff, boys, will you please stop squabbling like children!" Chhotomama said with some irritation. "There are bigger issues at stake here than whether or not you two have been socialising with anti-socials."

Outside, the light was fading. The meeting in Chhotomama's office had started in daylight, and now it was getting dark, but the room light remained turned off. No one wanted to get up and switch it on. Cookie's banter felt forced. A seeping lethargy had descended on the room and its gloom suited Chhotomama's mood. Flocks of sparrows flew by like dive bombers in V-formation across the large window behind Chhotomama's desk. Their excited *kichir michir* chirps drifted inside faintly, like the cheers of a small crowd appreciating a cover drive in club match at the maidan. Someone blew on a conch shell in a house close by. Its deep and mournful wail sounded more like a call to war than what it was meant to be, a call to evening prayer.

"Do you realise how serious this is?" asked Chhotomama. "Do you boys understand how badly people can behave when there is so much money at stake?"

"I think we know a little bit about it, Chhotomama," said Cookie. "This is our world, this is what we see every day. Bodhi, why don't you tell Chhotomama about the Ghatak family in Sarsuna and what they've done to each other over their property? Or better yet, tell him about what happened on Holi in Patuli."

Bodhi shook his head. No one wanted to hear promoter stories at that moment. There was a time for such entertainments and this wasn't one.

"I have no choice then," said Chhotomama. "I have to talk directly with Mrs Rajeshwari Roy. As soon as possible. That lady needs our support. We have put her in danger and now it's our responsibility to protect her."

# 3

"What do you mean by hunger strike?" asked Cookie.

"You know what I mean," said Bodhi. "Like netas do on TV. Like Gandhi*ji*."

"A full-fledged one? No food, no water? They'll die in five days, dammit. There's not even a hundred kilos of flesh between the two of them."

"No, they'll be doing a relay fast," said Bodhi. "Chhotomama from noon to midnight, and the old lady from midnight to noon. With water. And the only food they'll eat is puffed rice with milk."

Bodhi was finding it difficult to explain to Cookie what Chhotomama had just told him. Chhotomama had had a private meeting with Grandmother Roy that morning. He didn't want to waste time detailing the subterfuge that had been needed to make the meeting possible. That was for another day. They had talked for over an hour. Chhotomama had called Bodhi to inform him of their decision. They—Chhotomama and Grandmother Roy—would begin a hunger strike, a fast unto death, as soon as all the arrangements for it were in place. Bodhi would have to take care of most of the arrangements. It was not a request.

"So they'll last for ten days. Two weeks at most." Cookie was aghast. He had never missed a meal in his life and couldn't imagine a feeling of hunger that lasted longer than a few minutes. He had no idea how long a human body could survive without food, but he was sure it couldn't be many days. "And what do they hope to achieve with this? Who are they trying to impress?"

"I think they have a two-point agenda. First, they want an undertaking from the Roy family that Raniganj Mansion won't be sold. Grandmother Roy wants her sons to put this in writing in such a way that they can't change their mind later on, when she dies. Chhotomama's goal is different. He wants the government to declare the building a heritage site and commit to its maintenance. He knows that even if the Roys can't sell Raniganj Mansion, if it isn't maintained it'll turn to ruins in a few years. He's seen this happen too often."

"Whose bright idea was this?"

"Chhotomama's of course. And the old lady didn't need much convincing I'm told. Both of them have a death wish."

It was a recurring theme in the culture. A martyr complex. Something to die for. To find a cause that was greater than the ordinary drives of money, sex, and power. It was a rare privilege because it required the rarest of attributes—genuine bravery. Not bravado, not bluster, not a line on a resume, not a conversation piece for social gatherings, not a slogan in the name of social justice, but the real, real thing. Chhotomama and Grandmother Roy had beamed when they made their announcement, as if they had been granted a boon of immortality.

Would they be able to carry through with their promise? When the body started to fail and the mind became faint, when hunger sparked hallucinations, would they be able to persist? They didn't know, but that didn't mean they wouldn't try.

Bodhi had work to do. He had been given the responsibility of erecting a stage in the front yard of Raniganj Mansion. The stage should be raised three feet above ground, and be large enough to seat a dozen people, and have a canopy wide and strong enough to provide shade and keep out heavy rains. It was a simple job for promoters because this was the most basic of construction projects.

The hunger strike would begin as soon as the stage was ready. Chhotomama and Grandmother Roy would make an announcement for the media from that stage, so it would be seen on the evening news. "Make it nice-looking," Chhotomama had instructed Bodhi. "Dignified and sober. Don't use colours. Only white."

"And who's going to pay for this?" asked Cookie.

"No one mentioned money, so I presume we will," said Bodhi. "I suspect it's our contribution to the preservation of our history. Our penance for our sins of destruction. That's how Chhotomama would see it I'm sure."

"Don't get fancy with me, Bodhi," said Cookie. "This is all your fault. We had the thing in our grasp. And now because of your muddled head, because you can't decide what you want to be, the thing is out of control. Remember Raja Harishchandra, three crores...and that's just what you would make from this. That's three hundred lakh rupees. Three with seven zeroes after it. More money than you'll need in your life. More money than all the money that all your family put together has earned through their entire lifetimes."

"Cookie, I beg you, but would you shut up just for once," said Bodhi. "Let's just build the damn stage and get out of the way." He rubbed his eyes with both knuckles. He had a splitting headache that felt like two.

~

The stage was built in two days. After careful consideration of the logistics and other requirements, it was erected under the portico that had originally been designed as a car-veranda. To place it on the lawn would require them to remove the water fountain with the fat cherub. Though the fountain didn't work, Chhotomama decided that a fast for preservation shouldn't begin with any destruction. Moreover, the portico had some advantages. A canopy wouldn't be required, saving time and money. The wide five-step stairs underneath the portico and the aged but still-handsome main door the stairs led to would provide a vivid backdrop for TV cameras. And it was the most central location on the site; a stage on it would block the main entrance to Raniganj Mansion. The rear entrance would remain accessible, of course, but the message would be clear—the Institute was not open for business.

Bodhi came in to check on the final preparations. The scaffolding underneath had to be safe and sound (Bodhi had assigned a reliable head carpenter to the project), but the surface details were important. This was what people would see. This could turn out to be the most visible project in the history of Heavenly Homes Ltd. Financially it was a total loss, like the night soil payments to the goondas and police, but their reputation would be on the line. Bodhi worried because all suppliers were unreliable. They would cut corners where they could. He wanted to make sure that the contractor had sent sheets that were white and unblemished, without stains from wedding receptions and cultural fiestas, or damp brown patches from sitting in the rain. He wanted to make sure that the flower supplier had sent fresh, white, long-stemmed tuberoses. He had designed the event like a death memorial. Sad songs would be sung. Everyone would look depressed.

Raniganj Mansion was as busy as a wedding morning when Bodhi arrived at mid-afternoon. Several workers were milling around. There were young boys of fifteen and sixteen in short pants and bare chests with rivulets of sweat trickling down their dark backs. There were older men in their thirties and forties in long pants and sleeveless undershirts giving instructions to the young boys. They were all talking too loudly and laughing too much, showing little appreciation for the gravity of the situation. Chhotomama and Bankoli stood in a far corner close to the rear entrance. They appeared to be having an argument. Their faces were angry and they were waving their arms around. Fingers were being pointed. Bodhi decided to stay away from them.

Neera came up to Bodhi. She wore blue jeans and over it a simple white kurta with dark green stitches at the wrists and around the neck. "I'm glad you're here, BB." she said. "There's something I need to tell you."

What now? Bodhi was tired of being told things he didn't want to hear.

"I will be fasting too," said Neera. "I thought you should know."

Bodhi couldn't decide whether he should be surprised. Probably not. "Oh," he said, "that's nice."

"I'm glad you approve. If one can't take a stand on this, what can one take a stand on? If one doesn't commit to a cause like this...well, there's not much to say about the convictions of those people."

"Indeed." Bodhi wasn't sure whether this was a critique of his lack of commitment to the cause of preservation or a self-critique of Neera's own record of a lack of commitment to anything. He was being too harsh, Bodhi decided, because he was in a bad mood from being pushed around by everyone.

"I will be fasting with Mrs Roy, from midnight to noon," Neera said. "She'll have some company and moral support. It can't be easy for her at her age."

"No it can't be easy for her. I hope she doesn't get into serious trouble."

"I'm worried about her health."

"Yes. And don't forget her sons. And that daughter-in-law. The old lady might not have a home to get back to at the end of this. They might throw her out on the street."

"That's impossible," Neera said. "No one can be that cruel."

Bodhi smiled like a man burdened by much wisdom, part of which was the understanding that he could communicate only little of that wisdom to lesser beings.

~

As Bodhi moved around the construction zone he had to go near the spot where Chhotomama and Bankoli were arguing. It couldn't be avoided. He stood at a discreet distance but still could hear their loud words. The subject of their argument was obvious—whether the inauguration of the fast could be made compulsory for the staff of the Institute.

"You don't have any right to demand any sacrifice from the people without proper authorisation from the Party," said Bankoli, "and speaking for the Party, I can state with utmost confidence that we do not support public mobilisation for such elitist causes."

"Preservation of one's heritage is not an elitist cause," said Chhotomama. "What would you preserve, Dr Bankoli, if not the best of what you have? What would you save if your house was on fire?"

"My house is not on fire and that's beside the point. Why don't you tell me, where is the class conflict here? What are the issues that concern the proletariat? Why should they be forced to divert their energies from the daily struggle to put food in their mouths for a reactionary enterprise such as this?"

"Are you asking as yourself or as a representative of the Party?"

"You can think whatever you want."

"If that is how the Party thinks I'll resign from it," said Chhotomama. "Thirty six years I have been a loyal member, but I will resign. Make no mistake about it. I'll do it."

"That would be unfortunate," said Bankoli, "but appropriate. I assure you that the Party doesn't have any place for deviant thinking of this sort."

"All right then," said Chhotomama, "I'll resign as soon as this is over."

"If you're still around," said Bankoli with unconcealed malice.

"Yes, that's true," said Chhotomama, "unless I die during the fast. Then the Party can expel me posthumously and expunge my pictures and my name from everything."

"There's no need to exaggerate. Don't think you're that important," said Bankoli. "Don't think that anyone will care that much. We're soldiers for the Party, professor, not generals. But you seem to have forgotten this basic fact. You're behaving as if someone promoted you to general."

Bodhi didn't want to hear any more of this. He moved out of earshot.

# 4

Chhotomama had his beard trimmed and nails cut the night before the inauguration of the hunger strike. He wore a clean and ironed pair of white kurta and pajama on the morning of the event. As Bodhi waited for him to get ready, Chhotomama read a section from his favourite volume of Antonio Gramsci's *Prison Notebooks: The Modern Prince*. "Political and military victories," he read aloud, "have a permanent and universal value, and the strategic end can be attained in a decisive way with general effects for the whole. On the ideological front, however, defeat of the auxiliaries and the minor followers has an almost negligible importance. It is necessary to defeat the eminent people. Otherwise you confuse a newspaper with a book and minor daily polemic with a scientific work."

Chhotomama was girded for battle. He was ready to take on eminent people, regardless of whether they were from the capitalist class of the city or within the Party. Bodhi marvelled at his uncle's capacity for total belief—first in one thing, then another. It was as if the object of faith didn't matter—the Party or Raniganj Mansion—what mattered was the depth of the faith. Bodhi felt that his own confusion was inadequate in its intensity. He didn't believe anything, but did so half-heartedly. Why couldn't Bodhi be more like his uncle? Was it a character flaw or did he have to wait till he was sixty before he could see things clearly enough to be decidedly indecisive?

Chandan drove Bodhi and Chhotomama to Pratapgarh to pick up Grandmother Roy. She too had dressed in white, as she had been doing every day for the last dozen years. She had packed a small jute bag with three pairs of white saris and blouses, some underclothes, a bottle of Jabakusum hair oil, a comb, and some prayer essentials—a small etching of Ma Kali in a gilded frame, a tiny bronze bell, brittle sweets, and gangajal. She didn't need a prayer book because she had memorised all the prayers she would ever need. She left the house with Shilpi Roy under the pretence of a quick visit to the corner store. She left the bag behind. Shilpi would bring it later, when the world and her family became aware of this final great adventure of her life and there was no need to hide from anyone and no way to stop her.

~

As Chhotomama had expected, the inauguration of the fast was not very well-attended. There were a dozen or so people around, most of them the staff of the Institute, who had shown up despite not being required to. Some came because they felt obligated to Chhotomama. He had been their boss for years and though they were aware that the incoming boss didn't want them to support the fast in any way, they were quite confident that he would have as little ability to order them around as the outgoing boss. They were union workers and they knew who had how much real power. Others came because they sensed that this had the potential to be a full-blown tamasha that could provide entertaining tales for social occasions for many years to come. Maybe they would be seen on TV.

The TV people were, of course, the most important ones, and since they were present the absence of a crowd didn't really matter. Video crews were sent by the two channels (Urgent News and Breaking News) that most frequently used Chhotomama as a guest expert on all subjects from malnutrition to gang rape. Neera's journalist friend who worked for the *Daily Wire* and had written the story about Raniganj Mansion was also there with a photographer.

Chhotomama gave a short speech. He described the history and significance of Raniganj Mansion and the existential threat to it, and ended with a list of their demands. Neera and Grandmother Roy sat quietly to a side. Neither had faced a TV camera before. The older woman looked petrified. Neera wore a creamy off-white sari with a wide red border, like a devotee at a temple. Bodhi thought she looked like a devadasi ready to pleasure a priest. He wished he could be that priest.

The journalists had a few questions, not many, and the whole information session was over in half an hour. Then, songs began playing on the PA system Bodhi's contractors had installed. A Tagore composition—a popular invocation to wisdom—came first.

Light a fire in this life
Purify this life, oh lord
Purify this life with fire
Raise this body of mine

Make it a lamp on your altar
Let that lampfire burn with song
Let the darkness be lit with your twinkling stars
Let that starlight banish the darkness of my heart
Purify this life, oh lord
Purify this life with fire

Cookie and Bodhi watched the proceedings sitting on folding chairs they had dragged beyond the pouting cherub, close to the boundary wall. They were as far from the stage as possible, like the backbenchers they used to be as students. And just as in those days, Cookie chattered away throughout Chhotomama's little speech.

"How many people do you think will care two hoots about this? This bewakoof hunger strike for preservation."

Bodhi didn't answer. He knew Cookie would provide it himself.

"I'll tell you," Cookie said, "ninety per cent of the people in this city won't even know this is going on."

"That can't be. There are two TV channels here, not one, and the newspaper," Bodhi said. "Word will get out."

"How many people watch TV news, gadhey? (Cookie didn't). Only the news junkies and retired old men. Everyone else is watching serials or cricket. And how many people read this stupid paper? (Cookie didn't). How many people can even read an English paper? So, ninety per cent won't even know about this. That leaves 10 per cent. Half of those people have no interest in what old people do. As soon as they see Chhotomama or Mrs Roy, they'll switch the channel or turn the page. The other half doesn't like any kind of agitation. They'll start cursing as soon as they see another bunch of people demanding some damn thing and blocking something. Especially when they find out what the agitation is about. Preserving an old building! For heaven's sake. Give me a break. That leaves what? Nobody. Nobody cares, mere kagaz ke phool. Nobody gives a shit."

~

Cookie was almost right. Almost no one cared. But, almost no one is not the same thing as no one. In a metropolis of fifteen million the difference between almost no one and no one could be several thousand people.

When Bodhi dropped in late next morning—officially the second day of the hunger strike—on his way to a meeting with a supplier of marble tiles, he was surprised to see that the paltry number at the inauguration of the fast had doubled. He had never seen any of the new faces before. All were middle-aged men wearing white kurtas and pajamas (like Chhotomama) as if a funeral procession had lost its way and wandered in. Some of the new people were sitting on stage with Chhotomama and Grandmother Roy. Others were strolling about, examining Raniganj Mansion. A banner had been hung from one of the windows. The large white letters on the deep blue canvas spelled out their identity—*Seniors Against Damage and Destruction of Environment and Resources*.

"They just showed up this morning," Neera said with a big smile. "They live in the Ballygunj area. They are thinking about joining the fast."

Bodhi had heard about SADDER from his father. They were regulars on the same morning walk tracks around the lakes that Baba and his group of regulars used. The two groups never spoke to each other. SADDER was made up of high-class people. They were all civil servants that had retired a decade or more ago after holding important positions in the bureaucracy. Retirement was a living death. While employed, each had had an official car with an official driver, an official gardener, an official durwan, and several official secretaries. Some of them had even been authorised to use official sirens to plough through traffic. They had tried to hang on to as many of the trappings of power as they could, but one by one all were gone, and the powerless days stretched endlessly on with nothing to look forward to except an occasional board meeting or guest lecture. They had turned to activism in the last few years and were focusing on architectural preservation and environmental conservation. SADDER was headed by a man who used to be a joint secretary in the education department. He wasn't here yet but was expected soon.

"Mrs Roy's sons came by this morning," Neera informed Bodhi. "They were polite at first but soon they started shouting at her. The younger one especially. He seems to be a complete boor."

The sons had tried to persuade their mother to stop this foolishness and come back home. This was a family matter and mother shouldn't have dragged it out into the street for everyone to see. What would people think? Their mother had refused to engage in dialogue or provide explanation. They got the good old silent treatment.

"Did Shilpi Roy come with them?" asked Bodhi. "The younger daughter-in-law?"

"I know who she is. I think she had to go to work."

"I hope she's okay."

"Why shouldn't she be?" asked Neera.

"I don't know. There's something about these Roy men that makes me uneasy. Like they could do something drastic without even thinking about the consequences."

The frustrated sons had gone to the tea stall in front of the boundary wall—Chaturanan Pandey's shop—and had spent more than an hour there.

"How's the old lady holding up?" asked Bodhi. "And Chhotomama? Are they in reasonable shape?"

"They are fine," said Neera, "don't worry about them. It's only been a day. And I'm fine too. Thanks for asking," she added. Bodhi was mortified. This was what he had really wanted to know—how was his delicate Neera holding up? But he couldn't ask that, could he, not when there were genuinely fragile people fasting with her? That would have been improper. That's the word—improper. Bodhi could bear to be called many names, but not *improper*.

Chhotomama was taking a nap, so Bodhi didn't bother him. He said hello to Grandmother Roy and left for his meeting with the supplier of marble tiles. The meeting didn't go well. Bodhi could barely understand what the man was saying. Fragments and phrases registered—'Jaipur white,' 'Jaisalmer yellow,' 'three trucks'—but not whole sentences. His mind kept wandering over to Raniganj Mansion and its odd menagerie of hunger strikers. He dropped in at Raniganj Mansion again on his way back from the meeting.

It was late afternoon. The sun was angling low on the grey horizon and beginning to grow redder and larger.

The crowd at Raniganj Mansion had grown larger too. There were more than a dozen new people bumping around on the front yard now. Most were in their early twenties, and unlike the group of elderly men that had shown up that morning, this group had about as many women as men. The young men all wore beards and long hair. The young women all wore saris and short hair. They all carried limp cotton bags on their shoulders. It looked as if a street theatre performance was about to begin.

These youngsters were members of a fringe political party—The Democratic Youth Federation for Social Justice—that operated mainly on college campuses and attracted leftist young men and women who didn't feel comfortable with any established leftist party because of the comfortable power those established parties enjoyed. The Democratic Youth Federation for Social Justice believed in revolution. They saw the Party as an ossified bourgeois machine. The grizzled veterans of the Party saw the Democratic Youth Federation for Social Justice as irresolute imitators; they had never walked barefoot on bramble nor slept a night in a grass hut; they had never seen the inside of a sweatshop, let alone organise its workers, nor developed calluses from working with their hands; they were children of well-to-do families acting out their revolutionary fantasies as college students; they would settle into well-paying professions in a few years. The Democratic Youth Federation for Social Justice had hung its own banner from another of Raniganj Mansion's windows. Its base was white and the letters were in bold red. *Capitalism is not in Crisis—Capitalism is the Crisis.*

Bodhi knew these youngsters well. Not these specific ones, but this type. He could have been one of them. He had briefly dallied with the idea of becoming one of them. The rallies he had joined in college against ragging in the hostels and American adventurism in the Middle East had been organised by this group. Many of the revolutionaries who had been leaders of Democratic Youth Federation for Social Justice in those days were now living in America.

"Didn't I tell you, Bodhi," Chhotomama said with a gleam in his eye, "that there's a strong undercurrent of support for us? Look at the turnout. Just look around you."

Bodhi couldn't recall any such prediction from Chhotomama but he let it pass.

"The people need to be woken up," said Chhotomama. "All they need is for someone to sound the alarm. Once they're awake there's no stopping them."

"You should join us," said Neera, sitting cross-legged beside Chhotomama on the dais. Her frizzy hair was lit like a halo by a flood-lamp behind her head. Her devotional cream-and-red sari, the same one she had worn at the inauguration, glowed like translucent amber in the half shadow. She looked so beautiful that Bodhi's goggling eyes threatened to pop out of their sockets, right through the lens of his thick glasses. He was so scared by desire that he wanted to run for his life. "If you don't do it now," Neera said, "you'll regret it later. That you gave up a chance to become part of something special. That you didn't answer the call."

They were giddy with success and dizzy with hunger. It was impossible to tell which was the stronger contributor to their irrational exuberance. There was no point trying to tell them now that they hadn't achieved anything yet.

As Bodhi was leaving he saw a crew from Breaking News arrive.

~

"Your Chhotomama was on TV again," Baba said as soon as Bodhi entered the flat. "He gave a live interview."

"Did he say anything new?" Bodhi asked.

"No. The same demands. Also, that two other groups have joined the agitation. One of them seems to be those people I've told you about, those snobby babus who used to work in the government."

"I know. I saw them."

"I want to go there tomorrow," Baba said. "Can you have Chandan drop me there tomorrow when you go to work?"

"Why? Just to see?"

"Yes, that too."

"Don't tell me you're going to join them!"

"I'm thinking about it," Baba said.

"What's wrong with you people?" Bodhi exploded. The need to shout at someone had been building for some days and who better than his father? "Don't you have anything better to do? Have you forgotten about your heart situation and your blood pressure? Is this how you want to die? For some stupid building?"

"There's no need to shout, Bodhi."

"And I have to take care of the consequences. Always me. Everyone does whatever damn fool thing they fancy and I have to clean up afterwards."

"What are you talking about? All I said is I want to go and see what's happening. Give some moral support to my brother-in-law."

"Didn't you say you're going to join the fast?"

"That I'll decide later," Baba said.

"By yourself! Unilaterally! Like your decision affects only you and no one else."

"*Ohff* Bodhi, please don't do a maidservant melodrama. You're supposed to be a college graduate. Behave like one."

"I'll take you there only if you promise not to start fasting," Bodhi said in a quieter voice.

"I didn't ask you to take me there. I asked whether Chandan could drop me. If he can't, that's fine. I'll take a taxi. I don't need you or your permission to go there. Don't get over-smart with me."

~

Bodhi reached his office two hours late next morning—the third day of the hunger strike—despite having left a half hour earlier than usual. It didn't take that long to drop his father. But events had taken a new turn at Raniganj Mansion.

The front yard of the building was now crowded like a sari store a fortnight before Durga Puja. Both groups that had joined the agitation the day before had multiplied their ranks. There were more elderly men from SADDER wearing white kurta-pajamas. There were more young men and women from the Democratic Youth Federation for Social Justice. Plus, there were curious strangers nosing around. The flower beds had been trampled. The gravelled parking lot was making brittle crunching sounds. Maids from the neighbourhood were trying to peer over the boundary wall from the sidewalk. They had children wearing school uniforms with them and had gripped their hands to stop them from bursting in and joining the fun.

But what delayed Bodhi was not the growing crowd inside Raniganj Mansion but a new front that had opened on the battle for it. Beyond the building's boundary wall Chaturanan Pandey's tea stall was buzzing like a set of a low-budget movie on underemployment. Grandmother Roy's two sons were there directing the actions of a couple of bare-backed boys. Mrs Anjali Roy stood next to them with her elbows splayed and her fists on her wide hips. The workers were cleaning out the space, removing oddments of plastic and discarded tea cups. The shelf with the jars of biscuits and sweetmeats had been moved aside. The drum-oven for making tea had been rolled on its side next to the shelf. The bench where the customers used to sit had been reoriented; it was placed against the wall, parallel to the street. The calendar photos of Radha and Krishna on a swing and the big-breasted bodybuilders in orange halter-tops had been covered with a new banner. It had a hastily written slogan on what appeared to be a white bed-sheet—*THIS LAND IS OUR LAND.*

"What's going on, Pandey?" asked Bodhi. Chaturanan Pandey was standing on the pavement across the street from his stall with a concerned look on his face. A young girl stood by his side. She was twelve or so, dark and thin, with a glittering blue bindi on her forehead and shiny oiled hair tied up in white ribbons swinging in looped pigtails. She wore a school uniform of grey shirt with black skirt and black shoes.

"What can I say Bodhi babu?" said Chaturanan Pandey. "Everything has gone upside down in a day."

"What are these people doing?"

"You don't know? They haven't told you? They're setting up their own hunger strike," said Chaturanan Pandey, "those two brothers and that…lady."

"Their own hunger strike! What for?"

"They say that this is their house and they want it back from your Chhotomama. They are agitating against your uncle's agitation."

Bodhi scratched his beard. He wasn't prepared for this but wasn't surprised either. Thesis and anti-thesis and anti-anti-thesis, power and resistance and resistance-to-resistance, it was all part of the natural order of things in his world, part of the circle of life. "In your shop?" he finally said, "and you're letting them do it?"

"What can I do? They said that your uncle is trying to turn this house into a museum. If that happens, if he succeeds, then they'll clean up this footpath and take down my shop. My business will be gone, that's what they said. But if the brothers get the house they promised to let me keep my shop. And they'll pay me five lakh rupees."

"Five lakh rupees! Really! Just for being on their side? Have they given you any money? Even a hundred rupees?"

"Not yet. I'll get the money only after they get possession of the house."

"And all you have to do is let them use your shop? As simple as that?"

"No," Chaturanan Pandey said sheepishly. "I'll have to join the fast. That's why my daughter is here. She'll be looking after me. Her mother insisted. Beti, do pranam to sahib." The pigtailed girl bent and stretched her right arm toward Bodhi's feet but stopped well short of touching them. Ritual over, she resumed swinging her oily pigtails.

"Why would you join their fast?" asked Bodhi. "It's not your property."

"They said that I have rights too. I've been running this tea stall for so many years that now I have a right to keep my shop here. The only way to get my right, they said, is to fight for it."

"These are not good people, Pandey," Bodhi said. "You've taken the side of bad people."

"I know, Bodhi babu. And I know your uncle is a good man. He has always been very proper with me. But what can I do? We're poor people, sir. We never have a choice."

By evening, the news channels had seized the controversy. Experts were rounded up from colleges and civil society. Environmental NGOs sent representatives, as did builders and promoters. Views were sought from the man and the woman on the street. Humanitarian arguments were propounded. Market proponents made their case. Tempers were frayed and voices raised and accusations hurled. The government was roasted and the building industry fried. Experts talked over each other, interrupted, taunted and harangued, and when they needed to make a point, shouted. Grandmother Roy ('a brave senior citizen of our nation') found supporters, as did Chaturanan Pandey ('our brother from the toiling classes'). Neither Chhotomama nor the Roys attracted much sympathy.

Bodhi watched at home as Baba kept switching between news channels. His depression was lightened by notes of silent self-congratulation. He had been able to persuade his father to not join the madness. To be honest, Baba hadn't needed much persuasion. And he felt some justifiable smugness over his foresight. As he had predicted to Neera, opportunists and crazies had emerged like scorpions from under rocks. They were taking over.

# 5

Bodhi avoided Raniganj Mansion as long as he could on the fourth day of the hunger strike. He refused to go there and refused to discuss the subject with anyone. The story was all over the office by then. The staff knew that Bodhi had close connections to it and naturally they were curious. How often does one have direct access to an event in the headlines? But Bodhi was in no mood to oblige either the staff or Cookie who, it was obvious, had things to say. He was sure that he didn't need to hear what Cookie had to say. He left the office as soon as he could and spent the entire day at their two construction sites in Behala and Garia. Was everything all right? one of the site supervisors was moved to ask, for he had never in his twenty years in the construction profession seen a promoter sweat for hours at a job site when there was no need to do so. Later, at mid-afternoon, Bodhi cooled off during an unannounced visit to the air-conditioned office of the architectural firm that Heavenly Homes Ltd. used for all its projects.

Neera phoned twice, Chhotomama once. Bodhi didn't pick up. He was certain that they weren't dying yet.

His resistance weakened by late afternoon and by early evening he was back in the Elgin Road neighbourhood. Chandan, his driver, couldn't find parking close to Raniganj Mansion. The street was never empty of parked cars, even on Sunday afternoons, but today there wasn't a space to be had. Chandan parked the Sumo in an alley two blocks away.

Raniganj Mansion looked like a fairground hosting a small circus—with clowns and dwarfs but without tigers or trapeze artists. It was crowded but not thronging, dense with people but not so congested that no one could move. Several vendors had set up shop during the day. A balloonwala (who also sold whistles and soap bubbles) had taken the prime spot, immediately to the left of Raniganj Mansion's gate. A bhelpuriwala and a paanipuriwala were doing brisk business out of their mobile stands next to the balloonwala. Chaturanan Pandey had restarted his tea business. His regular canopied stall to the right of the mansion's gate was occupied by the Roy family and their supporters, who numbered close to a dozen at this point. As a result, Pandey had had to set up his principal means of production, the drum-oven for boiling water, outside the canopy, underneath the open sky. His wife and both his daughters were with him, but even with the added hands he was finding it difficult to serve his exceptionally large number of customers in a timely fashion. His waiting clients were circling the other vendors to his right—a topiwala selling baseball caps and straw hats and an astrologer with a clairvoyant parrot.

Bodhi estimated that there were more than a hundred people there, classifiable into three non-overlapping groups. There were members and supporters of the two rival teams of hunger strikers—Chhotomama's and the Roys'—and as both had added to their ranks through the day, the social distinctions between the rival fasters were obvious to anyone with eyes. The preservationists—from Chhotomama to the crusty retired bureaucrats and the student revolutionaries—all wore loose-fitted kurtas or half-kurtas of a single colour; most were in white but some wore shades of red. They belonged to a visibly higher stratum than the destructionists, a flotsam of middle-aged petty clerks and bookkeepers and unemployed young men from the Roys' neighbourhood in Pratapgarh. They wore half-shirts of great diversity. The Roy supporters must have been paid, Bodhi guessed, or promised money to show up. Word must have spread about the crores the Roys were going to make.

Then there were members of the media; now that Raniganj Mansion was a bona fide controversy, the media of the city had decided to cover it with carpet bombing. There were representatives from half a dozen English, Bangla, and Urdu papers and more than a dozen TV news outlets (not all of them devoted to news all the time). Most members of the media were identifiable by the badges and tags they wore and the microphones and cameras they carried and the general air of entitled aggression they exuded.

And finally there were gawkers and tamasha-seekers, most of whom lived within walking distance of the event and who were treating it with the same uninvolved but intense curiosity they would bring to a traffic accident or murder in their vicinity. A little excitement had been inserted into their humdrum days. Families had come with children. Young men and women had come in groups. Flirtations were taking place.

The stage underneath the portico was creaking under the weight of the numerous people using it. Chhotomama was lying on his side with his head on a cushion. He appeared to be sleeping. Three days of fasting had already taken place and the strain was beginning to show. Neera was sitting cross-legged behind Chhotomama. Her head was down and her back was bent. She was wearing a brown sari with a thin and faint block-print of large flowers. It didn't appear to be something she would have bought herself. It could be a gift from a poor relative or borrowed from someone, maybe the household maid. A couple of elderly men sat next to her, quietly and pensively. Several young men and women from the Democratic Youth Federation for Social Justice were singing songs of protest with two guitars and coordinated handclaps.

> Oh seeker of the path of light
> do not stop here
> in this land of dark night
> Do not moor your hope
> on this island of blight
> Listen
> Open your ears and listen
> for the thundering invitation
> From fields and forests an ovation
> flooding away walls of discrimination
> But do not stop here
> in this land of dark night
> oh seeker of the path of light

Bodhi sat on stage next to Neera.

"You've come…finally," Neera said. "Why didn't you pick up the phone?"

"I was in meetings all day," Bodhi lied. "Where's Mrs Roy?"

"She's inside," Neera said. "We've turned the Reading Room into a resting room and she's there. This is hard for her. She's not been feeling well. Some dizzy spells."

"Naturally. How long can you keep this up?"

"As long as it takes, Bodhi, as long as it takes. There's no turning back now."

"Do you realise that you're playing straight into the hands of the Roy brothers? If Grandmother Roy falls seriously ill or dies, they win. The mansion will be theirs and this whole drama will be over."

"How can they let their mother die like this? That's inhuman. No one, not even they can let it happen. What will the world think of them? Don't they care about what other people think?"

Bodhi shook his head. It was like talking to an interplanetary alien. There were no concepts they held in common. Neera had no idea what a man like the younger Roy was capable of doing.

"What about Chhotomama?" he asked. "Has anyone from the government responded to his demand?"

Chhotomama turned his head to look at Bodhi. He was awake and had been listening to them. "Dr Bankoli is speaking for the government," he said, "and for the Party. The government apparently has no interest in maintaining Raniganj Mansion even if they get it for free. Bankoli told me that the government is not an orphanage that it has to take care of any random motherless child that wanders by. It has plans and priorities. It will not respond to tantrums.

That's the word Bankoli used—tantrums. And the Party is issuing a show-cause notice to me. Probably tomorrow. I'll have to explain my anti-Party behaviour. Of course, my explanation is irrelevant. Bankoli said that come what may, I will be expelled."

"And you're fine with that?" Bodhi asked.

"Yes, yes. No question. This is not the Party I joined. This is not the Party I served for so many years. It's a rotten and bloated caricature of our ideals. These young people," Chhotomama said pointing to the singers of the Democratic Youth Federation for Social Justice, "represent those ideals far more than the Party. I won't even respond to the show-cause. Let them expel me. Let it be on their conscience…if anyone has a conscience left to worry about."

How would being expelled from the Party help Chhotomama's cause? Bodhi asked himself. He stayed with them on the stage for a while. The singers sang one song after another. There were hundreds of protest songs to choose from. People walked over to Chhotomama to congratulate him for his courage. Bodhi knew many of them—uncles and aunts and cousins and family friends—and exchanged greetings. Neera's father dropped by, looking distinguished and unhappy. He didn't stay long.

~

When Bodhi took his leave Neera walked with him to his car. "BB," she said after they were outside the mansion's gate, "I need a favour from you. My friend from America, the one I've told you about...he's coming." Bodhi's knees buckled and he stumbled. "He was going to come a little later but he changed his plans to accommodate this... situation. His flight is day after tomorrow. Around eleven at night. Will you please pick him up at the airport? He doesn't have any close family here. I would have gone of course, but how can I...in this situation."

Bodhi stared at Neera prattling away. Who was this person? Wasn't it just a fortnight ago that this person had walked hand in hand with him by the river? Didn't she just call him BB in the voice of a cooing dove? Was she completely guileless or was she evil incarnate? And what kind of a person was he to be in love with a person like her? His head felt like it would explode. A small groan came out of his mouth. Neera assumed he said "yes."

"Thank you, BB," she said. "You're a sweetheart."

Evil! Pure evil! There was no doubt about it now. No one with a shred of decency could say these things. No one could be stupid enough to say these things. Sweetheart! Even high society women couldn't be that naive. It had to be evil. Insensitive, self-centred, and manipulative evil. Bodhi felt the stirrings of an unfamiliar emotion. He felt like smashing something. Something large that would explode with a big bang and shatter into many pieces, as many as his heart had broken into. He would smash the thing with his bare hands if he could, but if he couldn't he wouldn't hesitate to use whatever would work. Bullets, dynamite, RDX. It didn't matter that he had never seen any of these objects except in movies. He had never touched any of them. Never mind. Something had to break.

By the time Bodhi fell asleep that night—after several hours of chain smoking on the veranda and changing channels on the TV with the sound off and lying in bed and sighing—he became unsure about his need to smash something. What good would that do? No, what he really wanted was to hurt Neera. Not physically, because Bodhi abhorred violence, but emotionally, inside her heart. It was the time-honoured Gandhian method; some called it the Devdas method. Do not retaliate when hurt. Let your abuser see your pain, feel your pain, and rely on the fundamental humanity of your abuser to understand his own inhumanity. This method could work only if the abuser had a heart that could feel the pain of others. Bodhi wasn't sure that Neera did, and if she didn't there was nothing he could do to hurt her. What then? Smash something of value to her? What *did* she value? Anything? Her little doggies Pomo and Poco? Those droopy drooly beasts. Could Bodhi kidnap and torture them? *Nah*, tempting as the thought was, Bodhi couldn't do it. He'd rather torture himself and make her watch. And so it went, round and round inside his head, fantasies of revenge alternating with visions of self-immolation till he fell asleep without having made up his mind about what to do next.

~

Bodhi saw a missed call from Neera when he got out of the shower next morning, the fifth morning of the hunger strike. He didn't call back. Why would she call other than to give him instructions on how to pick up her special friend?

Pay no attention to it. She called again during breakfast. Bodhi ignored it. Baba was reading the newspaper on his rocking chair. "They've been calling all morning," he said. "You should call them back." Bodhi laughed a dry bitter laugh. "Hah," he said, "when I'm good and ready." He ignored Chhotomama's call on the drive to office. But when Baba called soon after he reached office, he answered. He knew he shouldn't but he did.

"You're wanted immediately at Raniganj Mansion," Baba said.

"Why? What's the urgency?"

"Something big is going on. Your Chhotomama didn't want to talk on the phone but he sounded very excited. It's of the utmost importance. He insisted."

"I'm busy now. I'll go later when I have time."

"Don't be like this, Bodhi," Baba said. "I don't know what's happened between you two, but try to be nice. He's your favourite uncle isn't he? Whatever he's said or done to upset you, try to forget it. He needs you…and Cookie. He asked for the both of you."

Bodhi would have taken Cookie along anyway. He needed a buffer between him and Neera. If he needed to communicate with her he would do it through his friend, like fighting parents use their children. Cookie adjusted his schedule. "Just for an hour, okay?" he said, "and only because I can't bear to see you like this, scarecrow. Don't tell me what happened if that's what you want, but don't tell me nothing happened."

Raniganj Mansion looked like a house with a hangover. The area was littered with plastic and paper bags and burst balloons and broken clay cups. Two little girls in tattered frocks and matted brown hair were nosing through the litter, looking for things they could save and sell. There were few other people around. The balloonwala and the food vendors and the astrologer and his parrot were gone. Chaturanan Pandey was sitting on a rag spread on the footpath, dripping sweat from his virile moustache. The core fasters of the Roy team—the two brothers and the elder daughter-in-law—were dozing under Pandey's canopy, but their supporters had gone home. They would surely be back later in the afternoon. Shilpi Roy wasn't there. Bodhi realised that he hadn't seen her or little Maya at all after the duelling hunger strikes began. She hadn't attended a single fasting session.

The stage Bodhi had built for Chhotomama's team was empty. Its members were inside Raniganj Mansion, in the Reading Room on the upper floor where the fateful summit meeting had taken place not a fortnight ago that felt like a year. The room looked different. Things had been moved around and things had been added. Bodhi saw three folded camp cots propped against a wall at the far end.

Chhotomama, Grandmother Roy, and Neera were sitting around the long centre table of knotted pine that no longer occupied the centre of the room. They looked like second class passengers at the end of an overnight train journey. Not only were they unwashed and bedraggled, but the women wore perplexed expressions, as if they had gotten off at a station they couldn't recognise. Bodhi avoided eye contact with all of them. This was what he had planned to do, but the planning turned out to have been unnecessary, because sooner than his eyes had registered the presence of his one-time allies they were drawn to a striking new person sitting with them, blooming like a lily in the mud. This person was a plump and fair man in his mid-thirties, with a high, shining forehead and a clean shaven, jovial face. He wore a black suit with a red shirt and a yellow tie and managed to carry the outfit with grace. He was that rare man who makes stockiness look elegant, imminent baldness look insightful. The sight of him made Bodhi jealous.

He knew this man. So did Cookie and all the other small-time promoters like them. This man didn't know them but they knew him. His name was Pradip Kumar Muhuri (everyone called him PK). He was one of the most prominent promoters in the city. His projects had dozens of flats each. One legendary project on the Bypass, called *Blue Chip Lagoon*, had over 300 flats. It had three residential towers seventeen storeys high wrapped around a lake that used to be a fishery. *Blue Chip Lagoon* was the hallmark of quality in the city. PK Muhuri was a member of all the old clubs—the D Club, the R Club, the S Club, the M Club. He was a renowned partier in these clubs, reputed especially for an energetic shimmy that he had the ability to use with any musical accompaniment, from Sufi to rock-and-roll. He was also known to give generously to NGOs that provided services for children of sex-workers in Sonagachhi. PK Muhuri was a role model for Bodhi and Cookie, the antidote to the 'Peto' Mondols and 'Vat 69' Khans of their world, a promoter who had moved up to builder and now had the status of industrialist.

Bodhi and Cookie exchanged looks. What's this guy doing here?

"Ah, the boys are here," Chhotomama said. He looked tired. His voice was enthusiastic but there was a crack in it. "Bodhi, Cookie, you have surely heard of this gentleman. Mr PK Muhuri. He is very well known in your business. You know that, huh? Yes, I'm sure you do. Mr Muhuri, as I was saying, these are my nephew and his business partner. Their business is nothing compared to yours, but they are doing well, I'm not ashamed to say." That didn't sound like Chhotomama at all. Why was he being so obsequious? Everyone knew that he despised people like PK Muhuri.

"No shame in that, no shame in that at all," said PK. "Everyone has to start small. Rome wasn't built in a day. Every long journey begins with a single step. The great Dhirubhai himself began as a petrol pump attendant."

"Yes, yes," said Chhotomama, who despised Dhirubhai Ambani more than almost any other person he had never met. "The point is they know the business well. I think between the three of you, you can arrive at a fair value."

"So Bodhi," said PK, "if I may call you that…you look so much younger than me, like my little brother. Your uncle and I were talking about the market price of this property. How much do you think it is? How much would you pay for it?"

"I'm sorry," said Bodhi, "I'm afraid I don't understand what's going on. Is this some kind of test?"

"*Ho, ho,*" said Chhotomama.

"*Ha, ha,*" said PK. A dimple formed on his left cheek when he smiled.

Bodhi's felt a flush creeping up from his neck. He saw Cookie clench his fists.

"Let's worry about the whys and whats later," said PK, "just indulge me for a few seconds if you will and tell me what you'd pay for this. I'm sure you've done the calculations." He winked.

"Fourteen crores," Cookie said.

"That's it then, that seems about right," said PK Muhuri, "We'll offer fourteen crores to the Roy family."

"Please excuse my language, Chhotomama," Cookie said, "but what the fu… hell is going on here? Is this a joke or what?"

The harsh words seemed to snap Chhotomama back into character. Bodhi assumed that he had become lightheaded from hunger. He would never have behaved that way otherwise, like a rich man's yes man.

"I'm very, very sorry, Cookie," Chhotomama said. "This is not a joke and we shouldn't have joked about it. I'm very sorry." Cookie nodded without changing his fierce expression. "This is the thing. Mr Muhuri has brought us an extraordinary offer. It's so generous, so unexpected, that I lost my head. Mr Muhuri has offered to buy Raniganj Mansion from the Roys. He'll pay them fair market value."

"Excuse me again, Chhotomama," Cookie said, "but we could do that too. Haven't we always said that we could do that, Bodhi?"

"Yes, Cookie, I know that. But there's a big difference. You'd buy Raniganj Mansion to break it down. Mr Muhuri is going to buy it and preserve it. He won't touch one brick. And he'll set up a foundation that will pay for its upkeep. Isn't that amazing? This is exactly what we've been trying to achieve. This is a dream come true."

Bodhi and Cookie looked at each other. The same question was on both minds. Why would this random person do this? Out of pure generosity? That was just absurd. PK Muhuri was nothing but a very successful predator in the same ecosystem inhabited by Bodhi and Cookie. He hadn't become a successful predator by being nice to the other creatures in that ecosystem. "Please don't mind while I bite your head off." "Thank you for encouraging me to crush you like a cricket." Allegations of murder or extortion weren't attached to PK Muhuri's name—not that Bodhi had heard of—but that didn't mean he hadn't murdered or extorted. Who knew what he'd done to get where he was. He could fool others with his smooth ways but he couldn't fool them.

Cookie, who always preferred the most direct route to a destination, asked the question inside both heads. "But why would you do that Mr Muhuri. I don't think any of us have ever heard of a gift like this, have we Bodhi?"

"I can understand your scepticism, Mr Cookie," said PK, "I'd be just as sceptical if I were you." He winked again. "But, as I was telling the others before you came, I am not the casual stranger you think I am. I have a deep interest in this house. It's part of my family legacy. You see, Raniganj Mansion is my father's house."

"What!" exclaimed Bodhi. "Are you…"

"The bastard? Yes, I am and I'm not ashamed to say so."

So Shilpi Roy's story was true. This plump and prosperous man was the illegitimate son of Mr Prashanta Kumar Roy, the fruit of his busy loins with the mistress everyone had known about except his wife. His wife, the widow, who was present in this room, hearing all this. What was she thinking? She wasn't disputing his claim, so it must be true. Bodhi looked at Grandmother Roy. He had grown fond of the feisty and cranky old woman. Even if Mr PK Muhuri wasn't ashamed of his origin, Mrs Rajeshwari Roy certainly would be. She couldn't have imagined this turn of events. She appeared to be disoriented. She was licking her lips and muttering to herself.

Mr PK Muhuri had told the story of his life before Bodhi and Cookie arrived. It was a story of guts and glory. PK had turned the disadvantage of his fatherless birth into a motivational device. He had studied harder, worked harder, and competed harder than everyone around him. His father, to his credit, hadn't left his second family destitute. He had bought a house in Maniktala for his mistress. Till the day he died Mr PK Roy had provided generous financial support to PK Muhuri and his mother. PK had gone to one of the better-known missionary schools in the city. After that he got a degree in civil engineering. His first job was at a construction company where he learnt the ropes of the construction and real estate businesses. After a couple of years at this job, he broke away and borrowed against his mother's house in Maniktala and got into business himself. That had happened about a dozen years ago, just when the property market was beginning to boom. Success had arrived immediately and in these last years he had known nothing but success—at the rate of a twenty-five per cent margin of profit. So much success that he could throw away a fistful of crores on a whim.

"Oh, and there's one more thing you should know," PK Muhuri said. "I will change the name of Raniganj Mansion.

It's going to be called Protima Muhuri Mansion. It was my mother's last wish."

~

"Learn from a master, Bodhi," said Cookie, "bow down your head before a guru. This is how big shots become big shots."

"That must be the most brutal thing I've ever seen," said Bodhi. "My heart went out to the old lady. All this risk-taking, this entire jhamela with her own family, alienating her own children…for what? For this! Poor woman."

"What a bastard. He waited till the very end to make his move. After he had them eating out of his hand. Admirable, at some level, don't you think? When I grow up I want to be like him."

Bodhi thought about the scene from a few minutes ago. The calm disdain of PK Muhuri's announcement of the new name of Raniganj Mansion and the complete despair of Grandmother Roy. Bodhi thought she was having a stroke. She slumped in her chair and started shivering. She was almost seventy, had hardly eaten for four days, and had just been told in the coldest, most off-handed way possible that the thing she was trying to save, the building she was trying to preserve in her husband's memory, could only be saved by naming it after her husband's biggest shame, her own oldest enemy, her husband's mistress. Neera held Grandmother Roy by her shoulders and slowly walked her out of the room. Chhotomama sat frozen with a stupid smile.

"What's she going to do now?" Cookie asked.

"I don't know man," Bodhi said. "I don't see how she could tolerate this humiliation. I don't think she can continue to be on Chhotomama's side. She has to go back to her sons, eat humble pie, and agree to sell Raniganj Mansion. Not to Muhuri. Anyone but Muhuri." Someone not burdened by the weight of family history or motivated by revenge.

"Not only that," Cookie said. "I think this Muhuri fellow is a monster at another level. A level we cannot even comprehend. Chambal ka badshah ka baap, saala. I think there are two possibilities. One, that he has no intention of buying Raniganj Mansion. Never did. His only reason for showing up here today was to humiliate the old lady. He knows that she can't agree to the sale with this condition. And he has no intention of enriching the Roys with so many crores. Why should he? Let them suffer. But if somehow, for some bizarre reason, the old lady agrees to the sale—if greed gets the better of honour—Muhuri gets a prime piece of property. He names Raniganj Mansion after his mother, but only for as long as Grandmother Roy is alive. Just to torment her. The day she dies he breaks the building down and makes ten crores profit for himself. That's what I think. And if Grandmother Roy still has doubts about what to do we should tell her this. Tell her what's really going to happen."

"What are you saying, Cookie? Are you saying what I think you're saying?"

"You got it, tubelight. We're back in the game."

"Not so fast, Cookie. There's still Chhotomama. Even if Grandmother Roy abandons the hunger strike and goes back to her sons, he's not going to budge."

"Yes, that's true. Plus there's Neera."

"That doesn't matter. Neera doesn't matter anymore. It's over." Bodhi sighed.

Cookie looked at Bodhi's miserable face. He had guessed something was wrong between Bodhi and Neera. He had seen it in his friend's face in the morning. He had seen it in the way his friend had avoided Neera this last hour; he hadn't even said hello. Cookie had many questions but didn't ask any. He was sensitive about these things. Bodhi would tell him when he was ready. "Are you absolutely sure?" Cookie asked. "You better be absolutely sure."

"*Hnooo.*" Bodhi's eyes were fixed on a faraway point on the horizon. He took a long drag on his cigarette and let the smoke leak lazily out of his nostrils. They were walking in slow meandering patterns on the roof of Raniganj Mansion, choosing their steps with care to avoid slipping on the mottled mossy surface. The sun was in mid-sky. Heat rose from the roof in shimmering waves. There was no place to take shade. The heat didn't bother Bodhi or Cookie. At the end of the Muhuri meeting they had abandoned whatever plans they had for the day. They needed to figure things out. They knew that this was the decisive moment. Calculations weren't necessary. It was pure instinct.

"If Neera doesn't matter then Chhotomama doesn't matter at all," Cookie said. "I don't think he ever has. No court of law will take him seriously. He doesn't have any standing in this affair except that he's standing in the way of an inevitable outcome. Raniganj Mansion is history. One way or another it's coming down. Take pictures now because there won't be another chance." He grinned. "In fact, what

Chhotomama is doing is deeply undemocratic. He's against what the people want. Let's tell him that. That'll get him confused. Make him question his righteousness."

Cookie made the case for immediate action. With Grandmother Roy back on their side the Roy brothers would sell the mansion as soon as possible. But not to PK Muhuri, who surely didn't have any real intention of buying it anyway. To whom then? Who were the only promoters the Roy brothers knew? As far as Bodhi and Cookie were aware, they were it. Before the Roy brothers could look around for other promoters Bodhi and Cookie could pounce and swing a deal. It was true that they had some fences to mend, some relationships to repair, but the imminence of a large handful of crisp crores had a way of smoothing over such bumps. But there was no time to waste. If they delayed they would lose this window of opportunity. The Roy brothers would find some other promoter. Who knew better than them that there was no shortage of promoters in this city.

"No more dithering, Bodhi," Cookie said. "You can't be all things to all people all the time. This is your story, but everyone else is hogging the stage. It's about time you did something. It's time to act."

~

The Roy brothers were sitting under Chaturanan Pandey's canopy. Grandmother Roy was with them. As expected, she had switched sides. Her older son, Pankaj Kamal Roy, was holding her bony, wrinkled hands and weeping. His wife, Anjali Roy, sat at the end of the bench with her face turned the other way. Her younger son, Pijush Kanta Roy, glared at Bodhi and Cookie with bloodshot, hostile eyes. He may have been fasting but that didn't mean he hadn't been drinking. It was a potent combination, even for an alcoholic.

Bodhi began by inquiring after Grandmother Roy's health. Was she okay? All this fasting and then the blow of the Muhuri visit. How insulting it was. How impertinent. He was…they all were…concerned. At first the conversation didn't go well. The Roys felt betrayed. They felt that their innocence had been taken advantage of by everyone. Their innocence and their lack of income and connections. They were wiser now and wouldn't trust anyone. Mrs Anjali Roy emphasised the theme of betrayed innocence. Her morality had been outraged.

Fortunately, Cookie and Pijush Kanta Roy were able to talk to each other. They were kindred spirits that had seen and were comfortable with the dark side of life. They were also both very interested in the bottom line. And the bottom line was this—Raniganj Mansion had to be converted to an apartment building. Everyone agreed on this point. For that to happen, the Roys had to sell it to some promoter. They agreed on this point too. Then why not talk man to man, landowner to promoter?

They haggled over price. Cookie offered fourteen crores, the same price, he pointed out, that PK Muhuri would have offered. Pijush Kanta Roy wanted twenty. No promoter could pay them twenty, Cookie explained, because that would leave no profit for the promoter. He knew. It was his business expertise. They split the difference. Seventeen crores. It was going to be a hardship for Cookie and Bodhi, they might not be able to make a profit at all, but in light of all the difficulties the Roys had endured they were willing to go this far. Somehow they would manage. Cookie tried to make it sound like a sacrifice.

But why should the Roys sell to Bodhi and Cookie? There were many promoters in the city. Why shouldn't they shop around and test the market? Mrs Anjali Roy was clear on these fundamentals of capitalism. Go ahead, Cookie said, and see if you can get a better price. Make sure, however, that this other promoter offering a higher price would also take care of the Chhotomama problem. Cookie reminded them that Chhotomama was the original problem and he hadn't gone away. He was as determined to save Raniganj Mansion as before, maybe more so. He was a very stubborn man and had connections too. He could singlehandedly hold up the sale of Raniganj Mansion for years. Hadn't they seen how many supporters he had attracted? Didn't they know how long it took to settle cases like these through the court system? How many years...how many decades...were the Roys willing to wait?

They puzzled over the Chhotomama problem for a while. What was motivating that strange man? Why couldn't he just be bought off? Pijush Kanta Roy wanted to know. It was well known that every man had a price. How could he be beyond this universal law? Give Chhotomama a crore and ask him to get out of the way, Pijush Kanta Roy said. You are his family, he said to Bodhi, you should be able to work this out with him. Bodhi tried to explain, as best he understood, his Chhotomama's actions. He was a man with principles, he said.

"Are you saying that we don't have principles?" Mrs Anjali Roy's personal morality was outraged again.

"No, no," Bodhi said, "I'm not saying that at all. We just have different principles." He had given the matter some thought, and was sure of his ground, but knew that he couldn't communicate his understanding to the Roys. How could he explain the inner workings of a man who was utterly unmotivated by money to people who were motivated by nothing else? This was where the common rational world reached its limit and banged its head against the immovable rock of irrationality. Rational people could talk to each other but not to irrational people. "He's like a suicide bomber," Bodhi said. "The only thing that will give him joy is his own death for his chosen cause."

"Creepy," Mrs Anjali Roy shuddered. "I hate terrorists."

"And what about that other woman?" Pijush Kanta Roy wanted to know. "The fancy one. Doesn't she have to call off the hunger strike too?"

"No one knows what she is thinking," Bodhi said. "But we don't have to worry about her. She doesn't matter. If Chhotomama can be stopped, that will stop her too. She's not going to die for a building." He was sure of this.

They came to an agreement. Bodhi and Cookie would take care of the Chhotomama problem. How they did it was their business. The Roys would sell Raniganj Mansion to Bodhi and Cookie for seventeen crores. The whole sum would have to be paid at one time. No instalments. And no partial payment in kind, through flats in the new building, the usual way small-time promoters did their business.

They haggled over this for some time, but Pijush Kanta Roy didn't budge. He wanted to see the money. All of it together. Bodhi suspected it was so that he could disappear with his share as soon as possible. That would be good for everyone—his wife, his daughter, his mother. "All right," he said, "let's do it." It was a gentlemen's agreement and as good as the word of gentlemen, but just in case their memories didn't match up later they would immediately get this memorandum of understanding notarised on stamp paper at Alipur Court.

Cookie took Bodhi aside. He promised to do all the running around to gather the money. Seventeen crores was a lot. They would have to pool all their resources, all the money in their two running projects, sell or mortgage what property they had, Bodhi's flat, Cookie's flat, plus what they could borrow...and even that wouldn't be enough. They would probably need to bring in one or more partners—relatives, friends, other promoters—to raise the whole amount. Cookie would do all this, he said, as long as Bodhi did the one thing that would make everything possible—solve the Chhotomama problem.

"You have just one thing to do, scarecrow," Cookie said before he left with Pijush Kanta Roy to sign the memorandum of understanding, "get Chhotomama out of the way."

# 6

Everything had gone wrong. Nothing had happened the way Bodhi had wanted it to happen. Everyone had behaved as if no one else existed, as if their own desires were the only ones that mattered. So much ego. Such blindness. Chhotomama had behaved as though his views on preservation were the last word on the subject, every other interested party be damned; as if by holding a job in Raniganj Mansion he had been bestowed with proprietary rights to it. Grandmother Roy had acted as if the only thing that mattered was her dead family's honour; her living family be damned. Her sons weren't able to see anything beyond the money sunk underneath the three hundred tonnes of that bloody building, their own mother be damned. Cookie, blessed Cookie, cared for Bodhi and what Bodhi wanted and had been trying to keep his own desire in check, but he wanted this as much as anything he had ever wanted. This single deal that would make him the equal of his father. And Neera? Even now Bodhi couldn't understand what she wanted or that she really wanted anything at all or that she even knew how to want. Anyway, it was as clear as a driving manual that whatever she wanted it wasn't him. The shock of that realisation had started at his knees but the pain had now spread all through his body and came, when Bodhi couldn't stop it, in wrenching waves through his heart and his head. Bodhi was reminded that it's possible to feel physical pain without being physically hurt. He remembered the sudden chokes he used to feel in his heart in the months after his mother died.

Bodhi stood on the veranda of his flat and lit one cigarette from another. It was well after midnight. The neon tube on top of his building's gate flickered like the ardour of an inconsistent lover. The blinking light fell on the street dog regulars, the self-appointed guards of the mohalla, as they strolled about with intent. The night guards had ended their stick-beating rounds and gone to sleep on someone's driveway. Mustaque, the dhobi, and Ansari, the cigarettewala, were sleeping on Mustaque's ironing table. Faint voices came from the direction of the main road, probably from drunken men staggering home. The night looked and sounded like any other. But inside Bodhi's head, a cyclone raged.

What was the result of all this unregulated desire? Chaos. Absolute and complete disorder. Wasn't there supposed to exist some invisible hand that would coordinate all these conflicting desires into a happy and orderly outcome for all? None that Bodhi could see. There was no invisible hand. Even if there was, it couldn't erase what the moving finger had written. A visible hand was needed and it had to be Bodhi's hand. He finally knew what he had to do. All through this escalating mess he had set aside his own needs to satisfy everyone else. As always. But no one had noticed and no one had cared. As always. This was the way of the world and it was time for him to be as worldly as everyone else.

~

Next morning, Bodhi phoned Chhotomama and made one last attempt to persuade him to give up his hunger strike. He knew he wouldn't succeed but he had to try. He gave Chandan a holiday and took the day off from work himself. Cookie did too. Both had other things to do.

At ten-thirty that night, around the time he was supposed to be at the airport to pick up Neera's special friend, Bodhi drove over to Raniganj Mansion with two ten-litre canisters of kerosene. He parked the Sumo in front of the building. It was easy because there was no crowd to contend with. The Roy team had disbanded, so they and their supporters from their neighbourhood in Pratapgarh were missing. Chaturanan Pandey had gone home last evening after five days of hunger and hungama. He had gone home happy because Bodhi had reassured him that one way or another he would get the five lakhs he had been promised by the Roy brothers. Chhotomama's hunger strike was also sputtering. The defection of Grandmother Roy had significantly diminished public interest in it. The number of Chhotomama's supporters had dwindled into single digits. The media had disappeared because there was no controversy to cover. The fight, as far as they were concerned, was over. A smallish crowd had gathered earlier in the evening but now it was bedtime and everyone had gone home. The only people left in Raniganj Mansion were Chhotomama, Neera, and a security guard.

A light drizzle had started around eight. This was the first rain of the monsoon. Small drops of rain splattered into smaller droplets on hitting the edge of the stage underneath the portico and found their way on to the stage. Chhotomama and Neera had retreated to the Reading Room inside Raniganj Mansion. This room had been serving as the bedroom for all three hunger strikers for the last four nights. The centre table had been pushed to a side to clear a large rectangular space close to the middle. Three camp cots made of folding metal frames and canvas-backing were laid out in this rectangle, each below one of the ceiling fans hanging from long poles attached to the high ceiling. Grandmother Roy's empty cot was in the middle. Chhotomama was lying on his cot at the far end from the stairs. His eyes were closed and his right wrist was on his forehead, as if he was taking his temperature. Neera was sitting on a chair reading a book. She had put her feet up on another chair. Her right elbow was on the centre table. She was wearing the same saffron kameez and white salwar she had worn all day. She was planning to change into a nightdress in a few minutes, after Chhotomama fell asleep.

This was what Bodhi saw when he reached the top of the stairs with the first canister of kerosene: a makeshift refugee camp occupied by an ailing father and his exhausted daughter.

"Bodhi," Neera exclaimed, "what are you doing here?"

"Wait," Bodhi said, and went downstairs to bring up the second canister of kerosene.

"Bodhi!" Neera said when he returned with the second canister. "What's going on? What are those things?"

"One minute," Bodhi said. He carried both canisters to the door of the Rare Documents Room. He pushed the door open with his left foot and switched the light on. The tube blinked twice and flared into a bluish whiteness. Six dark wooden cabinets with glass covers lined three walls of the small room. The custom-made cabinets were crammed with brittle old books, maps, and handwritten manuscripts of odd shapes and sizes. Several of these objects were unique, the only known copies in existence.

Bodhi unscrewed the cap on one canister and discovered a small hitch in his plan. He should have brought a mug or some small vessel. He didn't want his hands to get smelly with kerosene. "Is there a mug somewhere around here?" he asked.

"There should be one in the men's bathroom," said Chhotomama, now sitting up on his camp cot and watching with puzzled interest.

Bodhi returned with the mug and poured it full of kerosene. He splashed the contents on the nearest cabinet in the Rare Documents Room with a flick of his wrist. The dark brown wood of the cabinet turned black with wetness.

"What the hell are you doing Bodhi?" Chhotomama tried to shout but his voice was hoarse and papery.

"What do you think I'm doing?" Bodhi tossed another mug-full of kerosene.

"I don't know, I have no idea, but please stop. Those things you're throwing water on, they are irreplaceable. They are invaluable. Stop behaving like a vandal."

"This isn't water, Chhotomama, this is kerosene. Can't you smell it? And I'm not trying to make your precious books and things wet. I'm going to burn them." He heaved what remained of the first canister of kerosene on the largest cabinet in the Rare Documents Room.

Neera's jaw dropped. Bodhi could see her pink tongue glisten from ten feet away. He wondered how it would taste—of mint maybe, or cinnamon, or strawberry jam—

and regretted that he would never find out. Chhotomama jumped up from the camp cot. "Oh my god," he said, "What madness is this, Bodhi? What's gotten into you?"

"This isn't madness, Chhotomama. This is blackmail. Two can play at this game. I'm doing exactly what you're doing. You've made Raniganj Mansion your hostage. Well...now these books are my hostages. If you want your precious things back you have to give up your hostage. You have to let Raniganj Mansion go."

Chhotomama howled and held his head in both hands. "Let it go to whom? That bunch of hooligans! That family of usurpers! Those people who exploited and stole everything they possessed! Give it to them so that they can tear down the one valuable thing that was created from their thievery! They don't deserve it and you know that very well."

"Who are you to decide who deserves what? Who made you judge and jury, Chhotomama? Who deserves anything? Look around you and tell me that you see anyone who actually deserves what they have. The rich get rich by stealing and exploiting. That's what you've told me all my life. Their children get rich just by being born. Do any of them deserve to be rich? Does anyone deserve to be poor? Or do they have a choice in the matter? Don't talk to me about who deserves what. It's all bloody luck. A wheel of fortune. Nobody deserves anything, so everybody deserves everything."

"Bodhi, I'm too old to learn philosophical niceties from anyone, especially you. I know what I know and that's what I know. I'm not giving up."

"No, Chhotomama, you have to. Otherwise I'll burn down this precious collection of yours. How long has it taken to build this collection? Fifty years? Sixty? It'll burn in six minutes. I'm serious. If you think I'm bluffing, just try your luck. You have to let Raniganj Mansion go to its rightful owners. Who appointed you the guardian of this house, Chhotomama? You yourself did. Nobody asked you, but does that matter? No! You don't care what anyone else thinks or wants. You don't care that your Party doesn't support you. You don't care what the Roys want. They are all the same to you. As long as the grandmother was on your side she was a good Roy; now that she isn't, you don't care. You don't care that if you don't stop your agitation she and her younger daughter-in-law may be in real danger. Your ego is out of control Chhotomama. You think you know what's best for everyone and you want everyone to bend to your will. That is simply not acceptable. Raniganj Mansion isn't yours and you have to let it go."

"Don't lecture me, Bodhi, don't you dare," Chhotomama hissed. "You're a fine one to talk. All you want is money. That's all you've ever wanted. You forced your parents to give up their house so that you could become a promoter. A low and dirty middleman. Don't think that just because we don't talk about it we don't remember what happened. How you were born in this family I don't know. None of us do. Your only interest is in the money you'll make from this building."

"Actually, you're wrong. You always are and you're wrong again. It's true that I'll make money…if all goes well, fingers crossed, *Joy Ma Kali* and all that. But I'll happily give that money away to a charity of your choice. I'll give the money away, Chhotomama, believe me. There was a time when I wanted to make a lot of money from this house, that's true, but I'm beyond that now. Let everyone else make out from this wheel of fortune—the Roys, Cookie, Bankoli, your Party, whatever...I don't care. I'll give my share to Mother Teresa's orphanage. Oh, but you don't like Mother Teresa. To Ramakrishna Mission then? No, you don't like them either. You don't like anything to do with any religion, do you Chhotomama, because you like to play god yourself. No, what I really want is for you to stop playing god and for Neera to stop playing goddess."

He took out a cigarette and lit it with shaky hands. He was having trouble thinking clearly. Where had these words come from? He hadn't planned this part of the speech. Would he really give away three crores? Just to spite Neera? Oh heavens, he did love her madly. He was a disgusting, despicable man. A fool. Bodhi's head swam. He picked up the second canister of kerosene.

"Bodhi!" Neera screamed, "you're mad." She rushed toward him. Perhaps she thought she could physically stop him. Bodhi let her come. He felt powerful. The kerosene fumes heightened his sense of invincibility over these frail and starving people. Neera grabbed his arm holding the canister of kerosene and it fell to the floor with a flat thud. Bodhi almost toppled over. In his euphoria of invincibility he had forgotten that he had the ability to trip over his own feet from a standing position. Bodhi had to hold on to Neera to stop himself from falling and found himself in the position he had been dreaming about for months. Neera was in his arms. She was a warm and wriggly thing, throbbing and panting and beautiful. Bodhi put his nose on top of her head and took a deep breath. Ever since he had seen that unruly mass that promised wildness and abandon he had wanted to bury his face in it. Neera hadn't washed her hair for days. It smelled like damp peanuts.

Bodhi pushed her away. "Don't come near me, Neera," he said, "and listen. Don't interrupt, just listen. For your information, I've not gone mad. If anything, I've come to my senses. I was mad before…to be in love with you…to think that you had any feelings for me…to think that we could actually be together. Everyone told me I was wrong but I didn't listen. Baba said that you and I are like oil and water, we'll never mix. You'll always be an upper class something or the other and I won't, regardless of how much money I make. He's never met you but somehow he knew. Cookie said that you're too airy fairy. Too self-absorbed. That you'd give me a run-around but never let me get close. He was right but I didn't listen. I was so mad that I went along with this mad scheme of yours. Well, it's Chhotomama's scheme but it might as well have been yours. I thought that you understood me a little and you'd see how much I was bending…twisting…to support your madness. But no. You can't see anyone but yourself. You and Chhotomama, you're alike. Narcissistic, egotistical and indifferent to the needs and wants of others. The most selfish creatures on earth. And you dress it up as selflessness. What hypocrisy! You know what, Neera, you should go to America with your special friend. There are lots more people like you over there and we'll be better off without you over here. Good riddance."

Bodhi felt free. The thing that had stuck in his throat like a fishbone was gone. He had swallowed it himself. He was master of his own fate again.

Neera stood as still as a painting. Her slanted eyes swelled with tears. Chhotomama stood next to her. "Stop being an ass, Bodhi," he said. "Don't say anything else that you'll regret forever."

Bodhi brought his right hand to his mouth to take a drag from the cigarette he had lit a minute ago. But there was no cigarette in his hand. It had been knocked out of his fingers during Neera's assault. He turned around and saw the cigarette lying on the floor and a pool of kerosene spreading slowly toward its glowing tip. He watched immobilised as the pool reached the cigarette and lit up in a blue and orange flash. *Bhoop*! A small flame about ten-inches high burned for a few seconds on the marble floor and jumped to the side of the cabinet closest to the door. There the flame stood on its toes, looking around, deciding where to jump next. In less than a minute half the cabinets were on fire.

Bodhi fought the fire, first with his bare hands and sandaled feet. Then he took his shirt off and used it to try to beat down the flames. He stutter-stepped forward and back waving frantically, like a matador trying to catch the attention of a distracted bull, his scrawny arms whirling out of a white undershirt tucked into his pants. Neera ran to the bathroom with the mug that Bodhi had used to spray the kerosene and ran back with water in it and threw it on the largest flame. She did it again and again, going back and forth between the Rare Documents Room and the bathroom. It was hard to tell whether their efforts were having any positive effect.

Bodhi seemed to be fanning the flames and Neera's water dousings seemed to be distributing the kerosene into new spaces. The fire spread to the other cabinets.

The security guard heard the commotion and saw the smoke and ran up. "Get the fire extinguisher," Chhotomama shouted to him. The guard didn't know where it was. He didn't even know what it looked like. Chhotomama didn't know where it was either but he did know what it looked like. They ran down the stairs to the ground floor as fast as their old legs could carry them. They bustled through every room they found unlocked—the kitchen, the canteen, the mail office—and found it in a corner of the supply room. The guard ran up with the extinguisher. Bodhi took it from him and let the foam fly. The fire was out in seconds. From beginning to end it had lasted for seven minutes.

The Rare Documents Room looked as if a riot mob had marched through it. A swirling mass of grey smoke played hide and seek with cabinets wet with water and covered with foam. The security guard opened the windows in the room and was about to take the unused canister of kerosene downstairs when Chhotomama stopped him. "We shouldn't disturb the crime scene," he said.

Not one of the six cabinets had fully burned, but two were seriously damaged. The thin glass windows on these cabinets had cracked and shattered from the heat, and first the fire and later the foam had entered through those openings. The damaged cabinets contained out-of-print books on Buddhist and Vaishnav philosophy from the Bengal school and facsimile copies of handwritten scrolls from the time of the rise of Chaitanya Vaishnavism in the sixteenth century. They appeared to be ruined beyond repair. Chhotomama inspected the cabinets with tears in his eyes. He ran his fingers over the broken spines and charred pages like a braille reader.

A police inspector later told Chhotomama that things could have been much worse. Everything in the room could have burned. The cabinets could have really caught fire. It was a combination of luck and environment and ineptitude that had limited the damage. The cabinet wood was exceptionally damp, perhaps because of age, perhaps because the room never got direct sunlight, perhaps because of the rain that had been falling all evening and the supersaturated atmosphere it had created. Moreover, the inspector said, those cabinets were built in a different time, when people knew how to make things, not like these days when everything was made of plywood and burnt like dry cow-dung. The cabinets were built like steel lockers, he said, with a solid heavy teak that would need more than a layer of kerosene to catch fire. Kerosene was well known to be an inefficient fire starter anyway. It was the fuel of the poor. And it evaporated quickly. Much of it had fumed away during Bodhi's speeches. Had Bodhi focused on pouring the second canister of kerosene instead of making speeches the whole collection would have turned to ashes.

Bodhi had burns on both his hands. He had to go to a hospital to get them treated. "I'm so sorry, Chhotomama," he said before leaving, "I didn't mean for this to happen. You know I wasn't serious. I was never going to light the fire. You know that, don't you!" he pleaded.

"Only you and your heart know what you were thinking, Bodhi," Chhotomama said. "But you go and get your burns looked at now. We'll talk later. Neera, why don't you also go home? Get some food and rest. I'm going to go home and think. We all need to think about what we've done," he said nodding his head. "But I'll wait till the police get here. I have to tell them what happened."

# 7

The next morning was grey and overcast. Low, slow, monsoon clouds hovered with threatening intent throughout the day. There were some isolated drizzles, but not so much as to put a damper on the bandh called by the Party to protest the anti-people atrocities and injustices of the Opposition party and global capitalism. The police spent much of the day managing the bandh. There were skirmishes and clashes at a few prearranged spots where TV crews had set up in advance. Over three dozen people were arrested. They were delighted with the outcome and joyously screamed slogans of social justice and eternal revenge while being bundled into dusty black police vans. Things went so well that the Party was able to declare the bandh an unqualified success.

The city was in a festive mood. This random holiday was a gift the residents had come to expect and knew how to use. Young men and boys played galli cricket through the isolated drizzles. Families flew kites from rooftops during the dry stretches. Mothers prepared the favourite meals of their oldest sons. It was a day for social bonding, for affirming and renewing the ties that hold communities and families together. True, some housewives were irritated because their maidservants didn't show up to cook and clean, but their irritation was tempered by an acceptance of the inevitable. What to do? It was what it was. Might as well microwave the leftovers.

As was routine with bandhs in the city, by late-afternoon it petered out. Buses and autos got back on the roads. The local bazaars opened for evening shoppers. The food courts in the malls began serving egg rolls and coffee. Multiplexes began running evening shows. And, after congratulating themselves on another bandh successfully managed, the police gradually resumed their regular work.

By the time the contingent assigned to arrest Bodhi reached his neighborhood it was almost dark. The rainy day had turned into a misty evening. Tiny globules of moisture hung in the air like a translucent powder and attached themselves to anything solid. Lamp posts perspired like long-distance runners. Lamplight glowed through shrouds of soft glittering wool. Everything was wet and cold and slippery, like a freshly embalmed corpse.

Bodhi surrendered meekly. He had waited all day for this. At the Lake police station he was booked by the officer in charge, sub-inspector Abdul Rehman, who had some difficulty spelling his name. What kind of a name was Bodhichitto, he asked, and what happened to the regular old goonda names like Fata and Chaku and Peto? Bodhi gave him an embarrassed smile but had no explanation for this reversal in the social order of the city.

~

Cookie arrived an hour after Bodhi was booked. He paid the going rate—three hundred rupees—to sub-inspector

Rehman for the privilege of visiting his friend inside the lock-up. He found Bodhi sitting on the floor of the cell with a handkerchief tied around his nose. There was a toilet inside the cell, separated by a wall three feet high and one brick wide, that hadn't been cleaned in two days. The cell smelled of ammonia and freshly-cut radish. There was one other prisoner in the lock-up. He was sleeping on his side with his elbow under his head, on a thin bare mattress on the floor. He was snoring without pattern in the melancholy light of a single forty-watt bulb.

Cookie had made arrangements for a lawyer to represent Bodhi. His name was KP Seth, LL.B., he said, and he had a fearsome reputation. So fearsome was he that no one knew what his initials stood for and, for two decades, no one had dared to ask. KP Seth had kept Cookie's father out of jail many times. He was a wizard. He would be present when Bodhi was produced before a judge next morning. He would make sure that Bodhi got bail and never saw the inside of a jail again.

"Don't worry," Cookie said, "you'll be out of here tomorrow. What happened at Raniganj Mansion was an accident. Everyone knows that."

"What about the kerosene I brought?" Bodhi asked.

"How could there be an accident if there wasn't any kerosene? Don't be silly. Mr Seth will take care of all that. It's not a big deal. A few books were damaged, okay, but no one died and no one was injured except you. And you were injured only because you were trying to put the fire out. You could become a hero."

"What will Chhotomama say? He could send me to jail for a long time."

"Nothing. Chhotomama won't say anything that'll damage you seriously. After all, blood is thicker than kerosene, no?"

"He got me arrested, Cookie. And I tried to burn down his library. I don't think either of us cared about the density of blood then."

"He had to do that. There's insurance and other formalities he has to think about. You'd have me arrested too if I tried to burn your library."

"I don't have a library."

"But you will, scarecrow, you will. You can have as many libraries as you want. This is the big news. Chhotomama has withdrawn his hunger strike. He didn't give a reason why, just phoned the Roys after the police picked you up and told them so. The ruffian brother phoned me. He's thrilled to pieces. Our deal is on and he's in a hurry. The Roys now have a clear path to the possession of Raniganj Mansion and we have a clear path to crores and crores. In six months the house will be rubble. Payday, man, payday."

Bodhi pursed his lips. "There's another thing I screwed up yesterday, Cookie," he said. "I promised to give all my profit to charity. I said that I didn't care about the money."

"People say strange things when they're under stress. No one's going to hold you to it."

Bodhi shook his head.

"Did you tell them how much you're going to make? No? Then what's the problem? If you don't tell how can anyone know? Even the taxwallas won't be able to figure it out. You make three or four crores and tell them one. Then you donate one. That is, if anyone even remembers what you promised."

Cookie punched Bodhi on his shoulder. Softly.

"You did it, Bodhi," he said. "You pulled it off…with one masterstroke. You kicked the old man exactly where it hurts. I'm full of respect, scarecrow. You act like this namby-pamby goody-goody all the time, but when push comes to shove, you shove harder than anyone thinks you can. That's what you did with your father's house. Remember? If you hadn't rammed it down his throat we'd still be selling Xerox machines. Heavenly Homes wouldn't even have existed. Deep down, man, you're ruthless. You and I know that, don't we, even if no one else does."

"A man's got to do what a man's got to do," Bodhi said weakly. Was it true? That deep down, from where the unfathomable urges came, urges that couldn't be explained or denied, he was a ruthless man? Bodhi needed to think about it. He was a little ashamed that he was almost thirty years old and still didn't know what kind of a person he truly was…deep down.

"It *was* an accident, wasn't it?" Cookie asked.

"Of course it was. What do you think? That I set the fire on purpose. Is this what you think of me?"

"With you, chhupa rustam, who knows."

"I'm shocked that you'd even think that. With friends like you, who needs enemies?" Bodhi huffed. "Anyway, can you please go to my house and talk to Baba and explain things to him. I didn't tell him anything and I don't think I can face him right now. And take care of him. See if he needs anything."

"Wah, what dialoguebazi," Cookie said. "I'll go see him, no problem, but you'll be out of here tomorrow.

There isn't a jail strong enough on heaven or earth to keep Bodhichitto Banerjee behind bars. *Ha ha ha.*"

~

Bodhi sat on the floor and pulled his knees up between his elbows and hung his head between them. He thought of curling into a ball and disappearing into himself. There was a strange sound in his ears, a dull throbbing beat, *dhup dhup dhup*, like a pile-driver in rapid motion. Somewhere, maybe in the next room, men were laughing. What were they laughing about? What was there to laugh about in the world? Bodhi wanted to shout at them to shut up. But that would require some effort and Bodhi had nothing left in him. He saw a cockroach approach his ankle like a scout for a hidden army, its antlers combing the air for the subsonic frequencies of fear and failure. Its hard brown shell brushed his little toe and he shivered in disgust. He thought about sending the repulsive little thing flying with a flick of his finger, as he would have in any other setting and not given it a moment of thought. But what was the use here? There were dozens more where this turd had come from. This was their domain. He had to learn to live with them. He had tried to force his way into a place where he didn't belong and as a result the remainder of his life would have to be spent among lower order creatures like cockroaches and snakes.

His descent into the underworld was interrupted by new sensory inputs. First there was a smell, nay a fragrance, that radiated slowly from some indeterminable direction and began to mix with, if not quite overwhelm, the stench of ammonia and radish. Then he heard a voice, soft and low like a goose-down quilt. "BB," it said, "are you awake?"

Bodhi jumped to his feet like a soldier caught napping on duty. His eyes widened and his mouth fell open. His cellmate woke up and rubbed his eyes in disbelief.

Neera stood outside the lock-up. She wore a dignified grey sari with a long-sleeve white blouse. Chunky green earrings swung from her big ears. Her hair was shinier and the maddening curls bouncier than last night. It smelled of something imported, not damp peanuts, like a perfumed garden of heavenly delight.

Bodhi felt quivers and shakes in several parts of his body. He didn't know what to say. He didn't think he had anything left to say. "I didn't think you'd come," he said. Neera cocked her head with a half-smile that said—life is full of surprises, isn't it?

She took a step closer to the bars. "How are the burns?" she asked. Bodhi held out his bandaged hands mutely, like a mutilated beggar seeking alms. She cradled his right arm through the rusted iron bars and blew gently on his open palm—*foo foo*. "There, there," she said. "That'll make the pain go away."

Bodhi choked. His lungs needed air. His throat needed water. "I'm sorry, Neera," he said, "I don't remember what all I said last night but I know it was cruel."

Neera smiled benevolently. She had forgiven him.

"And I'm sorry I didn't go to the airport to pick up your friend," Bodhi said. "I hope he made it in okay."

"Actually, it's good that you didn't go," Neera said, "because my friend didn't come. He couldn't come. Got stuck with some last minute emergency. I was going to tell you, but you weren't speaking to me."

The quivers and shakes in Bodhi's body became rumbles and quakes. His heart leaped and cartwheeled. The poet's lines from a hundred years ago started playing inside a far corner of his head in an endless loop, like a long-playing record stuck in an everlasting groove, but Bodhi couldn't hear it over the pile-driver going *dhup dhup dhup*, the volume rising with every strike, till he felt his heart popping out of his ears.

Oh hope, you sorceress
bless your treachery and illusions
that enthral us mortal fools

They couldn't say any more to each other because sub-inspector Abdul Rehman marched in to the beat of his lathi clacking on the floor. Moments ago he had been so befuddled by Neera's superiority that he had been unable to demand the money that was due to him from all visitors. His timidity now irritated him. He insisted that Neera must leave. It was past time, he said, to turn the light out in the lock-up.

But Bodhi couldn't sleep at all. He entered a new state—neither awake nor asleep—in which ordinary worldly laws no longer applied. His mind separated from his body. It floated like a thing with feathers over sun-dappled valleys bursting with spring, and for once, for just once in his anxious and muddled life, didn't worry that it would lose its power of flight and crash to earth.

Bodhi never knew how long he spent in that state in which the downward pulls of history and character didn't exist. And it was impossible for him to know when those downward pulls would return, as return they would. All he knew was that he was happier that first night in jail than he had known it was possible to be.

# Acknowledgements

I have adapted the words of accomplished writers here. In order of appearance, the compositions are—lyricist Sameer's song 'Crazy Kiya Re' from the movie *Dhoom 2* (2006); Gauriprasanna Mazumdar's song 'Ei to Hethaye Kunjo Chhayaye' from the Bangla movie *Lukochuri* (1958); Rabindranath Tagore's poem and song, 'Aguner Parashmoni' (1914); Salil Chowdhury's poem and song 'O Alor Pothojatri' (1949) and fragments of two poems, one from Sukumar Ray's story *Drighangchu* (1916) and the other from Nabinchandra Sen's poetry in 'Polashir Juddho' (1875), which is the last translation in this story. The Gramsci quote is edited from the *International Publishers* edition (11th printing, 1957). There are several other unknown creators whose snippets and parodies I have borrowed. I cannot acknowledge by name these ethereal authors whose earthy words are embedded in the vernacular culture of Bengal. But there are other names I must acknowledge. Sheemantika Nag and Phil Yanella read the manuscript as it was being written and didn't stop me from finishing. Kanishka Gupta taught me—after I had completed writing—things all writers should know before they start. Pallabi, of course, kept the whole thing going.